a novel

Chaos

JENNIFER LOCKLEAR

Chaos
by
Jennifer Locklear

Published by Locklear Books
http://www.locklearbooks.com
info@locklearbooks.com.

Enchanted Publications

Enchanted

PUBLICATIONS
www.enchantedpublications.com
enchantedpublications@gmail.com.

Library of Congress Control Number: 2018908404

First Edition: May 2018
ISBN 978-0-9978607-4-0

Praise for Constellation

"Constellation is nothing like I expected! I was ready for more of Jennifer's trademark brand of intellectual romance laced with quick wit. Instead, I found myself in the grips of a hauntingly emotional love story. It's equal parts wildly erotic and heartbreakingly angsty."

~Agents of Romance

"Jennifer Locklear has set up a sexy, suspenseful story; a story of two broken people, two broken families, and the torturous journey they undertake with the hope of becoming whole."

~Passionate Reads

"I was incredibly sucked into this story and tremendously moved by its characters. The author approaches heavy subjects with such maturity and delicacy, and I appreciate the realism. A soulful supernova."

~Raven, Amazon Review

"Jennifer sets the pages on fire with Kathleen and Jack. Her words made me feel. I cried, and I cheered."

~Melissa P., Amazon Review

"A modern classic in the making. I'm not ashamed to say I wept at some of the passages. The emotions pour off of the page."

~CATHERINE H., AMAZON REVIEW

Praise for Exposure

"Morgan and Jennifer have masterfully crafted a quirky love story that is smart and witty. Don't miss this fabulous fusion of passion and humor…"

~Agents of Romance

"I adored this book. The plot and the characters were engaging, fresh and unique. These two authors have made a fan of me and I would definitely recommend this book to romance lovers. If you are looking for something a little outside of the box with enough punch to keep you hooked - Exposure is just the place to start."

~Cassia Brightmore, Author

"Exposure is a great ride, a hilarious adventure, a warm and witty character study of the egos and eccentrics who make the movies and television shows we love to watch."

~Serendipitous, Amazon Review

"Egos, drama, divorce, movie set, lights, camera ... action! An engaging story that flowed nicely and delivered satisfaction on a silver platter."

~Sugar and Spice Book Reviews

"Remember those old screwball comedy movies? It's one of those. It's sexy, frustrating (in a good way), and funny. Get it and read it. Then gift it to your friends for Christmas."

~Morgan R., Amazon Review

Dedication

For Melissa and MJ

Chaos: A distinctive area of broken terrain.

Prologue

"AFTER THE first time we made love, you trembled in my arms and you asked me a question. Do you remember?"

My hands shook as I waited for Kathleen to answer. We'd been distant for weeks, our fragile relationship strained by the circumstances surrounding my daughter's brush with death. I needed Kathleen back in my arms like I needed air to breathe, but I had to settle for her voice on the phone.

"Yes. I'll never forget it."

I closed my eyes and summoned my courage. She was on her way to a job interview in Colorado, on the verge of leaving me, her family and her hometown for good. I couldn't stop her from making the trip to Denver, so I was doing my best to make her understand what she meant to me. "Then you remember my answer," I continued with a powerful mixture of caution and anticipation.

"Yes."

Encouraged, I turned toward my office window, ignoring the view of the Cascade Mountain Range. "Nothing has changed since the first time I held your beautiful body to mine. I will always feel that way about you."

She was at the Portland International Airport while I was one hundred sixty miles away in my office in Bend. She wasn't responding to my last statement, and although it was too late to

1

take anything back, I second-guessed my choice of words.

"Are you still there?" I asked her.

"Yes. Thank you, Jack. You don't know how much I needed to hear that."

I plopped down in my office chair. "Just as much as I needed to say it. I love you, Kathleen."

"I love you. I do. I'm not doing this to hurt you."

"I understand that now. I'm not trying to talk you out of going to Denver." I leaned forward and rubbed my temple. I was such a liar. I didn't want her getting on that fucking jet, but I didn't have the right to demand otherwise.

"I know that. They're getting ready to board the plane. I better go."

Familiar knots tightened in my stomach as I was forced to acknowledge the inevitable. "Have a safe trip," I said.

"Jack?" Her voice held a mild tone of anxiety. For the first time in that long and miserable autumn, we were emotionally united, even if only by a mutual sense of unease.

"Yes?"

"Robert asked me to think about things for a few days before I make any big decisions. I want you to know that's exactly what I'll do."

Kathleen was always true to her word. I'd learned this in ways both pleasurable and painful. Her statement held determination. She was intent on exploring her options, but her declaration also held promise.

"I believe in you, Kathleen."

"Thank you for saying so. I'll see you next week."

"Bye."

She disconnected the call as soon as I uttered the word. I should have said more, but I was at a loss. It had been several days since she'd blindsided me with the announcement she was flying to Colorado. I hadn't lost her for certain, but she was a strong candidate for any job in the advertising profession. I was running *out of time.*

While Kathleen boarded her flight, I tossed my phone onto the desk and leaned against the seat back, my work forgotten as I sorted out my thoughts.

Allison was staying in my home, helping our seven-year-old daughter, Heide, recover from traumatic injuries sustained when a baseball backstop crushed her. I would never deny Allison access to our child, and Kathleen agreed with me about my ex-wife's vital role as Heide's mother. I didn't want to be with Allison, but until she returned to Maryland and Heide's injuries didn't require my undivided attention, Kathleen was going to stay away from me.

She was sacrificing her own happiness to ensure my daughter's. I admired her strength of character but saw now that the prolonged isolation was alienating her. She'd endured a childhood tragedy and had told me in gruesome detail about the suicide of her mother. Kathleen's developing fear for her own well-being horrified me. I was scared that I had the potential to destroy her spirit.

I wanted Kathleen Brighton, and although she had bravely shared her biggest secret with me, I had stupidly hesitated to provide her with the same level of intimacy. If I had any hope of salvaging my relationship with her, I was going to have to tell her everything she wanted to know when she returned from Denver. It was a tremendous gamble.

I would lose her for good if I continued to avoid the truth. These were the ongoing consequences of my actions and I was forced to bear the responsibility of them once more.

After work, I drove straight home. My hands clenched the steering wheel as I took a few deep breaths. I couldn't go back into my house without my wits intact.

It was a strain on Allison and me to keep things civil for the sake of our only daughter. We were good parents, but terrible partners. Heide's strength was my biggest source of inspiration. If she could overcome her challenges with minimal fuss, I should be able to do the same.

I tried my best to set aside my worries about Kathleen as I left the solitude of my BMW and walked into the house. Heide was resting on the sofa with her tablet in her hands and the stuffed Minecraft zombie toy from Kathleen at her side.

I smiled as I approached, leaned down and kissed her forehead. "Hey there."

"Hey, Dad."

"Where's your mom?"

Heide screwed up her face in concentration as she fought to focus on her game. "In the kitchen. Making dinner."

"Thanks." I straightened up and listened for my ex-wife's greeting.

Allison either hadn't heard me come in or didn't care. Either way, I took advantage of the opportunity and went to my bedroom, closing and locking the door behind me. I removed my charcoal gray blazer and set it down on my bed. As I unbuttoned my work shirt, my eyes came to rest on one particular dresser drawer.

Kathleen was in Denver by now. Knowing she was far away made me miss her even more. I made my way over to the dresser. Inside were her garter and stockings, a memento from our first night together.

I recalled how deliciously pleasing it was to discover the elegant lingerie underneath her tailored work clothes. With her long blond hair and tall yet curvy figure, I wasn't the only man in the office who found Kathleen Brighton sexy. I was, however, the only one who knew what tantalizing silks and satins habitually adorned her stunning body. And I loved that she had left some of those items in my care.

Anxious to reconnect with her somehow, I opened the drawer and discovered the stunning truth.

Her lingerie was gone. It was as far from my presence as Kathleen was.

Disappointed, I closed the drawer quietly. Of course, Kathleen had removed her underwear along with her other possessions before Allison's return to Bend. She hadn't wanted my ex-wife to come across any evidence that I'd brought a new lover into my bedroom. I'd lived the life of a monk during my marriage to Allison. I didn't want to live like one after my divorce.

Even so, what troubled me wasn't that Kathleen had moved the items. It was how long it had taken me to realize her treasures were gone.

chapter One

"MR. EVANS? I'll show you to the conference room now."

"Thank you, Tracie." I smiled at the receptionist. The young woman with short and spiky black hair was an excellent first impression of Aurora Advertising. She was stylish and friendly with a bubbly voice. I was a stranger to everyone in this town, but she made me feel welcome instantly.

I stood up from my chair and buttoned my suit jacket as I followed her down a short corridor. When we reached the conference room door, Tracie turned to me.

"May I offer you anything to drink? Water? Or coffee perhaps?"

"Water would be wonderful. Thanks again."

She gestured to the doorway and I stepped into the room. Tracie followed, and walked toward a small counter in the back corner. There were only two other people seated at the large conference table—an older man and a younger woman. The man I recognized as the owner and current CEO of the agency, Robert Brighton. He rose from his seat, dominating my attention. He made his way over to me, extending his hand in greeting.

"Welcome to Oregon, Mr. Evans."

"Thank you for the opportunity, Mr. Brighton. It's an amazing place."

"You have a pick of empty seats here. Please take whichever

one you'd like."

The table was long, and the space was large, so I chose to occupy the empty chair next to Robert. My back was to the window and my spot was directly across from the unfamiliar woman, who was too busy taking notes to look up. I unbuttoned my suit coat and prepared to sit down.

"Here you are, Mr. Evans. Is there anything else I can get for you?" Tracie delivered a glass of water, complete with a fresh slice of lemon.

"No, thank you. This is great."

"You're welcome."

The receptionist closed the door behind her, and I turned to look at the mystery woman in the room. She had yet to say a word and left me wondering how much influence she might have in who was hired. I was uncertain if I should go ahead and sit down, but when Robert returned to his chair, I followed his lead. I placed my hands on the table and waited for the job interview to begin.

"Allow me to introduce Kathleen," Robert said. "I've asked her to sit in on the conversation."

I glanced from Robert to the woman who now had a name.

She paused her note-taking and nodded politely. "Hello, Mr. Evans." Her voice was soft and pleasant. She had long, golden hair that absorbed the incoming sunshine. Her face was hidden from view either from a bashful nature or a preoccupation with her notes.

"Hello, Kathleen."

I decided she was Robert's administrative assistant. As he launched into the interview, I gave him my attention and we fell into a comfortable discussion as he tested my various skill sets. We spoke for twenty minutes before he turned to look at the woman across from me. She had been so quiet I'd forgotten she was there.

"Kathleen?"

She abruptly halted her note-taking and looked at Robert.

"Why don't you ask Jack a question?"

Surprised with his curveball, I shifted toward her and waited for what was next.

A faint blush appeared across her cheeks. She appeared flustered by Robert's request. Maybe she wasn't prepared to ask me anything. It was a potentially awkward test for us both. I decided that no matter what she asked of me, I wouldn't take offense at her lack of preparation. Instead, I was more curious about what had motivated Robert's impulsiveness.

Maybe it's a West Coast thing.

Kathleen set her pen down and leaned back in her seat, raising her head up and away from her notes for the first time since the interview began. She made eye contact and her sparkling green gaze distracted me. In addition to their vibrant color, her eyes held both astuteness and true femininity.

She's pretty. The thought flashed unbidden through my brain, but I'd been married long enough to tune such frequencies down.

"You live in Baltimore now?" she asked me.

Easy question. Easy answer.

"Yes."

"Are you from Maryland?" she pressed.

She should have been able to figure that out from my résumé. She must not have seen it. I couldn't decide what her role was in this interview, and until I could, I was going to answer her inquiries with minimal detail. "Not originally, but I've been there for almost ten years."

"Are you from the Pacific Northwest?" she prodded just a bit further.

If these questions had been coming from anyone else, I would have begun fidgeting with impatience. However, we were both improvising this part of the interview, and I couldn't deny that I was enjoying this game of twenty questions. The tender lilt of the woman's voice was soothing.

"No. This is my first time out here."

"Why now? Why Bend?" she asked.

Suddenly I perceived a deeper reasoning for her geographic inquiry. As I began to formulate my response, she offered up her own theory.

"I think Portland or Seattle would be more appealing to you."

"You do?" I asked. "Why do you think that?"

She studied my face before she regarded my chest with her green eyes. There was something intimate in the way she studied me. I reached for my glass of lemon water, enjoying her contemplation.

"You look a bit too polished for life in a mill town."

I should have taken her remark as a compliment, but coming from Kathleen it stung.

"Bend is much more than a mill town these days," Robert said, startling me.

As soon as I heard the reproach in his voice, I forgot my disappointment from Kathleen's conclusion. His tone was disproportionately harsh. My knee-jerk reaction was to speak up and defend her, but I managed to hold both my tongue and my poker face.

I took another sip of water, hoping it would cool my rising temper. As I did, I watched Kathleen and saw she was staring right back at me, unfazed. She completely ignored Robert, her attention set on me. I was impressed by this glimmer of her inner strength. She hadn't reacted to her boss's chastisement, and I realized that she was both intuitive and disciplined.

I set my glass back down on the table as I debated how to answer her. I was having personal problems, but I wasn't about to disclose my marriage woes in a job interview.

"Sometimes... it's good to make a change."

The answer was evasive. I was nervous and stalling.

"Bend is very different from Baltimore," she pressed.

"Yes, it is. In this case, I think Bend may be choosing me. I'm not set on moving to any one place. The opening just appeared at the same time I decided that my life needed something new."

"So, you'd basically go anywhere? Bend isn't so special after all?"

Fuck. Walked right into that one.

Kathleen had put me on the spot, but rightfully so. Now I was in the position of convincing both my potential boss and this woman why their home city was an exciting possibility.

"Bend has many attractions," I began. "The outdoors, for example. The opportunity to enjoy the high desert, or the mountains. My family could use some time away from city life."

Robert connected with my response and resumed the interview. He was telling me the story of how he'd moved his family business from Portland and the advantages that had resulted from his decision. The story was interesting, and I hoped that Kathleen would contribute more, but she had apparently served her purpose. Robert never gave her another thought, and she went back to her note-taking without missing a beat.

When my allotted time was up, the three of us rose from our seats. I reached across the table to shake Kathleen's hand.

"It was nice to meet you, Mr. Evans."

"Likewise, and please, call me Jack."

She nodded and offered a friendly smile that illuminated her entire face. "Have a safe trip home, Jack."

chapter  Two

"DAD!" HEIDE charged full speed into the entryway as soon as I opened the front door, the incoming breeze lifting her blond hair from her shoulders. I had just enough time to drop my shoulder bag to the floor before she leaped into my eager arms. I kissed her forehead and lowered my own to rest against hers.

"What a nice surprise." I smiled at my blue-eyed little girl. "I thought you'd be fast asleep by now."

"Nope. No way. Not until I saw you." Heide wrapped her arms around my neck and offered the strongest hug she could. I stood still, reciprocating her affection. Her love and high spirits reinvigorated my own after a long day of cross-country travel. By the time Allison joined us and closed the front door, I felt like a new man.

My wife leaned in for a quick, chaste peck on the lips. "How was the flight?" she asked with a subdued tone. Not "What was Bend like?" or even "Did the interview go well?"

"Both flights went well. I had a two-hour layover in Vegas."

"Oh yeah? What did that cost us?"

"I actually won a little bit on the airport slots. It was great. We should go sometime."

"Maybe."

I studied Allison's face for a few moments. "Are you feeling all right?"

She shrugged but smiled at our daughter who clung to me like a koala bear to a eucalyptus tree.

"Mom's ready for bed," she declared.

"So am I," I commented with a wink in my wife's direction.

"Jack…" Allison's chastisement was punctuated with a frown.

I decided to turn off the charm and be of some help. "I'll get Heide settled and read her a story. Why don't you go relax?"

Allison's mood shifted slightly in my favor. "I've been dying to take a shower."

"Then go do it," I encouraged. "I'll get everything squared away out here and we'll catch up after you're done."

Allison smiled gratefully and hugged Heide and I both as she wished her good night.

After I put Heide to bed, I entered the master bedroom and smelled the perfumed scent of Allison's bodywash. The water was off, and the smallest bit of steam lingered from her shower. The door to the bathroom was mostly closed so I unpacked my bag and then stripped down to my green boxer briefs.

I was in a good mood. Despite the small hiccup in my back-and-forth with the young woman, Kathleen, I believed the interview in Oregon had gone well. If I was fortunate enough to reach the final round of the hiring process, I'd decided I would bring my family out to Bend with me. Once she saw the majesty of Oregon for herself, I was convinced my wife would find the enthusiasm for the move.

Allison came out from the bathroom, her blond hair mostly dry and her face devoid of makeup. Her radiant beauty was intact no matter the circumstances; however, she wore a simplistic pajama T-shirt and bottoms, and I was deflated. Over time, I'd come to accept this nightwear as uninviting. It was equivalent with declaring she had a headache.

Sex was completely out of the question.

Allison pulled back the covers of our bed without a word. With nothing better to do, I went into the bathroom to dispose of my laundry, remove my contact lenses and brush my teeth. By the time I returned, she had settled herself in bed. Her bedside lamp was off, and her back was to my side of the mattress.

I removed my briefs and replaced them with a new pair. She didn't want me to sleep naked in our bed now that Heide was older. Our daughter was in first grade, but still entered our bedroom at night when the need arose.

I turned off my lamp, reclined on my back and waited. Allison's breathing indicated that she wasn't yet asleep, but she didn't initiate conversation. After a few minutes, I could no longer stand the silence.

"Are you awake?" I prodded.

"You know I am," she mumbled.

"Is everything okay?"

"Yeah. Just tired. I started my period this morning."

"Do you need anything?"

"About a week's worth of sleep."

I rolled onto my hip and reached for Allison's lower back. I began to lightly massage her muscles, knowing she tended to have back aches during her cycles.

"That feels great," she said. "Thanks."

"Of course."

I focused on the task until my wife was relaxed.

"Can I tell you about Oregon?" I ventured.

"Hmm," she murmured.

"The interview went well. The CEO and I have some common interests and he realized it. I'm sure I'll be a finalist."

At this, Allison moved onto her back with an exasperated sigh. The tension between us was profound, but we kept the conversation going.

"That job is such a big change," she began. "Aren't you nervous about that?"

"What's to be nervous about? The job would be a step up in my career—both in responsibility and pay. With my track record,

I'm confident I can negotiate my asking price."

Allison was quiet.

My annoyance set in, but I spoke with careful deliberation to keep my wife from noticing. "We've talked about doing this many times," I reminded her. "I don't understand your hesitation."

"I don't know." She sighed and took in a deep breath. "I assumed that you'd look for a job on *this* coast. I never expected to move to the other side of the country. And besides, it's Oregon. Who lives in Oregon?"

I rubbed an eye in mild frustration. "Bend is bigger than you realize. It's just as large as any of the suburbs here, but not as congested. The mountains are nearby. You can see several at once. And if you must get to the city, Portland is only a few hours away. You could even get to Seattle or San Francisco within a day."

"What about Heide?" Allison challenged. "She just started school."

Bringing up Heide's well-being was a good tactic. If I were having any doubts about moving away from Maryland, they would have to do with her.

"If this goes according to plan, Heide can finish the first grade here and start second grade in Bend. If we're going to do this kind of a move, now is the time. We should do this before she becomes too attached to things here. She makes friends everywhere she goes. She'll be fine. Besides, Bend is an outdoor paradise year-round. We could keep her busy with different activities."

Allison's silence deepened.

I tried to fill the void in our discussion. "I could be home more, like you've asked. I wouldn't be commuting as much, and we could buy a bigger house. Maybe we could even think about having another baby once things are settled."

Allison's head whipped in my direction, her hair brushing loudly against her pillow.

"Another baby?" Her tone was harsh. "Since when have *we* been thinking about another baby?"

"I know that's a big step, but I'm open to the idea. Giving Heide a sibling is something we should consider. I'm not getting any younger here."

She chortled. "I beg your pardon. Is your biological clock ticking?"

"I just don't want anyone at kindergarten to think I'm the child's grandfather. Think of how much it would embarrass the poor kid."

"Good to see your priorities are intact."

We both chuckled at the thought, but her tone grew somber once more. "This is happening so fast. Something about this idea just makes me nervous. We don't know anyone out there. You'll be at work. Heide will be in school. Where does that leave me?"

"You could go back to television," I suggested.

"A new job and a new baby? Be serious."

"I am."

"I don't imagine Bend has a plethora of television studios, Jack."

"Actually, there are a few."

She was dubious. "You've already considered this? Why would you do that?"

The question was ridiculous, and my patience waned. "I work in advertising," I snapped. "I needed to study the local market for the interview."

"Who's going to hire me, Jack? I haven't worked since Heide was born and I don't see any station manager putting a forty-two-year-old woman on the air when he can have his pick of young college graduates who will work for much less money and put up with a lot more bullshit. Besides, I'd have to start over in a new market. I'd be doing the weather. Or the traffic. Or those god-awful four a.m. live stories. Out in the woods. With bears. Or Bigfoot."

She shook her head, huffed, and rolled away from me.

"It's too much to think about tonight. You just need to take things one step at a time. Don't start making life-altering plans right now. Wait and see if you get another interview before you start figuring out how the rest of *my* life is going to go."

"Our lives," I muttered, hurt.

Allison never responded to this. When it became clear the conversation was over, I pulled away from her. She fell asleep after a few minutes while I continued to lie wide awake, furious.

chapter Three

SEVERAL DAYS later, I was speaking with a male colleague when my cell phone rang. I'd kept a close eye on my calls, always careful to keep my phone nearby. I couldn't risk anyone at the firm figuring out I was seeking other employment.

I retrieved the phone from my khaki suit jacket and glanced at the display. The call was from the 541 area code, in Oregon.

I peered back at my coworker. "I apologize, Colton. Do you mind if I answer this?"

The younger man nodded and held up his hand. "Sure. No problem."

"This shouldn't take long. I'll catch up with you in a few minutes?"

"Sounds good."

I swiftly returned to my office, closed the door and secured my privacy before connecting the call.

"This is Jack Evans."

"Hello, Jack," a female voice answered. "This is Kathleen from Aurora Advertising. We met when you were here for the interview."

I smiled. "Yes, Kathleen. I recognize your voice. How are you today?"

"I'm well. Thank you. Is this a good time? Do you have a few minutes to speak with me?"

"I do," I confirmed as I settled into my desk chair.

Kathleen's tone relaxed as she eased into our discussion. "Did you have a good trip back to Maryland?"

"I did. Yes. Thanks for asking."

"Wonderful. Robert asked me to convey his appreciation for making the long trip to interview here in person."

"It was no trouble. I'm a bit old school in that regard. I prefer to hold important meetings face-to-face."

"Most of the candidates opted to hold their initial interviews via Skype." Kathleen's voice held the warmth I'd glimpsed at the end of my interview. "I commend you on your decision. Robert isn't easy to impress, but you did an excellent job."

"Thank you."

"We've had an extraordinary pool of applicants for the position. We interviewed fifteen during the first phase, and we'd like a second interview with you before we make our final decision."

I welcomed Kathleen's news with a mixture of excitement and relief. "That's great. May I ask how many candidates are left?"

"There are four of you."

"Excellent."

"Although you've been to Oregon, we require the finalists to visit Bend for this phase of the selection process. You'll be meeting with more of our staff and some of our clients. Is that something you can do?"

"Yes," I answered without hesitation.

"Great. We would need you here for a long weekend, beginning on Friday the twenty-second at nine in the morning. In your case, I would suggest flying in either Wednesday or Thursday. Plan on returning to Baltimore on Monday."

"I can manage that. That's perfect, actually. I'd like to bring my wife and daughter with me, so they can see how wonderful Bend is."

"That would be fine. I just need to verify your e-mail address and I'll send along the itinerary. I'll also send along some lodging suggestions so that you and your family can rest in comfort."

"Sure. I'll have you send it to my personal e-mail address."

"Yes. Go ahead."

I recited the information, finding myself eager to receive her message.

"That should take care of things for now," she said after verifying the address. "Do you have any questions for me?"

I tapped my finger on my desk as I considered indulging an impulse. "I hate to admit this, but I never got your last name during the interview. I was wondering what you do for the agency."

My inquiry had nothing to do with the upcoming business trip. It was, in fact, pure curiosity about the woman I'd met a few days earlier. Thankfully, she didn't take offense.

"My last name is Brighton." She revealed this surprising fact with minimal pageantry.

"The same as Robert?"

"Exactly. He's my father."

"Oh. Okay." I flinched at my poor choice of words.

"I've been with the agency since I graduated from college. Well, longer, but I'll spare you those boring details. I'm the senior target marketing strategist."

"So, you're a third-generation executive. That's fantastic."

"Any other questions?" Kathleen's voice was businesslike once again. Her interest in discussing her personal life had clearly faded.

"No. That will do it. I should let you get on with your day. Thank you for the great news. I'm excited to return to Oregon."

"You're welcome, Jack. We'll see you in a couple of weeks."

That evening, I fidgeted. I was resisting the urge to blurt out my news to Allison. I'd struck a compromise with her, agreeing not to speak about the possibility of leaving Baltimore in Heide's presence. As a direct result, I tried to rush my family through our dinner and evening routines.

Allison was perceptive of my efforts. The more I tried to hurry things along, the more my wife insisted on slowing things down. When my impatience triggered hers, I retreated to my home office to focus on my preparations for the final interview at Aurora Advertising.

I had applied for the job in Oregon after finding the posting by chance. But as I continued to explore the opportunity of working and living in the Pacific Northwest, I couldn't deny that I found the prospect appealing. I stayed in my office until Allison put Heide to bed and called for me to say good night to our daughter.

I'd hidden from Allison that evening, but I'd kept myself away from Heide as well. Ashamed of my behavior, I made my way to her bedroom. Her door was wide open, but I knocked on it anyhow, so I wouldn't startle her. Heide was sitting cross-legged in the middle of her bed. She halted her conversation with her stuffed snowman and looked up.

"I came in to say good night."

"Where were you?"

"In my office."

"You had some work tonight?"

I nodded as I took a seat next to her on the mattress. "A little bit. How was school today?"

"Good."

"Anything happen I should know about?" I watched my daughter's expression carefully, looking for any hint of unhappiness. As usual, I detected none.

"I don't think so."

"Do you want to do something this weekend?"

"Like what?"

"You tell me."

Heide tilted her head. "Can we go to the library?"

"Sure."

"Cool."

"Let's get you tucked in."

"Okay." She scooted toward her pillows and I pulled the blankets around her. I also removed various books and toys from her bed, so she'd have room to stretch out during the night. Then, I kissed my daughter on the forehead and smiled at her as I pulled back.

"You look good, Dad."

I was so surprised by her words I laughed. "I do?"

"Yep. You look happy again."

My smile disappeared, but I kept my tone friendly. "What do you mean by again?"

Heide shrugged and turned bashful. "I don't know."

I watched her as I debated whether to push her. I decided to prod just a little more. "Have I been looking unhappy?"

Her eyes met mine. "Maybe. A little."

"I didn't realize that. I'll have to pay better attention."

"I can let you know." She was eager to help.

"It's a deal," I said. "If I ever look unhappy, you'll have to elbow me or something."

Her eyes grew wide. "Really? I can?"

"Within reason." I held up my hands in surrender. "Don't clobber me."

"All right."

The matter seemed resolved for now. I'd been frustrated by the lack of direction and passion in my life. It was unsettling that things had gotten to the point where even my little girl had noticed my somber moods. Our conversation about my life had been short, but I took Heide's inquisitiveness about my newfound happiness as an optimistic sign.

"I have to go talk to Mom about something. Do you need anything?"

"Nope."

"Good. Thanks for letting me work tonight. We'll go to the library this weekend and pick out some books."

"Can we play checkers, too? Remember they have that huge table of them at the library?"

"Yes. That'll be fun." I stood up and made my way to her bedroom door. I halted at the threshold. "Good night, sweetie."

"Night, Dad."

"I love you."

"Love you, too."

I stepped back out into the hallway and wandered to the family room. Allison was sitting in her favorite spot on the sofa. The television was on, but she wasn't absorbed in the program. She was finally available for a talk.

I took my usual place near Allison but not sitting right next to her.

She glanced in my direction, an annoyed look cemented on her face. "What is the matter with you tonight?"

"Nothing's the matter," I responded tersely. "I got a phone call from the agency in Bend this afternoon."

In an instant, she understood. She sighed and tried to turn her attention to the television set. "I take it you're headed back to Oregon."

"We *all* are," I emphasized. "I'm bringing you and Heide with me. We're flying to Portland on the twentieth."

Allison dropped her head and shook it with determination. "We can't. You'll have to go alone."

I was dumbfounded. "What do you mean? Why?"

"Heide has school on the twentieth." Allison's justification was devoid of emotion or merit.

I crossed my arms. "That's ridiculous. You need to stop acting like Oregon is on the other side of the world. She'll miss a grand total of four days."

Allison fixed me with a severe stare. "Exactly my point, Jack. I don't want her missing an entire week of school just so you can scratch your midlife itch."

"For God's sake, Allison. She's in the first grade. It's not like she has midterms looming."

My wife glared at me, and her increasing anger further deepened my determination.

"Talk to Heide's teacher tomorrow. If there's work she can bring with her on the trip, I'll take the time to help her with it."

Allison had no rebuttal to my suggestion, and she knew it. She looked away from me and sighed. "So, on top of everything else I do around here, you'll need me to book the flight, find a hotel, rent a car. All that nonsense."

I intended my words to be kind. I wanted to be helpful, but my annoyance poisoned my tone. "You don't have to worry about any of the details. I've reserved us a hotel suite and a car. I also booked our flight."

"You did what?" she snapped. "Why would you do that without talking to me first? Why don't I have any say about this, Jack?"

"You know what a great opportunity this is," I barked back. "How many times do we have to go around on the subject?"

We were both angry now. Allison rose and stormed off to the kitchen. Within moments, I heard the sound of slamming drawers and cabinet doors. Her mulishness incensed me, and I was fed up with her resistance, but I also wanted to convince her that I had our family's best interests in mind. I got up and entered the kitchen where Allison was preparing Heide's lunch for school the next day.

"Look." I struggled to keep my voice even. "Things are getting out of hand."

"You think?" she mumbled with thick sarcasm.

"Please. Try to treat this like a family vacation. When was the last time the three of us went anywhere for a week?"

Allison was preparing a fruit bowl for Heide and angrily slicing fresh strawberries. She didn't interrupt her progress to look at me, but she did respond.

"I suppose if things go your way, this will turn into a permanent vacation."

"We've both known this kind of thing was inevitable, Allison. I've achieved everything I can at GKV. There is nothing more I can gain by staying there. Without a bold move, we'll just end up treading water financially. As it is, my career isn't satisfying, and I want more for you and for Heide. I want to give you both everything I can offer."

Allison was unresponsive, still focused on assembling Heide's fruit bowl.

"Please. Just try to be open-minded. I promise not to make any other decisions without speaking with you first."

Allison set her knife down on the cutting board and placed her palms on the granite countertop. When she lifted her head and made eye contact with me, her expression was serious.

"I've heard that before, Jack. Why should this situation be any different from a thousand others you've put me through?"

"It will be," I answered, weakly.

Allison glared her disbelief. She turned away and moved to the sink to wash her hands. The action was a distraction, not a necessity. When she turned off the water and grabbed a dish towel, she said, "I'm so tired of being the last one to know everything."

chapter Four

WE LEFT for Oregon as planned. I'd taken the extra step to book a direct flight from Baltimore, wanting to make the trip as easy as possible on Allison. She had chosen to sit in the aisle seat, declaring it would be best for her to go with Heide on the inevitable bathroom breaks. I sat next to the window and our daughter was in between us, oblivious to the growing tension.

As our plane made its descent into Portland, we were treated to a spectacular view of Mount Hood. The snow-covered mountain loomed large in the small, round window. The peak was so bright and so close that I unbuckled Heide's seat belt and pulled her onto my lap so she could see it. Allison raised a disapproving eyebrow, but otherwise stayed silent. Heide had never seen a mountain of this size and it made an immediate impression on her.

"Wow," she whispered in awe.

"That is the biggest mountain in Oregon," I explained, "but it's not the only one. There are lots of them here."

"Like how many? More than ten?"

"Yes. The town we're going to has at least four nearby. Wait until you see a bunch of them right next to each other."

"Awesome!" Heide turned her head to draw Allison's attention. "Did you know that, Mom?"

"I didn't," she admitted.

"Do you want to look?" Heide asked but had already turned

her head back toward Mount Hood. The plane began to turn away from the peak and she strained her neck to watch as it disappeared.

Allison grinned. "That's all right. I'm sure I'll see it after we land."

After a few moments, Allison began to fret. "Jack? Heide should go back to her seat now."

I tapped Heide on her back, and she bounded back to her spot. I helped her with her seatbelt as Allison watched with maternal interest.

Heide believed the trip to the Pacific Northwest was a family vacation. We'd also told her I would have to attend a few meetings while in Oregon.

Allison had been quiet for much of the trip. She'd alternated her time between reading and resting her eyes, but I hadn't taken offense. I understood she was gathering her energy for the new few days. Just like me, she was doing her best to hide her moodiness from Heide.

Once we'd landed and were making our way through the terminal toward baggage claim, Allison asked me a pointed question.

"Why didn't we fly to Eugene?"

It was a valid question. Landing in Eugene would have shortened our car trip to Bend.

"It's a vacation," I reminded her as Heide switched hand-holding partners, moving from me to her mother. "This will give us a chance to enjoy more of the scenery."

"Are you sure we can get there today? Maybe we should stay in Portland tonight. We could find a hotel near the airport."

"It's fine. We'll be settled in Bend in time for dinner, and we won't have to travel again tomorrow. I'm up for it. Let's just get there so your weekend can begin."

The final push to Bend took several hours, but I was determined to grow Allison's enthusiasm for Oregon by pointing out the many spectacular sights on the long drive from Portland.

I'd even rented a luxury SUV for extra comfort. Heide and I enjoyed every moment as we traveled from the city through the Willamette Valley. Eventually, we began to wind our way through forest and the volcanic landscape of the Cascade Range. Allison played along for our daughter's sake.

Late in the afternoon, we arrived in central Oregon and pulled into the parking lot of the Riverhouse. Kathleen had recommended the hotel via e-mail, and after looking at the website, I booked a suite for our stay. The Riverhouse was located right in town, and yet the Deschutes River ran through the center of the property. Following another suggestion from Kathleen, we flew to Oregon on a Wednesday, allowing me a full day of rest before my final interview began on Friday morning.

After settling in our room, I sent Kathleen a brief e-mail to let her know I was in town and to thank her for her guidance. As I drafted my message, my fingers hovered over the keyboard. I considered inviting her to join me and Allison for happy hour. I pondered the right choice of words, and when they didn't come, I decided it might be wiser for Kathleen to extend a personal invitation.

Within a few minutes of sending my greeting, Kathleen responded. Her message was polite, concise. She was glad we'd arrived, and she would see me on Friday. I closed my laptop and turned my attention back to Allison as she unpacked Heide's suitcase.

She was moving contentedly around the suite. Now that we were in Bend, she was beginning to relax. I opened my own suitcase and began to put away my things before Allison took care of it. I'd saved one last surprise for my wife by securing a room that included a Jacuzzi tub, and she was excited to try out the oversize bath.

"We've been on the go for hours. Do you want to order room service?" I offered. "You can take your bath."

She beamed and approached me for a quick kiss. "I'd love to.

What a treat! I don't remember the last time I had room service."

"That tub will take a while to fill. Why don't you start? Heide and I can finish unpacking."

Allison draped her arm around my waist, her fingertips brushing the top of my backside. Her spontaneous intimacy startled me.

"That does sound nice," she murmured.

"Go ahead. Take full advantage of my services." I winked, happy to share a playful exchange with my wife.

Dinner arrived while Allison was still in the tub. I helped Heide set out a blanket on the deck, so she could enjoy a spontaneous picnic. Next, I opened the bottle of wine I'd ordered and poured two glasses. I ventured to the master bedroom and sat on the edge of the tub. I handed Allison a glass and watched her as she sipped her pinot noir.

Her eyes drifted shut as she spoke. "I have to admit this is a great hotel, Jack. You're doing an excellent job of spoiling me."

I grinned, pleased that she was beginning to enjoy herself. "The river is great, isn't it? I want to slide the deck door open tonight so we can listen to it from bed."

"The trees are so big. I keep forgetting I'm in town and not in the middle of the forest."

The water swirled in the tub, obscuring a clear view of Allison's body, but her breasts were visible—glistening and pert. She had raised one leg up to rest of the edge of the tub. I set my wine glass down and grasped her foot with both hands. I began to massage her gently and she hummed her satisfaction.

"What are the plans for tomorrow?" she asked.

"Whatever we want. We can sleep in. We can stay here or go out. I'll leave it up to you."

Allison shook her head. "I won't be of any use there. You know way more about the area than me."

She'd all but admitted that her interest in Oregon was so minuscule she hadn't bothered to look for things to do over the long weekend.

This realization stung, but I pushed aside my disappointment and made a suggestion of my own. "There's a town called Sisters a few miles from here. It's built to look like something right out of the Old West. We could take Heide, have lunch and do a bit of shopping if you like."

"Sure." Allison's tone was mellow, but she sat up straighter in the tub. "That sounds like fun."

I rubbed her foot a few moments longer, before shifting my hand to her leg. I began caressing her calf with slow and sensual movements. We were both in good moods, and I sensed a genuine opportunity.

I cleared my throat. "With any luck, Heide will feel the jet lag soon. Maybe we can get to bed early tonight."

My gaze traveled up Allison's body until my lustful gaze met hers.

"It has been a while." She looked away, nervous.

I stayed silent. Patient. We hadn't made love in over two months, but I wasn't going to be the one to point that out. Her defenses were coming down, but I needed to tread lightly. Although we'd been married for years, sex between us had never been carefree. I always initiated the prospect with caution. It was dangerous to assume Allison would be open to the idea of having sex. There was never a guarantee.

"I don't want to make any promises. I don't want to tease you." The concern in her voice added to this rare display of vulnerability.

"And I don't want you to feel obligated," I reassured her.

"I know I've been withdrawn. I'll find my way back soon."

I patted Allison's knee, hoping to convince her that I understood her dilemma.

Allison's eyes darted to the doorway. "Should we check on Heide?"

We both rose, and I reached out to take my wife's arm. The

last thing I wanted was for her to slip and injure herself. She stood inches from me—naked, wet and dazzling—and I'd barely touched her skin in weeks.

"I want you," I said, not pausing to think. "I want to be inside you all night."

She swallowed and withdrew her arm from my grasp. "I want to give that to you, Jack. But please don't expect anything tonight."

"Why not?" I asked, more from bewilderment than hurt.

"We're sharing this suite with Heide. I won't be able to truly relax. Not with her sleeping so close by. It's not an ideal situation. Especially for what you want from me."

Disillusioned, I nodded. My wife had made up her mind. This was to be the direction the rest of our weekend would take. There would be no lovemaking for us in Oregon. I had crossed the line. I'd been too aggressive. Regardless, I couldn't allow Allison's lack of desire to ruin this trip. I needed her in good spirits to achieve success during my interview.

Later that night after Allison and Heide were both asleep, I took a shower. Fresh memories of Allison's bath consumed my thoughts. Soon, I was aroused and roughly satisfied myself. I experienced no embarrassment or shame. I was a married man who masturbated more than I made love with my wife. It was never ideal, but it was the nature of our relationship. For better or worse, I had committed myself to her. I held out hope that we would resolve our challenges.

After my shower, I was wide awake and threw myself into preparing for my final interview with Aurora Advertising. I sat in a wingback chair in a corner of the master bedroom and turned on my tablet. I put the polishing touches on my assignments and soon the device had my full attention. I decided to search for information about Robert and Kathleen on the internet. I wanted to learn more about the Brighton family.

There were many articles featuring Robert, both local and statewide. He was an innovative leader, a rogue, who'd moved a successful business away from Portland and grew it outside Oregon's major urban centers. There was also a marriage announcement that was nearly a decade old, but no wedding photo was attached. I made an important mental note that it was crucial not to mistake Robert's wife for Kathleen's mother.

When I searched for Kathleen, I found her LinkedIn account but no other form of social media. Her online presence was limited to work, and from all appearances, she was one of the most successful businesswomen in the region. Articles that featured her specifically were harder to come by, but I did read one that highlighted her work with the local hospital. She didn't appear to serve on the hospital's board, but her credentials qualified her to do so.

By the time I set the tablet aside and settled into bed for the night, I'd made up my mind. Heide's astute observation about my rediscovered state of happiness spurred me on. Aurora Advertising and the Brighton family impressed me, and I would accept nothing less than an offer from *this* firm.

I wanted to be in charge of my own destiny. I wanted to begin a new life in Oregon.

chapter Five

ON FRIDAY morning I returned to Aurora Advertising as scheduled. After chatting with Tracie for a few moments, she escorted me past a group of cubicles. We stopped outside the office of a completely bald man working at a stand-up industrial desk. He wore dark-rimmed glasses and was dressed in a gray dress shirt and a dark necktie.

He looked up and moved from behind his desk. "Hello, Mr. Evans. I'm Austin Vogel." He extended his arm toward me and we shook hands. "You'll be job shadowing with me today."

"Happy to meet you. Please, call me Jack."

"Thank you, Tracie," he said with a kind smile.

She took her cue and made her way back to the reception area.

"What's on the agenda today?" I asked.

"We'll be meeting with three clients before attending the reception tonight."

"What time is the first appointment?"

"We need to leave in twenty minutes. Did you have breakfast yet?"

"No. I decided it might be wise to hold off."

"Perfect. We have a breakfast meeting with a couple of folks from Emerald City Coach."

"They're based in Eugene. Right?"

Austin nodded in appreciation. "You've done your homework.

Good for you."

He provided me with a brief tour of the entire office. As we wandered through the agency, I kept my eyes open for Robert or Kathleen, but both were absent. When I made mention of this, Austin nodded.

"On a day like today? Robert is conducting his business on the golf course."

"And Kathleen?"

"She's overseeing the last-minute arrangements for this weekend. Robert prefers her hands-on approach, and she's excellent at planning."

Austin paused in the hallway and turned toward me. "Do you like sushi?"

"Yes."

Austin nodded and resumed his tour. "Kathleen reserved a private space for tonight at 5 Fusion. It's really good."

The day went by fast, and Austin was able to show me a great deal of Bend. By the end of the afternoon, I was getting my bearings and was more at ease with the city. When we met up with the rest of the staff and the other job candidates at 5 Fusion, I was more convinced than ever that I was on the verge of a great adventure. There was just something about Oregon, Bend in particular, that lifted the weight of the world off my shoulders.

Austin pointed to a dark-haired man standing across the room. "I need to check in with an associate about a project."

"Should I go with you?"

"No. Why don't you head over to the bar? Treat yourself to one of our local microbrews. I'll only be a couple of minutes."

"Sure. Thanks."

I ordered my drink, scanned the room, and tried to decide who to approach first. After a few moments, I recognized a familiar face. Without hesitation, I strolled over to her and when her twinkling green eyes met mine, she rewarded me with a friendly smile.

"Hello, Jack." Kathleen Brighton wore a white knee-length skirt and a white chiffon, long-sleeved, lace shirt. I was accustomed to the dark or neutral business clothes that most women wore at my office in Baltimore. Her choice of outfit was like everything else in Oregon—a breath of fresh air.

"Hello, Kathleen." I resisted leaning in to kiss her on each cheek because the gesture was not as common between mere acquaintances in the Pacific Northwest. I wanted to be professional, so I offered her my hand instead. Kathleen's hand was light and smooth within my grasp.

"It's wonderful to see you again," she said.

"You, too." I withdrew my hand to gesture around the room. "I'm told you're the one to thank for tonight's reception. This place is great."

She looked down and shrugged, almost hiding her grin. "I can't take much credit. All I did was reserve the room. The rest was up to the restaurant."

"Well, you have impeccable taste. I'm sure that applies to all areas of your life."

"I don't know about that, but it's kind of you to say so." She took a small sip of her San Pellegrino water. She was so composed, even her drink was a fashion accessory.

Kathleen glanced around the room. "Is your wife here?"

I shook my head. "She's back at the hotel. With our daughter."

"You've had a long day," she commented. "You must be ready to head back and join them for dinner."

I didn't want Kathleen to believe that I was looking for the first excuse to leave. The atmosphere was warm, and the alcohol was flowing, but this was still part of the interview process. People like Kathleen and I were always networking. I had no doubt my people skills were being evaluated.

"We had a relaxing day yesterday. I wasn't sure how late this would go, so they're going to eat without me tonight."

"I wouldn't hold it against you if you wanted to stop for the day. If you'd like I can help you sneak out."

I didn't know Kathleen well, and it was difficult to know if she was being genuine or baiting me. I opted for directness.

"As a finalist for the job, that can't be the wisest move. Thankfully, I'm with very pleasant company."

Kathleen paused, and her expression softened. She blinked once, her long eyelashes brushing the edge of her high cheekbones. "As I recall, you were looking forward to seeing the sights with your family. How are they enjoying Bend so far?"

"It seems to agree with them. We spent some time in Sisters yesterday, and they both like the Riverhouse. Thanks again for that suggestion."

"You're welcome. I used to go there for dinner sometimes during the summer."

"Did you sit out on the patio?"

"Yes. My mother used to take me there." Kathleen hesitated as if she had shared something without intending to. After a beat, she added, "I love to sit outside right next to the river. There are just enough rocks to make the water fascinating. You forget your troubles."

I took a sip of my beer as I weighed Kathleen's statement. "My wife keeps forgetting we're in the middle of town."

Kathleen's face lit up. "Exactly. It's an oasis."

"My daughter looks for any excuse to cross the covered bridge." I chuckled. "I think we've been back and forth about fifty times in the past two days."

Kathleen maintained her smile. "That's sweet. That must make her very happy. From now on, I'll think of the two of you whenever I see that bridge."

The buzz and bustle of the cocktail hour receded as our conversation progressed. The more I spoke with Kathleen, the more I enjoyed her company. During our first meeting, I'd been surprised by her intuition. This evening, I was surprised by both her modesty and her poise.

We both fell into a brief yet comfortable silence. I took another drink of my beer before picking up our discussion. "I don't know if I should mention this, but I almost invited you over to join us for happy hour last night. I chickened out at the last moment."

Kathleen appeared surprised by this. "I would have been tempted." She looked over my shoulder and leaned in. "But then I would've had to do the same thing with the other candidates. You know, to be fair."

We both laughed.

"Hello! Jack!" The booming, authoritative voice of Kathleen's father broke through our intimacy, and she pulled back.

I turned to Robert. "Hello, Mr. Brighton."

He shook my hand with strength and confidence. "Welcome back. How did things go with Austin today?"

"They went well. Thank you." I was eager to summarize my day, but I was also concerned that Robert hadn't acknowledged Kathleen's presence.

"I've seen the best of the city today, including this place." I gestured in the direction of Robert's daughter. "I was just complimenting Kathleen on her choice of venue."

"I've never understood the sushi craze," Robert remarked dismissively. "But since when does my opinion matter?" Robert tucked a hand inside a trouser pocket, adding a dramatic flourish to his question.

His remark confused me and rendered me speechless.

Kathleen's mouth twitched, and she looked nervously around the room. I'd suspected awkwardness between the two on my first visit to Oregon. Now my suspicions were confirmed.

"There are other menu options," Kathleen replied in a clipped tone. "There's plenty of variety to choose from."

Robert grumbled, "Let me know where I can find it."

Before she could respond, Austin reappeared. "I heard my name from across the room," he said to Robert, good-naturedly. "I had to make sure I wasn't in trouble."

Kathleen's reaction was quiet, but decisive. She stepped away from her father and moved to stand behind me. Robert paid no attention to this, shifting his focus toward Austin.

"Tell me what you think of Jack," he pressed Austin. "Is Bend ready for someone like him?"

Kathleen stepped out from behind me at my other side, her expression growing severe and dark. This was only the second time I'd been around Robert and his daughter, but each time his presence had rendered her silent.

"He was prepared for today," Austin replied, "even when I tried to throw a couple of surprises at him."

Kathleen's sudden mood shift did not disturb Robert, and so I tried my best to navigate the unfamiliar territory. Not wanting to offend anyone, I nodded and smiled at Austin.

"He's a great mentor," I told Robert. "After today, I feel right at home."

"Agreed," Robert smirked. "I keep telling him he should be the senior strategist."

At the mention of her current job title, Kathleen cleared her throat—angrily—drawing a sharp gaze from her father.

"I'm sorry, Kathleen. Do you have something to say?"

I exchanged a nervous look with Austin as we awaited her reply. Kathleen turned her head slightly in my direction.

"Not especially," she mumbled.

"I thought as much." Robert's voice was ice cold. Bitter.

Kathleen was now struggling to mask outright hostility. No one could deny the animosity between the two, but I pretended not to notice.

Kathleen detached from us. With a wordless retreat, she strolled over to another group of her colleagues. She never looked back. Attempting to move the conversation forward, I relayed my impressions of the businesses I'd visited during the afternoon. Once that was done, I offered my good wishes and wandered away with Austin, returning to the bar.

He nudged a full bottle of Inversion IPA in front of me. "Hey, I apologize for not paying better attention there," he began. "I saw far too late you'd been thrown into the lion's den."

I exhaled and did my best to shake off the encounter. "Don't worry about it. That's what this weekend is all about, isn't it? Making a good impression on the bosses?"

"Boss. Singular."

Austin's tone held such conviction that I couldn't let his statement go.

"What do you mean?"

"Don't get me wrong. Kathleen's opinion can carry weight, but you shouldn't spend a lot of your time trying to amaze her."

"Of course, her opinion counts," I said in a defensive tone. Austin's remark put me on edge. "She's going to be the owner sometime in the next decade."

Austin kept his expression neutral but moved forward. "There's one thing you need to understand. When it comes to Robert, nothing is set in stone. You can't assume she's next in line."

Since walking away from Robert, I'd been thinking a lot about Kathleen and Robert's dynamic. Now, I saw a chance to speak candidly about it.

"I've noticed some tension there, but she's spent her entire career at the firm. She's a senior manager. She can't fake her way through that."

"They have an odd relationship." He gestured between the two of us. "Newer people, like you and me, know nothing about their personal problems. The few who do know and are still in town, say nothing. Whatever happened in that family, it wasn't good. Whatever happened between those two took place a long time ago, and the specifics aren't common knowledge. At least not anymore."

Austin didn't balk at my observations, and I appreciated his honesty. But still, I wondered if I'd pushed for too much information too soon.

"It's none of my business."

Austin offered a final piece of advice. "Just in case you're offered the position, there's something you need to know. It's good for your career to be aware of that situation, but not so good for you to acknowledge it. It's best to let things lie between those two."

"Don't ask. Don't tell. Is that what you mean?"

Austin nodded.

He had made his point. I turned away from the bar and watched Kathleen again.

"She doesn't strike me as cold."

Austin angled his body so he could watch Kathleen. "You're right. She's not. She's just… self-sufficient."

I recalled how Kathleen had stepped behind me when Robert unleashed his criticism.

"It's like she's protecting herself against something," I stated, more to myself than to my colleague.

"I'm pretty sure it's a result of having Robert Brighton for a father. He's difficult enough to work for. I can't imagine what it's like to be his kid."

I grimaced at this. I knew a warning when I heard one.

If I was going to work for Robert Brighton, I had to be ready to meet demanding expectations.

chapter Six

I DON'T remember how long I stared at the dresser drawer that once held Kathleen's lingerie. But it was a while.

Eventually, I left my bedroom to join my ex-wife and our daughter for dinner. I went through the motions of the mealtime ritual, but my thoughts and concerns about Kathleen distracted me. I hadn't heard if she'd arrived in Denver and was aware of her absence.

Despite our strained relationship, it was comforting to know I could see her at the office. As painful as our growing separation was, I'd held out hope for us. Since returning to work, I'd planned to seize every opportunity to nurture our love and find a way back into her arms. But now that she had gone to Colorado, there was nothing to look forward to.

I left my untouched dinner on the plate. I offered Allison an expression of regret and packed up my uneaten food for lunch the following day. I helped with the dishes, and when there was nothing left to do, I stepped outside and took a seat on the swinging bench I'd once shared with Kathleen.

At the beginning of the summer, we'd sat in this spot together and talked about Allison. I remembered with heartache how Kathleen promised me she would never interfere with my family. She never wanted to cause trouble between Allison and me. As far as I was concerned, Kathleen had kept her promise. The reason I was sitting there alone was because I hadn't followed her example.

I leaned forward, placing my elbows on my knees and resting my face in my palms. I missed Kathleen. I'd missed her for weeks, but with her away from Bend, I no longer felt whole. I worried she was gone for good. I hadn't experienced fear like this since the day of Heide's accident. I hadn't grieved like this since my father died. I didn't know how to win Kathleen back, but I didn't want to live the rest of my life without her.

"Jack?" Allison's soft voice at the same moment she rested a light hand on my shoulder startled me. Consumed in my own emotions, I hadn't noticed her approach. I sat bolt upright and realized I was crying. It wasn't something I was prone to, and I brushed a hand over my eyes to remove the evidence.

Allison sat next to me, angling her body toward mine. When I dropped my hand back to my lap, she cradled it in her own. It was a touch, a fit, I remembered well. It wasn't the hand I was desperate to hold; nevertheless Allison's offer of comfort was welcome.

We sat still, adjusting to the moment. I couldn't make eye contact with her. Instead, I distracted myself by looking at the recognizable outline of the Big Dipper.

"What's the matter?" she finally asked.

I hesitated to answer.

"Please," she persisted. "Let me help. Don't shut me out anymore."

I blinked, thinking of my past actions and Kathleen's need to secure a peaceful future.

"It's Kathleen," I confessed while continuing to watch the stars. "I'll understand if she's the last person you want to talk about."

"Will things be all right between the two of you?"

"Why do you ask?"

"Last weekend was the first time I'd seen her since we were in Portland."

I looked at Allison. "Where did you see her?"

"Here. She drove you to the house. You were drunk, so I asked her to take you to her place until you sobered up."

"Oh? I don't remember that."

"You were passed out in her car, so that's not surprising." Allison's grip on my hand tightened just a bit.

I waited to hear what she would reveal next.

"She asked me why I left you."

"What did you tell her?"

"Nothing, because the question means one of two things. You either haven't told her why, or she doesn't trust the information you gave her. Knowing you the way I do, I'm certain it's both."

I thought long and hard about Allison's conclusion. If there was anyone capable of understanding both my mind and Kathleen's, it was my ex-wife. I looked at her and took the leap of faith.

"She thinks I want you back."

Allison leaned back as confusion flashed across her face. "Who gave her that idea?"

"Me."

Allison's eyes grew wide. "You?"

"I fucked-up."

Allison eyed me with caution. "I'm not here to stay, Jack."

"I know that," I assured her. "You belong in Maryland. And I belong here."

"With Kathleen?"

"I hope so, but nothing is certain right now."

Allison nodded. "I've been thinking about her a lot. Objectively. What she's done for Heide. For you. For me. I should have been more grateful. I fucked-up, too."

We looked at one another, and Allison's grin was returned with one of my own. The silent exchange was filled with acknowledgement and significance.

Allison swallowed. "I'd like to go to lunch with her. Try to make up for some of the things I've said and done. I'd like to help you fix this with her. Do you think she'd let me apologize?"

I smiled at her offer. The moment was bittersweet. "I know she would, but she's not here."

"Where is she?"

I sighed as a new wave of heartache crashed inside me. "Colorado. She's thinking of moving there."

"What? Why?" Allison's disbelief reflected my own.

"Because I fucked-up." I rose from the bench seat and began to pace around the fire pit. Allison watched me complete several laps.

"You know, I've only seen you cry one other time."

Her unexpected declaration calmed my restless spirit. I halted and smiled in her direction. "The day Heide was born."

Allison beamed with motherly pride. "You were a goner from the moment they placed her in your arms."

"Heide is the greatest gift I will ever receive. I told Kathleen once that raising her will be a legacy of our time together. I wasn't a good husband to you, and I am sorry for that. I hope I can make up for my mistakes by being a good father to Heide."

"You're an excellent father. You once talked about having another baby. Maybe someday Kathleen can give you another child."

My smile disappeared as I shook my head. "She can't have children, but that doesn't matter to me. I just hope she'll decide to stay here. Maybe she'll give me another chance."

"I used to wonder why I wasn't your soul mate."

"I'm sorry, Allison."

"We both made mistakes. We both thought we would reach a point where we couldn't live without one another, but we never had that. We were both naïve. I see how deeply you love her. Now, I know. I'm not your soul mate because she is."

I fell silent. I didn't know how to respond to her revelation.

Allison rose up from the bench and made her way to the back door. Just before she stepped into the kitchen, she paused. "Heide's doing so well, don't you think?"

"Yes." I swallowed numerous emotions in one large gulp. "It feels like a miracle."

Allison offered me a generous smile. "If you speak to Kathleen, let her know that Heide misses her. That she's been asking why Kathleen hasn't come over to visit. If it will help anything, let her know how much better Heide is. Tell her that I'm thinking about going back to Baltimore soon."

"Are you?"

She nodded. "It's odd. The idea of leaving her here should make me sad, but I'm not. I'm elated because Heide is alive and healing. We could have lost her."

"We almost did."

"But we didn't." Allison squared her shoulders. "The emergency is over now. We made certain agreements when we broke up, agreements about how we were going to raise Heide. Tell Kathleen it's almost time for us to go back to what we planned."

chapter Seven

DESPITE THE unexpected Brighton family near-argument at 5 Fusion, the rest of the weekend was free of any incidents between Robert and Kathleen.

It wasn't so much that the two had made amends as they simply limited their interactions and stuck to work-related discussions. It was as though the two had long ago agreed to disagree and were both doing their best to abide by a feeble truce.

By Monday, my job interview at Aurora Advertising was over. I woke up that morning with Allison and Heide. We packed our suitcases for the trip back to Maryland before we went to breakfast in the hotel dining room. We sat at a table by a window with a view of the outdoor patio. The sun was shining in a bright blue and cloudless sky. I wasn't surprised when Heide made her move.

"Can we eat our breakfast out there?" she asked our server, pointing toward the patio. "It's our last day here."

"Is it?"

Heide nodded.

"I wish I could let you eat out there, but I'm afraid the deck isn't ready yet."

"Is there something I can do to help make it ready?" Heide pressed.

I reached across the table and covered my daughter's hand

with my own. "Don't push, Heide. You've heard the answer."

"Listen to your father," Allison said.

"I can't let you sit outside to eat, but if your parents say it's all right, you can go out there after you finish your meal."

Heide perked up at once. "Really?" She glanced between her mother and me. "Can I, please?"

"I want you to eat a good breakfast," Allison replied. "We have a lot of traveling to do today and tomorrow, and I need you to eat and rest when I ask you to."

"I'll eat my whole breakfast, Mom!"

"If we say yes, you can't go out there and run crazy." Allison glanced at our server's name tag. "You don't want Sara to regret doing such a nice thing for you."

"I promise!" Heide began bouncing in her seat.

I grinned at my daughter's easy enthusiasm. "I think you owe Mom an extra hug today. And I know you owe Sara a big thank-you."

"Thank you, Sara," Heide chimed.

"You're welcome. Now, what are you having for breakfast?"

True to her word, Heide ate every bit of her scrambled eggs, fruit and whole wheat toast. After paying the bill and leaving Sara a generous tip, I escorted Heide out to the patio while Allison stayed at the table, finishing her second cup of coffee. As Heide explored the spacious deck, I approached the railing and quickly became fascinated by the churning waters of the Deschutes breaking around the rocks jutting just above the river's surface.

I stood there and stared at the reflective river nearby and began thinking about Kathleen Brighton. I wondered how things were going for her at the office and realized I'd never know the answer. Within a matter of minutes, I would leave Bend for Baltimore. By the following morning, we'd be halfway through our flight home and I didn't know if I'd ever come back to Oregon. The thought of never returning saddened me. I wanted to dine on this patio one summer night, preferably while Kathleen was present. I wanted to see her enjoy her oasis.

I was distracted and lost in my thoughts. When I registered that Allison was calling my name, I had to admit I wasn't paying attention to my wife. I was also guilty of losing track of Heide. One swift look around the deck confirmed she was safe from danger.

"Are you all right?" Allison asked.

I nodded toward the river. "Sorry. I was caught up watching the water."

Allison held up my phone. I'd insisted on bringing it along to breakfast and set it on the table, so I could watch for incoming calls. But I'd forgotten about it once I accessed the outdoor patio. I muttered my thanks and took it from Allison. One glance at the display showed that I'd managed to miss a call from the agency in that small window of time.

I made eye contact with Allison and showed her the displayed number.

"They're calling you?" She sounded surprised. "First thing on Monday morning?"

"Yeah."

"This is it, then."

I nodded and studied Allison. I couldn't get a read on her emotions, so I offered up a suggestion.

"If it's the offer, I can ask them for some time."

Allison shook her head. "You shouldn't do that. It could lose you the job."

"What should I say?"

Allison's response was swift and surprising. "If the job is meant for you, then we should make a go of it."

I was in awe. I was elated, but the job wasn't a certainty, so I moved the conversation forward with a bit of caution. I took a few moments to take in the scenery around us.

"This is a good place for Heide to grow up. It can be a wonderful place for us, too."

My wife folded her arms and her expression hardened. "If I make this commitment, I want something from you in exchange."

"Name it."

"I want us to go to marriage counseling. And I don't just mean a session or two. If I commit to this move, I need you to commit to our marriage. No more excuses. No more distractions."

I struggled to answer her. The right answer was the obvious one, but I also knew the nature of my job. It required me to be on call at a moment's notice, to work late nights, weekends, even holidays. In this case, I would be obliged to travel from time to time. I never thought of my work as an excuse or a distraction, and this had always been a fundamental difference in philosophy between Allison and me.

She heaved a sigh when my answer wasn't forthcoming. "Is it so much to ask?"

I blinked. "Of course not. I'll go to counseling with you."

"Then why the hesitation?"

"The work is going to be demanding at first. You have to know that."

"I do. But if you want us to uproot our lives, you need to invest in this family just as much as you invest in your new job."

"You're right."

Allison's face relaxed, even though I had yet to commit to her request.

"You should call back. Good luck."

"Thanks."

I placed the call, anxious to learn what the future had in store for us. I reached out for Allison's hand, but she missed the gesture and turned to join Heide, who was eager to run across the covered bridge one final time. I dropped my arm back to my side just as someone answered the call.

"Robert Brighton."

"Hello, Mr. Brighton. This is Jack Evans. I'm sorry I missed your call a few minutes ago."

"Good morning, Jack." The animation of his voice was reassuring. "How would you like to work for us at Aurora?"

I turned my attention back to the Deschutes River. "I'd like that very much."

"Glad to hear that. Are you still in town?"

"Yes. We fly out tomorrow, so we're planning to drive back to Portland this afternoon."

"I always prefer to negotiate in person. Are you in a rush to get on the road?"

"Not really. We just want to be in Portland early enough for our daughter to get a good night's rest."

"Why don't you swing by the office? We'll talk numbers."

"Sure. We just finished breakfast, so I can head over now if that works for you."

"Perfect. I'll let Tracie know to expect you."

"Thank you, Mr. Brighton."

"Damn straight." Robert ended the call with this unconventional line.

I was ecstatic. Moments ago, I'd been lamenting a missed opportunity. Now, I rushed to catch up with my wife and daughter, secure in the realization that summer nights in Bend would be a certainty.

When I returned to our suite, I smiled and nodded at Allison before grabbing the keys to our rental car.

"Is it time to go?" Heide asked, confused. "I'm not done packing yet."

"You still have lots of time to pack. I have to go to a quick meeting."

"You're still going to take me swimming at the new hotel, right?" Heide crossed her arms in a challenging manner.

"Oh, yes. I promise."

I turned to Allison. "This shouldn't take long. Robert wants me to come in and discuss the compensation package."

"All right." Her voice held a note of finality, but it didn't feel like an acceptance. "This is happening."

With Allison's condition for moving still fresh on my mind, this was an opportunity to show her I was thinking of her well-being. "I'll make sure Robert knows we can't do this in two weeks. I'll give us as much time as I can."

She ushered me to the door. "We'll talk details later. We need to figure out how to break this news to Heide before she guesses what's going on."

I was so happy, I couldn't help but wrap an arm around Allison's waist. I pulled her in for a kiss, and although I kept it chaste in the presence of Heide, my lips lingered on hers. When I pulled back, I continued to hold her close.

"You won't regret this."

Allison didn't respond even as turbulent emotions churned in her eyes, but I convinced myself it was only because Heide was nearby. We'd talk once we were back in Maryland, and then we'd begin planning for our new life in Oregon.

chapter Eight

"I STILL can't believe Jack is leaving us," Elyse Bradford admitted as she stood next to me at the company's farewell party. Her dark, short hair was perfectly sculpted and framed her face without obscuring it. "After all these years, he's the colleague I expected would always be here. He's rock solid, loyal, smart, creative and generous. We began working at GKV together a decade ago, and he's always been a good friend with a great mind and a kind heart."

Elyse paused to suppress her emotion. Her bright blue eyes welled up with unshed tears, surprising more than a few. It wasn't like her to wear her heart on her sleeve and the room went silent as she raised her glass of champagne for a toast. Our many coworkers followed her lead. Elyse glanced down for a second or two, regaining her composure.

When she lifted her head, she resumed her speech. "Jack is leaving Baltimore for a spectacular opportunity in Oregon, and I know he's going to excel in his new job." She turned to face me with a warm smile, which I did my best to reciprocate. "We hate to lose you, and while I'd never wish bad luck on anyone, know we'll welcome you back should you change your mind about living on that other coast. To Jack."

The small crowd repeated her toast and sipped the champagne.

Over the next hour, I consumed two more glasses of champagne and exchanged final well-wishes with many. When there was a lull, Elyse reappeared and leaned in close to my ear. I strained to hear her soft request over the raucous conversation of my soon-to-be former coworkers.

"Jack? Could we speak in my office for a few minutes?"

I pulled back to study Elyse's face and recognized the sadness in her expression. I'd been expecting and dreading the forthcoming conversation, knowing it was all but inevitable. I nodded and followed her as she walked to the stairwell.

Her spacious office was located one floor above. The corridors and cubicles upstairs were deserted and dark. A small prickling sensation ran down the back of my neck and shoulders, but I ignored it.

She entered her work space without closing her door, but I took the initiative to push it shut. I wanted to ensure our total privacy. It would be our last good chance to say a proper farewell. I leaned against the door, uncomfortable with striding too far into Elyse's territory. I placed my hands in my pockets and waited to see what would happen next.

"Hi," she began. Her tone registered strong emotion.

"Hi." In comparison, my tone was robotic.

Elyse absorbed my mood and turned to look out the window of her office. She crossed her arms over her chest, stared at the evening skyline and took a few moments to collect her thoughts. I waited, wanting to give her the time she needed.

"This isn't my fault, is it?" She swung around abruptly. "I would hate to think I'm driving you away from the company. Away from Baltimore."

"It's not your fault, Elyse."

She nodded. Her anxious sideways glance conveyed she didn't quite believe my statement.

"There's so much I want to say," she told me, "and I've run out of time to say it."

I didn't know what kind of response she was looking for, so I kept silent.

"Why are you doing this?" she demanded. "I need an explanation. Why such a drastic change?"

"That's complicated."

"Try me."

I resisted. "This isn't a good idea."

She tried once more. "Whatever is bothering you, I'd like to help."

"I don't need your help with this."

She locked eyes with me, her expression severe. Her anger barely contained. "I hate that you've stopped talking to me. I'm used to it, but I hate it."

"I'm sorry."

"Are you?" When I didn't answer her, she shook her head. "Why do you have to be so damn cold? I'm trying to be your friend." Frustrated, and fighting a losing battle to resist her emotions, she turned away from the window and strode behind her desk. "Fine. Fuck the friendship. Name your price. Tell me what you need to stay here, and I'll make it happen."

I winced at her harsh declaration but answered her. "This isn't about the money."

"Do you want my help putting you on the path to partnership?"

"No."

"What can I do, Jack?"

"There's nothing you can do. This is something I have to do."

"Why?" she implored.

I stayed quiet yet again.

"You're avoiding me for a reason," she concluded. "Is there something wrong in your marriage?"

I couldn't lie to her, not with our history, but I couldn't bring myself to talk about my marriage problems with her. I sighed, painted into the metaphorical corner.

"I see," she uttered with contempt. She came around her desk and closed the distance between us. She stood in front of me and, with her high heels on, met my gaze at eye level. For the first time since entering her office, I fidgeted. I hadn't said anything outright, but she understood much more than I wanted her to. Armed with the information she craved, she rediscovered her confidence.

"She isn't the right woman for you, Jack. She never was."

I began shaking my head as Elyse finished her statement.

"Maybe you loved her once," she continued, "but I don't think you do anymore."

"Stop." I raised my voice to gain control of the conversation. I had to cut her off before she could dig too deeply. I paused to give us both a chance to gather our thoughts.

She didn't wait long to provoke me again. "You shouldn't stay with her just because of the kid."

"The *kid* is my daughter," I hissed. "My daughter's name is Heide, and Allison is her mother. We are a family, and that's never going to change."

"Allison makes you miserable."

"That's your assumption."

"I know you, Jack, better than anyone else here. Don't think for a minute you can fool me."

I held up a hand. "Allison is my wife. That's all there is to it. What happens in my marriage is none of your business."

"I get it," she snapped. "I lost you to her. I'm not trying to lure you away. Can't you just acknowledge that I once meant something to you?"

My jaw twitched. "I'm Allison's husband and I need you to respect that."

She narrowed her eyes and jabbed me in the chest with a finger. "You punished me for being the responsible one. I'll never respect that."

A ferocious response flashed through my mind, but I held my resolve. Even if I didn't like what she was saying, she wasn't wrong.

She shut down and retreated to another corner of her office to a small leather sofa. I expected her dismissal, but she didn't offer one. Instead, she stared at me, turning the discussion over to me without another word.

I'd expected a confrontation of some kind before leaving for the Pacific Northwest, and she hadn't disappointed. Regardless, I softened my stance.

"I don't blame you for being upset with me, but I don't want this to be how we say goodbye." I tried my best to be conciliatory.

Elyse studied me.

Seizing the opportunity, I reiterated my point. "Of course, you mean something to me. I don't want to leave here with bad feelings between us." I waited while she considered my words.

Eventually, she nodded. "I don't want that either. Jesus. I won't ever see you again, will I?"

"I don't know. I won't make promises either way."

"Can I hug you?"

"Elyse..." Her name escaped my lips with a warning and she flinched.

I drew in a deep breath to release my impatience. "What else can I do to leave this room on good terms with you? There has to be something else."

"Stay," she whispered in a pained voice. "Don't quit the firm. Don't leave Maryland."

It was the most vulnerable moment between us in years, and despite my best intentions, it drew me in. Shattered my defenses. I took one step forward, followed by more. When I stood in front of her, I reached for her hand. Her fingers seized mine, her grasp familiar and strong. She leaned toward me, her mouth upturned toward my own, inviting my kiss, but not demanding it. We hovered in this frozen state for several agonizing and uncertain moments until she reached out with her free hand and grasped my belt. Before her hand could drift down, I raised my other hand and took hold of the back of her neck. I tightened my grip and she stilled in response, even as her eyes filled with desire.

"We've known each other for a long time," I began in a strict tone. "I don't fool you, and you don't fool me. I could reach up your skirt and rip your panties off right now, and you'd let me. I could toss you on that desk, up against the window or down on your couch. Probably all three. We could fuck for hours and you'd love every second of it."

She nodded.

"There was a time when I would have done just that, and you remember it well."

"I think you still want to," she panted. "You just won't admit it."

I allowed her words to sink in. "I can't. I have a daughter now, and she depends on me to be a good man. What kind of father would I be if I fucked you tonight? What example would I set for her?"

Elyse flashed me a wicked grin. "Your love for your daughter is undeniable. Your wife, on the other hand, I'm not so sure."

If there had been any uncertainty in my decision to leave Baltimore, Elyse's actions ended it for good. I couldn't leave the East Coast soon enough, and I didn't plan on ever returning to Baltimore.

I didn't want anything unresolved when I left Maryland, and so I briefly caressed Elyse's skin. She relaxed. I leaned in and brushed my lips across her forehead, before detaching from her.

"I have to go."

She stared at me in stunned disbelief as I turned and left her office.

chapter Nine

LESS THAN an hour after fleeing Elyse's office, I returned home from my last day of work at GKV. I was in an agitated state and planned to avoid Allison. Heide was asleep and, for once, I was thankful to come home so late.

Allison was busy in the kitchen, removing dishes from the cupboards and packing them away. I strode right by her without my usual greeting. My irritation must have been noticeable, because she stopped her work and followed me to our bedroom. She didn't say a word or try to halt my progress as I stripped out of my work clothes. I was relieved. Truth was, I couldn't wait to get them away from my body.

I acknowledged Allison with a glance before pulling my undershirt over my head.

"You're home earlier than I thought you'd be." Allison's voice conveyed her curiosity.

"Yeah," I mumbled, uncertain how many of the evening's details I should share with my wife.

"Did something happen?"

"No."

I was naked now and stomped toward the bathroom. I wanted to take a shower and forget the miserable encounter with Elyse. Allison followed and watched with a fair bit of skepticism.

"Jack?" Her voice was stern.

I yanked the shower door open but stayed on the bath mat. I stared straight ahead at the tiled wall, conflicted.

"What is it? What's the matter?" Allison pressed.

"I need sex," I answered bluntly, my eyes still trained on the inside of the shower. "Can you accommodate me tonight?"

Out of the corner of my eye, I saw her take a step back. I turned and saw just how much her face registered shock. She crossed her arms, and I knew my less than romantic overture offended her.

When she answered me, her voice was frigid. "I'm not interested in being your consolation prize."

My anger flared. "Please give me some fucking credit!"

She turned and left me to my own devices. I stepped into the shower, pulling the door closed behind me. I ducked my head under the steaming water and wrapped my hand around myself as I tried in vain to forget my unhappiness.

I went to bed right after my shower, overcome by the exhaustion of the day. I slept hard, and when I woke the next morning, Allison wasn't with me. Her side of the bed was made, leaving me to wonder if she'd slept elsewhere.

She was cooking breakfast and I was hungry, so I dressed in a white T-shirt and jeans and made my way to the kitchen. I took my seat at the table with more caution than usual, pondering how best to gauge her mood. She poured some coffee into my favorite cup and sat next to me as soon as she set the mug down on the table. She took my hand in both of hers, surprising me.

She spoke with delicate care. "I haven't seen you this upset in a long time. It worries me."

I squeezed her hand, hoping to offer reassurance. "I'm better this morning."

"Only a little bit."

I looked down at our hands just as Allison moved a finger over my wedding ring with tenderness.

"You never take this off," she remarked. "Not when you're working around the house. Or taking a shower."

I swallowed the lump of emotion that seized my throat. "That's true. I've worn it since the moment you placed it there."

Allison's smile held a mixture of fondness and heartache.

"Did Elyse try something with you?"

I blinked at Allison's directness and didn't respond right away.

"This is important," she added. "Don't hold back from me."

"I don't want to upset you," I said with sincere honesty.

She nodded and looked me in the eye. "I know you didn't fuck her. That's pretty obvious."

"I haven't fucked her in almost seven years."

Allison trembled, but only just a bit. "Did you want to?"

"Absolutely not."

"Are you having second thoughts about leaving here?"

"None."

"Okay," she said with determination. "I believe you."

"Thank you."

We both remained still, and I wondered if we were both waiting to see whose anger would flare up first. She was the one to break the silence.

"When we get to Oregon and start therapy, we're going to have to dredge up some ugly things."

I wanted to say I understood this, but I froze in place.

"It's the only way for us to move forward," she said. "You need to put the past behind you physically. I need to do so emotionally."

With this stark revelation from my wife, I nodded. "Elyse thought she had an opportunity. She tried to take advantage of it, but she has nothing I want. I walked away, and I'll never see her again."

Allison leaned forward and kissed me on the cheek. Then she released my hand and stood up from the table. She began to move away, and I wrapped my hand around her wrist to stop her. She looked at me with expectation.

I held her gaze. "You were right to say no to me last night. I acted like an asshole. I'm sorry."

"You came home when you could have chosen otherwise. Let's focus on that instead."

Allison pulled her arm from my hold, and I allowed my fingers to fall back down to my lap. She ran her fingers along my worried brow, a small, encouraging smile forming on her pretty face.

"We have a lot to get done before the movers arrive. Let's get to work."

"It's not too late," Allison murmured as she reached down to collect three bowls from the floor. "I could call Diana right now. I know she'd take the cat. She'd only be moving next door, and she could stay in the one place she knows."

I shook my head as I set our pet's transport crate on the floor. I kneeled to unzip the flap on the end. "No. She'd miss us."

"Heide and I, she'd get over by the end of the day. She'd wonder what happened to you, but she'd move on, eventually."

"We already bought her a plane ticket."

Allison chuckled. "Please don't remind me of that, Jack."

"I can't leave her behind," I admitted. "It's been almost ten years. We're her family."

"She's not young anymore. Aren't you worried about the stress of the trip? Flying cross-country on a noisy jet? Taking her to a new house?"

I shook my head with affectionate pride. "No. She's tough. You weren't there when I found her. She's a survivor. How many cats do you know swim around in Chesapeake Bay until a boat just happens by? She made sure I didn't drift by without noticing her. We've been together ever since. I won't leave her now."

"But Kitty Hawk on a six-hour flight, Jack? I'm not sure your relationship is that strong."

"Nonsense. The spirit of aviation is right there in her name. We'll be fine."

"I guess. I don't know why I'm worried about it. You're the one who gets to find out."

I smiled and wandered toward the closed door of the sunroom. It was the cat's favorite place to nap and the natural choice to keep her as the movers dismantled our Baltimore home.

It was time for me to leave for the airport and the cat was coming to Oregon with me. Allison and Heide would stay behind in Maryland for another four days. They were scheduled to arrive at our new home on the same afternoon as the moving van. After just two weeks on the market, our house was in escrow—much to my delight and some of Allison's chagrin.

Everything about the move to the Pacific Northwest had fallen into place, and I was positive it meant something good. Something right. During my salary negotiation, Robert Brighton had surprised me with a generous signing bonus. It was enough to help us put a down payment on a home in Bend with enough left over to lease a new car. I'd sold my aging sedan to one of the other neighborhood fathers, who was looking for a safe automobile for his college-bound daughter. It was August, and we would be able to settle in Oregon just in time for Heide to begin the new school year there.

Even Kitty Hawk was cooperative, running right to me when I entered the sunroom. She allowed me to lead her into the pet carrier, just as I'd trained her. I'd spent my last night in Maryland and was prepared and eager to leave for our new home in Bend.

It was all unfolding perfectly.

chapter Ten

"MOTHERFUCKER!" MY voice echoed off the walls of our empty home in Bend, and I looked down at Kitty Hawk just as her ears flattened back against her head.

"The movers are running behind," I said to the cat because there was no one else to talk to. "They won't be here for another day." I set my phone back down on the window sill.

I glanced around the living room in frustration, my gaze landing on the airbed situated on the floor in the middle of the vacant space. The mattress was large enough for Allison and me to use in the master suite. But I was going to have to get clever when it came to Heide.

I'd hoped to have her room put together by the time I picked her and Allison up from the airport later that afternoon. I wanted my daughter to be happy. She'd accepted the reality of our move but had occasional bouts of anxiety in the days leading up to our departure. Her comfort in our new home was vital, so I grabbed my car keys and went in search of a solution to this unexpected problem.

Several hours later, I finished pitching a small tent in Heide's room. I also unrolled a brand-new sleeping bag inside, hoping her first night in the new house would be a memorable adventure. I'd even bought a poster of the local mountains and displayed it on the wall across from the tent's opening. I wanted Heide to see it from her spot inside the tent.

Allison wasn't going to be happy when she heard the moving van was delayed, but she wasn't going to be surprised either. According to her, nothing had gone her way this summer.

With extra consideration and heightened nerves, I selected an outfit for my first day of work. The office was professional with an air of relaxation and informality that I wasn't used to. I didn't want to overdress, but I wanted to make a certain statement. I chose navy trousers, a white dress shirt and one of my newest silk neckties to add some color. I rounded out the outfit with cream-colored suspenders for another bit of contrast.

I was selecting a navy blazer from the closet when Allison approached me, still dressed in her pajamas. She smiled at me and I returned in kind.

"Very handsome this morning," she said, surprising me.

"Thank you." I glanced down at my necktie. "I'm wearing your anniversary gift for good luck."

She closed the distance between us and lifted her delicate fingers to smooth out the tie. I was desperate to flirt with my wife but held back, knowing it could send her into immediate retreat. Instead, I savored the closeness of her body to mine and waited as patiently as possible. She lifted her eyes and looked at me with warmth. My smile widened and I brought my hand up to caress her cheek.

Allison swallowed and parted her lips to speak, but the words weren't forthcoming.

"What is it?" I asked her.

"I'm anxious to begin counseling..." Her words drifted off again.

My forehead furrowed. I didn't know what words I expected to hear, but these weren't it. "I know."

"I don't want to pick someone at random from a website. I want someone with a solid reputation."

I didn't like the direction her words were leading. My body tensed along with my voice. "What are you asking me?"

"We need a referral."

I dropped my hand away from her face and took a significant step back, my incredulity and anger on the rise.

"You want me to ask around the office for a therapist? On my first day? What the hell kind of impression would that make?"

Allison leveled me with an icy glare. "I don't know, Jack. One that says you care about your family more than your job?"

I pointed an angry finger at her. "That is not fair!"

"Don't tell me what is and isn't fair. We made a deal, and I've held up my end of it! It's your turn now."

"I will take care of it, but don't put demands on me. Don't tell me to march into work on my first day and inform everyone that my wife thinks I'm the world's shittiest husband."

"That's not what I said, Jack."

I threw on my blazer with a sense of defiance and marched back to her. She held her ground as I held up one finger in front of her face.

"Just once, Allison,"—I shook my finger for emphasis—"I would appreciate it if you'd put some fucking faith in me!"

"Are you kidding me right now? That's all I've ever done! And what do I have to show for it after all these years?"

I stepped around her, ready to put some distance between us. Just before I walked through the bedroom door, I turned to address her one last time with exasperation and ire.

"I'm tired of your complaints. I work a good job. You and Heide are well taken care of. I'm home every night and all I want in return is for my wife to love me once in a while. So why don't I just make this simple? I call your bluff. If you're so fucking miserable with me, then figure out something else. If your life with me is so terrible, then change it!"

Allison was silent. I was satisfied. And so, I left for work without a backward glance.

I was preoccupied with arranging my new office. Although I'd never admit it to anyone, I couldn't work with clutter surrounding me, physical or otherwise.

I would receive a few days grace period while I settled into the routine at Aurora Advertising, but I wanted to put my best effort forward and that wasn't going to happen until my personal workspace was comfortable. I was absorbed with sorting an abandoned box of files when a light knock landed on my open door. I held up a finger while I kept my eyes focused on the document I was reading. Once I was content with my findings, I glanced up.

Kathleen Brighton was standing in my doorway, a polite grin on her face. As always, she was dressed stylishly and the random thought that she was wearing another skirt drifted through my consciousness. I had yet to see her pleasing legs fully covered.

"Good morning, Jack. Welcome to the firm."

"Hello, Kathleen. Thank you. Sorry if I kept you waiting."

She shook her head, her mild amusement holding firm. She gestured at the surroundings. "I hope your office is to your liking."

"It's great. Much nicer than my last one."

"Good. I like to hear that. I wanted to make sure you knew about our staff meeting. We hold a briefing every Monday morning."

"Yes. I got that e-mail. I was just organizing some stuff while I had a few minutes."

"Since it's your first day, I thought I'd walk with you, if that's all right?"

I offered my friendliest smile. "Thank you. Yes."

As we weaved our way through the office toward the break

room, Kathleen spoke again.

"You should know, Robert asked me to introduce you during the meeting. I don't know about you, but I hate when I'm blindsided by things like that."

I recalled Kathleen's tendencies toward bashfulness. At one time, I had battled those same predispositions, but my time in college had changed that.

"I figured there would be something. I'm prepared."

She kept looking ahead as she asked her next question. "Is there anything you'd like me to mention? Or not mention?"

"No. I can't think of anything," I said. Then impulsively, I muttered, "There's not much to me."

We arrived at the break room door just in time for Kathleen to respond to my last statement. She flashed me a brilliant smile as her eyes met mine. "I disagree."

Tracie pulled Kathleen away with a question about a pressing deadline. By the looks of things, Kathleen and I were the last ones to arrive for the staff meeting. Some faces I recognized from my earlier visit, but most were new to me. All the seats in the room were occupied so I wandered to the side and leaned against the wall.

Kathleen and Tracie walked side by side to the front of the room, their heads close together as they engaged in muted conversation. Kathleen laughed and placed her hand briefly on Tracie's upper arm in affection. When Tracie broke away and Kathleen turned to face everyone, the room silenced.

"Good morning," she began.

Those gathered in the room, including me, returned her greeting.

"As you can see, Robert is away today. He's over in Boise to see about expanding his empire to Idaho."

Many in the room chuckled.

"Before we begin with project updates, we have a new employee joining us today." Kathleen extended her arm in my direction and I was surprised that she knew where to find me. As people turned their heads in my direction, I slid my hands into my pants pockets, attempting to appear relaxed and casual.

As everyone scrutinized me, I watched Kathleen and waited for her introduction. She hesitated and avoided meeting my gaze. Instead, her green eyes shifted to my torso, and I froze when I realized her stare didn't repulse me, as Elyse's often did.

Without thinking, I pulled my hands from my pockets and rested them on my hips. Kathleen's gaze drifted across my body and came to rest on my left side. She blinked twice and then looked away as her cheeks took on a rosier hue. I glanced down and realized why.

Against the dark material of my trousers, my gold wedding band was on full display, shining brightly under the overhead lights. Remembering my argument with Allison earlier that morning, I made a mental note to focus my efforts on finding a marriage counselor.

I looked back up as soon as Kathleen resumed the meeting. "Jack Evans is our new media director. He's just moved to Bend from Baltimore, so be gentle with him. This is bound to be an interesting transition."

More chuckles filled the room, including my own.

"We are incredibly lucky to have Jack join the team. He comes to us after having worked for one of the leading advertising firms on the East Coast and, make no mistake, his arrival signals how far Aurora has evolved. To be able to secure someone of Jack's experience and caliber from across the country is an amazing achievement for us."

My own cheeks began to warm as the room broke into spontaneous applause. Kathleen grinned and joined the rest of the group in clapping. She nodded in my direction, cueing that it was my turn to speak. Once the greeting died down, I straightened up from the wall.

"Thank you for the warm welcome. And thank you, Kathleen,

for those kind words. What can I say? My family and I are thrilled to be here. We are new to the Pacific Northwest, so we have a lot to learn, but everything we've seen here so far is beautiful, and we're excited to begin this new adventure. There's just something special about this place. I haven't exactly put my finger on what it is yet, but I know the journey is going to be incredible. Please know that my door is always open, and if you have any thoughts about how Aurora can best connect with the audiences of our clients, I welcome those discussions."

I nodded toward Kathleen in deference, and she smiled at me one last time. As the meeting progressed, I did my best to follow as many details as possible, but my thoughts kept wandering to Allison and our troubles. I wanted to chalk up our latest argument to the stress of the move and the new job, but the truth was we were fighting more than we were getting along. We weren't communicating, and we weren't having sex. Days without intimate contact had evolved into weeks, and weeks had now developed into months. Our marriage was in real trouble, and like it or not, I only had one alternative to try and save our relationship.

Given the choice between approaching Robert or Kathleen for some personal help, no debate was necessary. I regarded her again as the staff meeting ended. My decision made, I waited until the buzz of the exodus was in full swing before cutting a path toward her.

"Great job," she greeted me.

I nodded, intent on my goal. "Do you have a couple of minutes to talk? I'd like to ask you about something."

Kathleen's expression was curious, but also decided. "Sure. Why don't I meet you in your office in a couple of minutes?"

"Perfect."

I turned and began the walk back. I did my best to appear at ease whenever someone greeted me, but thoughts of what was happening outside of work dominated my thoughts. Thankfully, Kathleen didn't keep me waiting long and even closed the door without my prompting her to do so.

"What can I do for you, Jack?" she asked as she took a seat in front of my desk. She leaned back and crossed one leg over the other in a move that was polished by years of practice.

I scratched my chin. "I wondered if Aurora has any medical professionals as clients. I read a little bit online about your work with the hospital here. Is St. Charles a client, by chance?"

"Yes. We do work for St. Charles."

"Is the Bend hospital independent or part of a larger chain?"

"St. Charles is its own health system. There are four hospitals under their umbrella."

"Are they all located in central Oregon?"

"Yes."

"They must be a significant employer for the region, then."

"The biggest, actually."

"Do you think you could help me arrange a meeting? Perhaps a lunch and a tour? It would be a good idea for me to become familiar with their operations."

"Are you looking to establish local medical care for your family?"

Once again she surprised me with her quick and direct assessment. She may not have figured it out, but she was certainly going down the right path. "Yes."

"Just primary care? Or do you need something more specific?"

I hesitated. "Primary care is fine. I also need to find a pediatrician for my daughter."

"How is Heide doing? This has to be a tremendous change for her."

Once again, I was astounded. Kathleen remembered my daughter's name. Thinking about Heide brought me a much-needed moment of lightness.

"It was a little hard for her to leave Maryland, although she likes it out here. She starts school next week. Once she meets a few kids, she'll settle right in. She's always been able to adapt. Better than me, anyhow."

"You're all going to do just fine."

I'd thought so too before leaving Baltimore, but I was having my doubts. "Thanks."

Kathleen rose from her seat, ready to put her words into action. "I'll get that tour arranged for you. I'll send out an e-mail and introduce you to some people at the hospital."

"I appreciate anything you can do for me."

"Happy to help." Kathleen opened the door and waved on her way out into the corridor.

It seemed like a perfect solution. Tour the hospital, visit the various physicians there and pick up a few business cards along the way, including some therapists. I could bring some cards home and pass them along to Allison. Then she could do the research and make her own choice.

Problem solved.

chapter Eleven

WHEN I returned home from work, I discovered moving boxes strewn around the living room. I paused as soon as I closed the door and took a long look around. Many of our household items were scattered and piled among the carnage of cardboard. It was as though everything had been unpacked hurriedly and then abandoned. The house was far too quiet for my comfort.

I moved toward the bedroom with a fair bit of caution and confusion. The door was closed, so I glanced toward Heide's room. Her door was wide open, and I could sense her presence inside. I couldn't see her, and I couldn't hear her, but I knew she was there. And something felt off.

Heide's bed had been set up, but the tent remained. She'd been having fun camping in her new room, and I hadn't had the heart to take it down. The flaps of Heide's tent were zipped shut, and my worry increased when I heard a distinct sniffle from inside. I set my messenger bag down on the floor and knelt at the tent's entrance. I didn't want to frighten her, but I couldn't knock on the nylon material either. I took extra care in speaking with a gentle tone.

"Sweetheart?" I reached for the fastener, but hesitated. "Can I come in?"

"Okay."

I unzipped the tent carefully, not wanting to alarm her in any way. I moved into the space and settled myself on the floor. When I did, I studied Heide. She was sitting in the back corner of her tent, holding a doll. Her intense focus was on fixing the toy's hair. She wouldn't look at her father and this bothered me.

"Where's Mom?"

"In your room. She's been in there all day."

"Yeah?"

"She doesn't feel good."

"Headache?"

Heide nodded. She finally looked at me and I registered the longing on her face.

I held out my arms to my daughter. "Come here."

Heide dropped her doll and scrambled over to my lap. She burrowed up against my chest and wrapped her arms around me.

"Are you all right?" I asked as I began to stroke her hair. There was no more important question to me than this one.

"I'm sorry, Dad."

"For what?"

"I wanted to help Mom. I wanted to surprise her. I took everything out of the boxes but then I didn't know what to do with the stuff and now there's a big mess. I made things worse. I didn't mean to make them worse."

I squeezed her. "You know what? Moving is hard work. There's always a big mess when you take your things from one house and put them into another. The big mess is part of the process. Please don't worry about it."

"I know what the things are, but I don't know where anything goes here."

I pulled back so Heide could see my smile. "That's because we haven't decided yet. Do you want to help me with it?"

Heide nodded.

"Good. First, I'm going to check on Mom. Then I'm going to change clothes and get us some dinner. After we eat, you and I will go through everything you unpacked and find a place for it. I'll tell

Mom to keep resting, and then we can surprise her when everything is put away and looking nice. How does that sound?"

"Good."

"Mom is going to be so amazed at all the help you gave her today. I promise."

"Okay."

"We might have to stay up a little late tonight, but I'm ready to work on it if you are."

"I'm ready."

With the matter settled, I tapped Heide on the back and she pulled away from me. I made my way back out of the tent and grabbed my bag.

"Let me spend a few minutes with Mom. All right?"

Heide nodded and smiled. I was relieved to see her happy once more. If only it was that simple with Allison. Why wasn't it?

I left Heide in her room and opened the door to my bedroom. The room was dark, the blinds were drawn shut and the lights were off. Allison was in bed, asleep. I approached her quietly. Her breathing was deep and even, and she had an eye mask over her eyes.

I glanced at Allison's bedside table and saw the things she used when she fought a migraine—a glass of water, medicine and a discarded cold compress. She was wearing the same pajamas she'd had on during our argument that morning, but there was a bath towel lying on the floor beside the bed. The matted nature of her hair confirmed she had taken a hot shower prior to her nap.

Allison's migraines had always been stress induced, and they'd reached epidemic levels during the past six months. I'd even taken her to the emergency room twice when her pain became too excruciating. I hated that I was a contributing factor to her suffering. Neither one of us seemed capable of fixing things. One would try while the other inevitably resisted. It had always been this way between us, but this was different.

The division between us now was as wide as it had ever been, and I was clueless how to find a way back to Allison. I suspected she didn't want me to bridge the gap. If it was just the two of us, our relationship would have ended a long time ago, perhaps even before we married. Heide had kept us together and kept us trying to find ways to live and love one another, but I was fearful that even our devotion to our daughter's well-being wasn't enough. The domino effect was well underway.

Allison was sleeping, and I understood that the best prescription for her migraines was rest. So, I moved through our bedroom in silence, selecting some clothes I would be comfortable in for a long evening of housework. I stepped into the bathroom and changed. Then I left Allison to her sleep.

We would talk later, once she recovered from her migraine and was able to give me her full attention. My focus shifted back to Heide, who had returned to the living room and was busy placing the empty boxes along the wall.

"That's a great idea," I told her. "I'll get started on dinner while you finish putting the boxes together. After we eat, we'll flatten the boxes and put them in the car for the recycling center."

"Then we'll have more room to work," she chirped.

"Exactly."

I went in search for the ingredients needed for chicken stir-fry. Having taught the recipe to Allison myself, I knew it well. If Allison woke up, I would make sure to have a plate ready for her, too, although it would take a couple of days for her full appetite to return.

My mother had always been a forward-thinking woman and insisted her children learn how to cook for themselves. As a teenager, I'd been embarrassed by the amount of time I'd spent with her in the kitchen, but now I was grateful. Cooking was relaxing and a good, creative outlet for me. I'd come up with some of my best ideas while prepping a meal. Allison had taken over the duty in our marriage, and in this moment, I realized it was something I'd missed doing.

Unfortunately, there wasn't much food in the house yet, so I grabbed my phone and ordered a pizza. Allison's headache must have thwarted her plans to go grocery shopping. Perhaps I would talk to her about splitting the meal preparations during the week. Maybe that would lower her stress levels.

chapter Twelve

AFTER A solid night's rest, Allison recovered from her migraine. I followed her down the hall and studied her cautious movements as she made her way toward the living room. She froze behind the sofa and took a slow look around. The area was clear of boxes and the unpacked items had been arranged in their proper places. True happiness lit Allison's face for the first time since she'd arrived from Maryland.

"You must have been up all night," she said with a hint of admiration. "Did you sleep?"

"Heide helped me, so it didn't take as long as you might think." I edged past Allison, pausing to kiss her forehead on my way to the kitchen. "Follow me. Let me make you some breakfast."

Allison complied and took a seat at the breakfast bar. She squinted as her eyes adjusted to the brightness of the morning sunshine filtering through the bay window.

"Just some toast, please," she said. "I'm not ready for anything else right now."

I kept my voice quiet on purpose. "How about some hot tea?"

She nodded, taking care not to move her head too much. After filling the tea kettle and setting it on the stove, I approached Allison and massaged her scalp. She didn't resist me. She even leaned into my touch and closed her eyes in relaxation.

"I'm sorry I can't stay home with you today," I told her. "If this wasn't my second day…"

"It's all right, Jack. I promise to take it easy."

"I could take Heide to work with me. That way you can rest more."

"I appreciate it, but she'll be fine here."

"I'm sorry we fought yesterday." My apology to Allison was long overdue and woefully inadequate, but I didn't want to cause her further distress by pushing.

"Me, too."

"Are you able to look at me for a moment?" I asked.

She took her time opening her eyes, but once she focused on me, her gaze was full of curiosity.

I kept massaging her scalp as I spoke. "I made a promise to you when you agreed to let me take the job here, and I can see how much we need to go to marriage counseling. We don't have to go into everything now, but I don't want you to worry about this anymore. I'm working on finding us a therapist. I just need a few more days for everything to fall into place. Can you give me a week or so?"

Allison nodded and smiled, concentrating on my massage. I sidelined the conversation and kept stroking her hairline until her light breakfast was ready. I washed my hands and then prepared her toast and tea. I left her to eat so I could finish dressing for work.

That afternoon, I made good on my plans to tour the hospital. Thanks to Kathleen's connections, I was able to meet with healthcare professionals and methodically collected business cards along the way. After dinner, I took the stack of cards and placed them into Allison's palm.

"I want you to research these doctors and make the choice you're most comfortable with," I said. "I'm fine speaking with any of them."

"Should I make the appointment?" she asked me.

"Yes. Let me know when it is, and I'll set aside the time for it."

"Thank you, Jack."

Allison went ahead with her research and made a choice, but as new patients, we had to wait three weeks for our first appointment. This aggravated her, but she occupied herself by focusing her energy and attention on putting the rest of our new house in order. Within days, Heide began school and her first season of soccer. We settled into something of a normal routine.

One afternoon, Robert called me to his office. When I entered the room, he beckoned me to sit down. He was never one to beat around the bush and this encounter was no exception. As soon as I settled in my chair, he got right to the point.

"We're hosting a formal welcome reception for you. I told Kathleen to make the arrangements. She's set up an after-hours event here with the chamber of commerce. She's also contacted the local media to cover it, so you can expect to be interviewed. Your wife should attend, too."

Bend wasn't a small town, but the community was close-knit and seizing opportunities to be welcomed into the circle was vital to my success at Aurora. "That shouldn't be a problem. What is the date?"

Robert glanced at a piece of paper resting on the surface of his executive desk. "Next Wednesday."

I hesitated. Allison had set our first therapy appointment for that same evening. "What time?" I asked.

"Five thirty. It should only take a couple of hours."

I gave my temple a quick scratch. "All right. Sure. We'll both be there."

"Excellent. That's all I needed, Jack. Thanks for popping in."

I went back to my office and closed the door for a few

moments of privacy. I picked up my cell phone and called Allison right away. This was a conversation I preferred to have sooner rather than later. And one I favored to have over the phone.

"Hi," she greeted me happily. "What's up?"

"We need to talk about something. Do you have a minute or two?"

"Yeah. Sure. Go ahead."

I told Allison about the welcome reception. As expected, my news was less than welcome.

"Did you explain that you can't do anything that evening?"

"No, Allison."

"Jack..."

"The whole thing has been arranged. People have been invited and the local news is going to cover it. It's beyond my control. From the sound of things, we were the last ones to find out about it. I'm sorry."

"Damn it. Fine. I'll call the doctor's office and change the appointment."

"Take whatever you can get. I'll make it work. I promise."

"All right. I'll call now and get back to you."

"Thank you for understanding."

"I understand. I'm not happy about it, but I understand."

"Thanks again."

I ended the call before the moment disintegrated for either of us. After I finished my day's work and drove home, Allison greeted me with two items of good news. Not only had she rescheduled our appointment for earlier in the day, she had also reached out to the mother of one of Heide's new friends. The two girls were going to have a sleepover on the night of the reception.

With this welcome surprise, I was hopeful that Allison was ready to resume our physical relationship. I looked forward to both the reception and the rest of the evening.

Things were picking up for me at work. Not only had I inherited a strong client base, Robert had tasked me with acquiring some long-sought-after prospects. Several days later, things took another surprising turn.

"Jack?" Kathleen called from her office just as I strolled by her open door.

I smiled, happy to have the opportunity to thank her for her work on the reception. "Hello, Kathleen."

"I just got off the phone with Kevin at the helicopter flight school. He heard about the party tonight. I invited him to join us and offered to introduce you. But he'd rather talk business now. He's opened some time this afternoon. I'd be happy to go with you."

"That's fantastic. When should we leave?"

"Is thirty minutes enough prep time? I hate to rush you. I can make a few calls and then we can leave."

"That's perfect. I'll drive. Just come back to my office when you're ready."

The meeting at the flight school was my first opportunity to watch Kathleen in her true element. As I stood by her side and watched her charm Kevin, I was impressed with her ability to interact with him without acting phony. She had lived in Bend for most of her life, and she knew the place and its residents very well. Kathleen's local knowledge complemented my industry acumen. Together, we secured the firm's newest client over pleasant conversation, a bit of creative brainstorming, and a tour of the school's fleet of helicopters.

As we made our way back to the office, it became clear to me that Kathleen's suggestion to attend the meeting was a smart move on her part. I was the stranger from the East Coast and Kathleen's inclusion and endorsement of me in front of any would-be client made for an exceptional seal of approval. She'd taken hold of an organic social opportunity and made the meeting happen. I owed her for this successful acquisition.

"I feel like celebrating," I told her spontaneously. "Are you in a rush to get back?"

She acted surprised but smiled. "I have some time."

Without putting too much thought into it, I drove us to the Riverhouse. When Kathleen realized where we were headed, she turned to me. "I haven't been here in so long."

"The good weather will disappear soon. It's such a nice day. I thought we could sit outside next to the river."

Kathleen looked away from me and gazed at the entrance to the lounge. She grew quiet but only for a few moments before nodding. "All right. Let's do it."

chapter

Thirteen

IT WAS *Monday morning. The weekly Aurora staff meeting was underway with Robert leading the usual charge. And Kathleen was nowhere in sight.*

I couldn't pay attention to a word Robert was saying as he updated everyone on the latest company developments, and I couldn't wait until the meeting was over before pulling my phone from my pocket.

After keeping my distance from Kathleen over the weekend, I couldn't take one more minute without saying something. I texted her, anticipating that her plane had landed in Portland the previous evening. Maybe she'd decided to sleep in this morning.

"How was your flight home?"

Kathleen texted me back in short order, but not in the way I expected her to.

"Sorry. I can't talk right now. I'll text you when I'm free."

"Are you in your office?"

"No."

"Is everything all right?"

"I'm fine."

Confused, I was now intent on seeing her. I texted her again, this time more insistent.

"I'm coming over to your place after the staff meeting."

Her reply was immediate and infuriating. "We can't see each other today."

"Why not? Where are you?"

Her next text took longer to arrive. After excruciating minutes, she answered back with just one word. "Safe."

"Fuck this," I hissed at my phone and then remembered where I was. Robert was still addressing the crowd but shot a brief glare in my direction. I shoved my phone in my suit jacket and concentrated on Robert's concluding remarks. I stayed stock-still as my coworkers avoided eye contact and filtered back to their work stations. Once the room cleared out, I wasn't surprised when Robert approached me. He stood in front of me and waited for me to speak.

"I apologize for my rudeness."

Robert's intense scrutiny soon had me averting eye contact.

He took a deep breath. "Let's go talk in my office." He walked away.

Not knowing what else to do or say, I followed. I focused on the short walk and entered Robert's office. He circled his desk and sat down as I closed the door behind us.

"Jack." His tone was somber, and authoritative. The impending conversation wasn't going to be between an employee and his boss. I needed to speak with Kathleen's father, and Robert knew it.

"What's happening with Kathleen?"

Robert gestured to an empty chair in front of his desk. "Sit down."

He was cautious, and even though I was determined to get answers about his daughter's whereabouts, I allowed Robert to set the standard for our discussion. He set his hands on the desk and drummed his thumbs on the surface as he contemplated his words. It was a rare display of subdued deliberation, and the gesture provided me with an unsettling insight.

Robert held my unyielding gaze and said, "When I opened your position here, I had one goal in mind—to alleviate Kathleen's stress. Things between her and me were spiraling out of control and I was helpless to stop it. Kathleen wasn't listening to me, and she sure as hell wasn't going to take advice from me. I was grasping at straws, hoping I could at least slow down her implosion. I expected your presence to ease things for my daughter, not complicate them."

My response to this revelation wasn't immediate. I processed Robert's words for several agonizing moments. "When I applied for this job, I was grasping at straws, too. I accepted your offer because I wanted to save my marriage. It wasn't my intention to move to Oregon and lose Allison. It wasn't my intention to move out here and fall in love with Kathleen either."

"Have you gone back to your wife?" Robert asked without mercy.

I shook my head. "It was never my intention to hurt your daughter, and it sure as hell isn't my intention to lose her. Not now. Not ever."

If Robert took any solace from my answer, he kept it hidden. The severity of his mood remained intact. "I haven't always been the father she needed, but that has changed now. While I still have a chance to make things right between us, I will do just that."

"I understand."

"Do you?"

I shifted in my chair and rubbed the back of my neck. I searched for a way to connect with Robert on a personal level and took a risk.

"Kathleen told me about her mother's death." I tried my best to strike a gentle tone.

Finally, there was a shift in Robert's demeanor. He absorbed my statement with widening eyes, leaning back in his chair as if to place some level of emotional distance between us. "She told you what happened?"

"Yes."

Robert appeared skeptical. "*Did Kathleen tell you what she saw that night?*"

"*She told me everything.*"

Robert froze. The lone sound in the office for the better part of a minute was his uneven breathing. I could only imagine what the weight of my revelation was doing to him. When he eventually responded, he couldn't look me in the eye.

"*She's never told anyone, Jack. In all these years, she's refused to talk about what she went through. I still don't know what happened between her and her mother... beforehand.*"

The significance of this moment was vital. I sat there, imagining how terrible it would be for Heide to withhold anything from me, let alone the most traumatic experience of her life.

"*I'm sorry about that,*" I said. "*It has to weigh on you, but please understand. I'm not going to betray Kathleen's confidence.*"

"*Nor would I ask you to,*" he said, his voice brimming with emotion. "*But this changes things. Give me a minute.*"

Robert rose from his chair, turned his back to me, and wandered over to the large window behind his desk. He didn't take in the view. Instead, he looked down at the floor and placed his hands in his pockets.

"*We'd been unhappy for years,*" he began. "*Her mother and me. I sought out an affair and then used it as the excuse to leave her. It was chickenshit. But then, so was I.*"

Realizing how difficult it had been for Kathleen to share her family's story with me, I expected the same was true of her father. I drifted into an uncertain silence as another one of the Brighton family secrets was exposed.

"*Kathleen doesn't know about the affair,*" Robert added as an afterthought.

"*Are you sure about that?*"

Robert turned and pierced me with a significant look. "*Why do you ask? Did she tell you otherwise?*"

"No. She's never mentioned one, but are you sure she doesn't know?"

"Besides me and the other woman, Kathleen's mother was the only person who ever knew. It was never serious, and it wasn't going to last. It ended right after the suicide."

"I see." I paused, haunted by the family tragedy a father and daughter had endured in isolated despair.

Robert and Kathleen had each extended a level of trust to me that was undeserving. Just as these two were finding common ground, my own inability to cope with disaster was driving them apart again. If I couldn't save my relationship with Kathleen, I could at least help bring her home.

"What would've happened if Kathleen found out?"

"Found out about the affair?"

I nodded. I wasn't ready to hear the answer, but I needed to know it.

Robert shook his head and turned his gaze toward the window. "I don't like to entertain hypotheticals, Jack. It's a waste of time."

"She was supposed to be at work today. Have you heard from her?"

"She's been in touch."

"I told her I wanted to stop by her place. She's clearly not in Bend."

Her father didn't deny or confirm my conclusion. "She's asked for a few more days."

"You will welcome her back? If she decides not to go to Denver?"

Robert looked over his shoulder, assessing me. "This was unexpected. But Kathleen will always have a place here. Never doubt that."

"What do you think she's going to do?"

Robert offered a sad smile. "Hypotheticals, Jack."

"Please," I implored. "I need to be prepared."

Robert sat back down at his desk. He pointed a long finger at me. "Before she met you? I could've answered your question with total confidence. Now... I'm not so sure."

"What would you have told me then?"

"Then?" Robert glanced briefly at the wall behind me. "That you'd have better luck breaking into Fort Knox than getting through her barriers. When her steel door closes, it's impenetrable. And God help you if you're on the wrong side."

"And now?" I asked. "What's changed?"

Robert considered this at length and I waited with mounting anxiety.

"Now? I don't know if anything has changed. Maybe the only thing that has changed is how she deals with those barricades. Maybe Kathleen doesn't know how to keep the vault door from locking any more than we do. Maybe putting some distance between the two of you keeps the door open."

My heart was pounding. "That sounds dangerously close to hope."

"Be patient, Jack. If she can forgive me, she should have no trouble finding her way back to you."

chapter Fourteen

THE BARTENDER at the Riverhouse greeted us with a hearty smile when I indicated our desire to sit outside. I opened the patio door and held it for Kathleen. I followed in good-natured silence as she chose a table close to the river. We were enveloped in late-summer sunshine and she lifted her face to the clear, blue sky. She closed her eyes and grinned, delighted by the warmth on her skin.

It was a quiet, weekday afternoon, so our attentive server approached just as soon as we took our seats. The college-aged waitress looked at Kathleen first for an order.

"I'll take an iced tea, please."

"And you, sir?"

"Do you have Inversion?" I'd discovered the local IPA soon after moving to Bend, and I still savored the newness of the microbrew.

"Yes, we do."

"That'd be perfect. Thanks."

I watched our waitress bound toward the bartender, wondering if she was old enough to serve alcohol. I glanced at Kathleen and noticed she was stifling a smile. I hadn't thought my order through and was chagrined.

"I'm sorry," I mumbled. "I should have asked if it was all right to order a beer."

"I'm not your keeper," she replied with a shrug as she leaned back in her chair. She was relaxed, and the thought warmed me more than the sunlight. I copied her posture and brought my hand up to rub my chin.

"Well. You kind of are. We've been on the clock this afternoon."

"I'm not worried about it."

Our drinks arrived a few moments later, and she lifted her glass for a sip.

"Do you drink alcohol at all?" I asked.

She set her tea down on the table and tilted her head. "Why do you ask?"

Her voice held no teasing note. No sense of playfulness. If anything, her question sounded apprehensive. I was still grasping the depths of her shyness, but I pressed forward. She hadn't changed the subject outright.

"No reason, I guess. I've never seen you do it."

Kathleen's grin returned and she nodded. "That's because you've never seen me outside of the office."

"That's an excellent point."

In the days since I'd begun working at Aurora, I'd chatted with Kathleen a multitude of times, but she always kept our conversations centered on work. Sitting outside, enjoying a beer with her blessing brought my inhibitions down.

"I hope I'm not upsetting you. This is as close to outside of work as we've gotten so far. And I'm curious about you."

Kathleen tilted her head. "Really?"

"Yes."

She dropped her gaze and circled a contemplative finger on the rim of her glass. When she brought her eyes back to mine, there was a determined set to her features.

I waited to see which way our conversation was about to turn.

"What do you want to know?"

"Plenty. For example, are you married?"

She held up her left hand, which held no ring. "No."

"Am I being too nosy?"

She grinned while leaning toward me. "Not so far, but honestly speaking, there's not much to me," she said, repeating my words to her before she'd introduced me at the staff meeting my first day of work. Pride flared. I'd made a memorable impression.

"I disagree," I bantered back, cementing an inside joke.

We beamed at one another and then fell into a mutual silence. During this time, Kathleen's eyes drifted to the Deschutes River. I recalled her referring to this spot as her oasis. She'd mentioned that she used to dine at the Riverhouse with her mother, but I also knew she hadn't been back in a long time.

On impulse I asked, "Your mother doesn't live in Bend anymore?"

Kathleen blinked but didn't take her eyes away from the white water rushing by just steps away.

"No. She doesn't." Her voice was quieter. I strained to hear her statement over the roar created by the river.

I leaned forward. "Where is she now?"

"Portland," she said, avoiding eye contact.

I wanted to ask her more, but stopped. The energy around us had shifted in a matter of a few words. There was little doubt that Kathleen was uncomfortable now. We both went still for a second time.

She took the lead and resumed the conversation. "How are you liking Oregon so far?"

"Still adapting." It was my turn to be on the defensive, although I'd earned a bit of her investigation.

"I've never been to Baltimore," Kathleen revealed.

"No?"

She shrugged again. "I don't get out of the neighborhood much."

"Where do you like to go when you leave the neighborhood?"

Kathleen's cheeks turned a bit rosier than usual. "My last vacation shouldn't count," she told me. "It was way out of the norm."

"That sounds interesting. Where did you go?"

"France."

"Why there? Was it on your bucket list?"

"I wanted to go somewhere far away, and I guess I was in the mood to see Paris."

"That's great," I replied. "What did you do there?"

"All of the usual things, I suppose. What did you like best about living in Baltimore?"

"I miss Chesapeake Bay. Once upon a time, I had a sailboat."

"Yeah?" Kathleen's tone communicated both her interest and her surprise.

I was suddenly at a loss for words. If I was going to be truthful to Kathleen, I would have to reveal that the sailboat was one of many quagmires in my marriage. I hadn't spoken about sailing in years and was surprised that I'd mentioned it. Of all the things I could have revealed about my old life, why had I started with that boat?

Stalling for extra time to prepare my answer, I took another sip of beer. "I gave it up when I got engaged."

"Your wife wasn't a fan?"

"Nope." I left it at that and Kathleen laughed good-naturedly. Despite the fine line I was walking, I was glad to get our conversation back on track.

"Have you visited the coast here?"

Here was a question I was happy to indulge. "Not yet. It's a bit of a drive, isn't it?"

She nodded. "A little over three hours. The highway from here is narrow and windy, but the drive is beautiful. There's plenty of scenery along the way."

"Do you go to the beach often?"

"Now and again. The coast was always too windy and foggy for Robert. He likes it here more than anywhere else."

Here was another obstacle when it came to Kathleen.

JENNIFER LOCKLEAR

Although I hadn't witnessed severe tension between her and Robert since the reception at 5 Fusion, I knew better than to ask about their relationship. I was running out of conversational avenues. Her mother was off limits and so was her father. She wasn't married and didn't have a family of her own, which eliminated any number of small talks we could have engaged in.

I tapped my beer bottle, focusing my attention on the nearby wooden bridge that crossed the river. I remembered Heide's joy there during our stay and smiled. I brought my attention back to Kathleen, confident I had discovered new territory to explore.

"Tell me what it was like for you growing up in Bend."

"What do you mean?" Kathleen's eyes narrowed.

Her expression bothered me. What trap had I stepped into this time? "I was just curious. I remember Robert telling me how he moved you here from Portland. Perhaps I just need some reassurance that I've done the right thing by my daughter."

Kathleen considered this at length. I wanted her to be honest about her childhood here, so I waited patiently as she collected her thoughts.

"I liked my school," she said. "I had lots of friends and I made the honor roll. Once I got on it, I never fell off."

"I can see that about you." I moved the conversation forward again by asking, "Were you bored here? After living in the city?"

Kathleen shook her head. "If it was boring here, I would have moved away after high school and never come back. Granted, Bend isn't for everyone. It's just like anywhere, I suppose. People love it or hate it, or they're indifferent and hang on until something better comes along."

"You didn't miss being a kid in the city?"

"No. To be honest, my memories of Portland are fuzzy."

"Fuzzy." I repeated the word, wondering if my daughter would someday recall Maryland in the same way. I supposed it was inevitable, but the realization was difficult to accept.

"We signed Heide up for soccer. She played in Baltimore. I

99

hope something familiar will help her adjust." I was beginning to ramble, something I wasn't prone to.

"You don't need to worry," Kathleen said. "New kids here always get an extra dose of attention. Everyone will want to get to know her. She'll have her choice of friends."

"That's good to hear."

"She'll do fine," Kathleen added with certainty and I believed her.

Before I could thank her, Kathleen's phone pinged. She picked it up from the table and checked her message. While she did this, I finished my beer.

When she set down her phone, she looked at me again. "We should head back to the office." She gestured for our bill. Our server returned, and Kathleen held out her hand for the ticket. Once it was in her palm, she set it down in front of her and moved to retrieve her wallet.

"My treat," I stumbled, flustered by her quick action.

She dismissed my offer without even glancing up. "It's on the company."

I persisted. "This was my idea. Let me take care of it. Please."

There was an insistence in my tone that surprised even me. She froze, half twisted in her seat with her hand still inside her purse. She looked at me again, and I pointed to the bill on her side of the table. The ticket was next to her left breast. One wayward glance and I was staring at the slight embossment of her nipple against her blouse. She pushed the black leather folder in my direction, and I scooped it up and stood to retrieve my wallet from my trousers. Mortified by my behavior, I hurried over to the bar before Kathleen could read my thoughts and slap me with a sexual harassment complaint.

We didn't speak on the drive back to the office. Kathleen occupied herself with her phone, responding to texts and e-mails. I was anxious and moody. I'd wanted to see Kathleen enjoy her oasis, and yet I couldn't help but feel it was a mistake taking her to the Riverhouse. She'd spent much of our social time acting guarded and suspicious. We'd had a great client meeting earlier that was vital to the firm and for me, but I fixated on those few fleeting minutes spent on a sunny, riverside deck.

I'd taken Kathleen's oasis and turned it into a mirage.

chapter

Fifteen

WHEN WE returned to the agency, the staff switched gears and was prepared for the evening's reception. I muddled through the rest of the afternoon, second-guessing our detour. I tried to distract myself with projects that were helpful but required little mental energy. I searched in vain for a way to forget my mistakes of the day.

Allison arrived at the reception twenty minutes behind the main surge. Given her former career in broadcasting, it wasn't like her to be late for anything, but I'd been so busy greeting one new person after another that I hadn't had any time to stop and think about that. When she found me, I was catching my first bit of respite. I was deep in conversation with Kathleen.

Allison approached us, dressed immaculately but looking out of sorts. I did my best to draw her into our conversation without derailing it. I had one goal in mind and knew that Allison was smart enough to realize when I was trying to strike a deal. I draped my arm around my wife's waistline, pulling her close to me in welcome.

"Kathleen. This is my wife, Allison."

Kathleen extended a happy smile and reached out to shake hands. "Hello, Allison. It's so nice to meet you."

Allison shook Kathleen's hand. "Hello."

"We had an excellent meeting this afternoon with a longtime

prospect," I told Allison and gestured to Kathleen with my free hand. "It was spontaneous, but Kathleen and I pitched it together and it was brilliant."

"Jack made the deal happen. All I did was set up the meeting and make the introduction."

"Not true at all," I disagreed. "Kathleen knows everyone and everything about Bend. She made the whole thing feel more like a neighborhood get-together instead of one of the biggest deals of the month."

"Of the year!" she beamed.

"We've stumbled onto something here," I told them both. "Having us tackle the meeting together worked to the firm's advantage. I was thinking about drafting up a proposal to Robert, asking if you and I could keep working together to take on some of these prospect assignments he's so excited about. What do you think?"

Allison tensed within my embrace as I waited for Kathleen's answer.

"I agree. I'll have no problem setting the meetings, and your advertising experience far exceeds mine." Kathleen glanced to Allison. "He thinks so fast on his feet."

"You have no idea," Allison responded. She smiled, showing that she was making a joke, but her posture remained rigid, and her hands were clasped in front of her body. She hadn't reciprocated my embrace, just merely tolerated its existence.

Just then, Tracie approached Kathleen. "Robert needs you to come say hello to Ted."

"Right. I'm sorry to dash away, but you haven't seen your husband all day. Have a glass of wine and catch up for a few minutes." Kathleen turned away and took a few steps before spinning back around and pointing in my direction. "Oh! But don't go too far, Jack. I'm guessing Robert's next move is to get you interviewed for *The Bulletin*. That's why he's calling me over now."

"Got it. We'll stay here."

Satisfied with my answer, Kathleen bounded off with Tracie. I turned to Allison and leaned down to kiss her temple. She stepped away from me before my lips could brush her skin.

I was perplexed but gestured to a nearby table with two empty seats. "Come sit with me. Was the traffic bad? You're late."

I began walking, but noticed when she didn't follow me. I stepped back toward her and took her hand in mine, leading us both to the table. She didn't resist and took a seat when I pulled out a chair for her.

"Let me get you a glass of wine. All right?"

Allison appeared conflicted but glanced around the busy room and nodded.

When I returned a few minutes later, I drew the other chair toward hers and sat close, trying to afford us as much privacy as possible in the crowded room.

"Is something wrong?" I asked in a low voice.

Allison's politeness subsided as soon as she took her first sip. "By now, I should know better. Why am I continually surprised by the things you do?"

"Me? I'm the one you're upset with?" I was astonished. "I don't understand. Everything seemed fine when I left for work this morning. You made me coffee. We talked about Heide's first sleepover. We didn't fight on the phone about this afternoon. In fact, this morning on the way out the door you..."

Realization dawned on me and my humiliation was immediate. If I'd screwed up my afternoon with Kathleen, it was nothing compared to what I'd just done to Allison. "Oh, fuck," I whispered. "Our therapy appointment."

Allison glared at me. No more words were necessary to convey her anger and disappointment.

I scrambled to apologize. "I didn't skip it on purpose," I stammered. "I just zoned out. I'm so sorry."

Allison looked at me in rage and disbelief. When she

responded, the low tone of her voice turned my blood cold. "You zoned out?"

My mind was blank. My wife seethed in her chair, waiting for me to respond, and all I could focus on was making sure no one else could overhear our argument.

"Jack!" Her demand for attention snapped me out of a stupor.

"We can't talk about this here," I told her, desperate to move on to neutral subject matter.

"We can't? Or you can't?" she challenged. "Here we are once again."

Against my better judgment, I muttered, "And where exactly is that?"

"In this place where you hurt me, and I'm just supposed to suck it up and be the forgiving wife."

"Not now," I hissed. I refrained from slamming a frustrated fist down on the table and glanced around at the crowd. My blood pressure receded once I saw that we had not drawn attention to ourselves. My eyes sought Allison's once more. "There is too much on the line here tonight. What's done is done and we can't fix it here."

"You're the one who's screwed things up." Allison jabbed my chest with a solitary finger. "You're the one who needs to fix things, not me."

"Fine," I told her, hoping to bring a semblance of peace back to the current situation. "I will take care of this. Please. Can we just move on to something else?"

Allison shook her head. "You're always so worried about what your colleagues will think. Your reputation is so precious when it comes to your career. If only your reputation as a husband was half as important. Why isn't it, Jack? Why do you care so little about what your wife thinks of you?"

"Your opinion matters, Allison," I said but with an exasperation I could no longer disguise.

Her eyes roamed the room until they came to rest upon

Kathleen Brighton on the other side of the lobby.

"If we were still in Baltimore, I'd know exactly who to blame for your distraction and why." Allison jutted her chin in Kathleen's direction. "Is she the one I need to be wary of now? I know she distracted you this afternoon with some big meeting, but please go ahead and tell me about how she did it. If she got you to forget about your marriage counseling, she must be my new competition."

Everything was spinning out of control, but I owed Allison an explanation, as lame as the truth might be.

"Don't be ridiculous. And don't blame Kathleen," I said. "This is my fuck-up. I didn't make it back to my office after lunch to review my schedule. That's what I usually do. I hadn't cemented the appointment in my brain for this afternoon, that's all."

"What are you telling me, Jack? That our marriage isn't worth thinking about away from home?"

I became flustered yet again. "Of course not."

"What you just said makes no sense at all."

"I really am sorry," I tried. "I don't blame you for being angry with me. But let's set it aside for now and talk when we get home. Don't make me say this again. I can't get into an argument with my wife in the middle of a party being held in my honor and filled with colleagues and clients."

Our glances both darted in Kathleen's direction just as she turned and beckoned me over. I rose from my seat and straightened my suit to occupy my negative energy. As I walked away to join Kathleen and the rest of her group, Allison glared.

"Don't keep me here longer than need be," she said. "The sooner we go home, the less time I'll have to sit here and stew about it."

chapter Sixteen

ON ITS surface, the party held in my honor by Aurora was a rousing success. As soon as I vacated my seat at Allison's table, it was impossible to find my way back to resume our conversation. Many of the firm's longtime clients popped in to meet me in person as did some prospective clients. The local press approached me for interviews, and Kathleen and Robert both appeared to be in good spirits. But I found it difficult to enjoy any level of triumph, knowing that Allison sat nearby, unattended and disappointed.

She had asked me to find a way to leave the party as soon as possible, but once again her request went unheeded. Three hours after her confrontation, we drove home in separate vehicles. I rode in absolute silence, allowing my thoughts to race unchecked. When we opened the door to our house, I was relieved that Heide wasn't there to greet us. I was no fool. Allison had rebuffed my romantic yearnings for months, and tonight she had ample reason to turn me away again.

As I locked the front door, she strode through the living room and down the hallway straight to our bedroom. I was a coward and dipped into the kitchen for a glass of water. I couldn't corral my fleeting thoughts, and the lack of focus fueled my irritation. I needed to reconnect with her, but I couldn't conceive of how. I waited in the kitchen and stared at my empty drinking glass, seeking inspiration.

It never arrived, and so I wandered to our bedroom, hoping a good night's rest would refresh us both. From my vantage point in the hallway, I could see Allison sitting on her corner of the mattress closest to the door. I only got one foot across the threshold of the master bedroom before she stopped me.

"I don't want you in here tonight," she said.

"Allison—" I began my apology, but she cut me off.

"I mean it, Jack. I'm furious."

"You don't sound furious." I said this with frank curiosity, because it was the truth. I'd never seen her so calm during an argument.

"Well, I am. And not just about today."

"No?"

She shook her head. dropping her eyes to the carpet. "I'm angry about every day I've known you."

I had no counter for her statement. We both knew she was being honest. My silence must have surprised her because she lifted her head and met my gaze as she rose from the bed.

"I gave up everything I had to make this marriage work. You can't even give me one afternoon."

I was chagrined and sulking. "I didn't miss the appointment on purpose."

"I don't care why you missed it. Whatever the reason, it doesn't change the fact that you couldn't be bothered to remember it in the first place."

Allison paced the room while I continued to stand halfway in and halfway out the bedroom door.

"I've left everything behind since I married you," she reiterated. "My career. My own family. My friends. Everything. I left it all to move across the country to a place I don't even know. And you know what, Jack?"

"What?"

"The more you force me to examine my life and ask myself why I've done such crazy things, the more I realize I only did it for

Heide. Not for me. Not for you. And certainly not for this pathetic marriage we've managed to trap ourselves in."

I thrust my hands into my pockets and shifted in place. She'd told me not to enter the bedroom, but I knew walking away from her wasn't the answer, either. "I have my faults," I concurred. "I've caused a lot of damage over the years. You deserve better than me."

Allison stopped marching and sat back down on the mattress. She rested her elbows on her knees and dropped her face into the palms of her hands, but she didn't cry. The silence dragged on, with only the sound of our anxious breathing filling the room. I had to remind myself we were fighting, because this argument was unlike any I'd had with Allison.

She resumed the conversation, albeit with her face still buried in her hands. "I'm so exhausted. Aren't you tired of this life?"

"I don't want to give up."

Allison chortled, causing me to wince. "That I know all too well. But at the same time, you don't want to change."

I straightened my posture in defiance. "I don't think that's a fair statement."

"No?"

"I'm not foolish enough to claim I haven't made mistakes. But Heide and you are my family."

"You're a decent man. But you have never been the husband I dreamed about."

"I know that. I'm sorry."

"We aren't right for each other."

"I can do better," I protested, but even I heard the halfhearted nature of its delivery.

Allison's head whipped up and she cast me a scornful look.

"Please," she implored me. "Do us a favor and stop trying to convince yourself to save face. We both need to accept that this marriage is one long mistake."

Allison's choice of words stung. "How can you ask that?" I

demanded in a pained tone. "Nothing where Heide is concerned will ever be a mistake to me."

She blinked hard at my rebuttal and lifted a finger to wipe a stray tear from her eye. "That's not what I meant. Heide is the light of my life and yours. You love her with your whole heart."

"I do."

Allison nodded with a sorrowful expression. "So do I. But truthfully, Jack. When was the last time you told me you loved me? I want you to think about when you last said the words to me. More importantly, when was the last time you told yourself that you loved me?"

It was a poignant question. And one I had no response for. The moments dragged as I tried to recall a recent declaration, and Allison was merciful when she could have exploded. It was an extraordinary moment.

"That's why I can't sleep next to you right now. We both have a lot of thinking to do."

Defeated, I gestured to the pillows on my side of the bed and stepped into the room to retrieve one. "I'll grab a blanket from Heide's room," I mumbled.

Allison held still, not even turning her head to watch me.

Within a few minutes I'd stretched out on the living room sofa, but sleep eluded me over that long night.

The next morning, Allison exited her room at her regular time. She found me sitting on the couch because I'd long since given up trying to rest. At her appearance, I stood up and made my way into the kitchen.

The calm between us was still intact as I brewed a pot of coffee. It was only after we each had our own cup in hand that we resumed our conversation.

"I need more time to think," she began. "Everything that happens from this point on has to be strongly considered. For Heide's sake."

"All right," I agreed. "What do you need from me?"

"I called my sister. I asked if I could go visit her for a couple of weeks."

"Back to Baltimore?"

Allison nodded but refused to look at me.

"Okay," I breathed out. "What about Heide?"

The mention of our daughter's name brought an immediate tear to Allison's eye. She wiped it away. "She just started school. She's settling in here. Don't you think?"

"Yeah."

"I'll only be gone a few weeks. I need the space to clear my head. It wouldn't be fun for her. She's better off staying here."

"I can take care of her."

"I know. You two will be fine. If I had to leave her with anyone else, I wouldn't consider doing this." Satisfied, she rose from the kitchen table to make her way back to the bedroom.

I stood and followed her from a cautious distance. "Allison?"

She turned to face me, her exhaustion on full display.

"When you come back, there will be no more fuck-ups. I mean it."

I recognized her familiar expression of reserved disappointment as it took hold. She'd heard me say similar words many times over the years. I was forcing her to consider them once again and that was when I saw something different—a newfound determination. I believed in my own words, but Allison was no longer interested in holding me accountable to such delusions of grandeur.

I could see it. She was beginning the slow, painful process of our separation and she didn't want to entertain any ideas that might convince her that returning to Maryland wasn't the best alternative for her well-being.

She'd made up her mind. She was leaving. And soon.

chapter Seventeen

ALLISON WAS gone.

Five days earlier, we'd attended my official welcome party at Aurora Advertising. I encouraged more conversation during the long weekend before she left. Allison held her ground. She wouldn't commit to staying in the marriage, but she hadn't declared that our reconciliation was impossible. She'd left for Maryland on Monday morning with a promise to come back with a plan. She'd left me with just enough hope to keep the peace between us.

I stood in the middle of the living room, alone. I wondered how to go on with the rest of my life, but the answers were evasive. After a few minutes, the silence in both my house and my mind was more than I could handle.

I went to work and attended the firm's weekly staff meeting. I fielded congratulations from coworkers and clients alike on the success of the reception. The night was a professional triumph, but a personal failure. Feigning enthusiasm for the team was an overwhelming task, but I managed to get through the day without drawing any unwanted attention to my growing anxiety.

Allison and Heide were never far from my thoughts. My marriage was on the line, and I was adamant that no one at work knew this. I wasn't going to utter a word about our family troubles while I still harbored optimism that my relationship with Allison could be salvaged.

With each passing minute, Allison was moving farther away from us both. As the day progressed, I grew more apprehensive to see my daughter. I wondered how their farewell had gone that morning. Had Heide been upset? Had she watched her mother's car as it drove out of sight? Was she as distracted at school as I was at work?

I returned home that evening, aware that Allison's plane was about to touch down in Baltimore. Was she relieved to be back in Maryland? Was she feeling secure in her decision to leave Heide in my care? Was she thinking about me as much as I was thinking about her? Was she going to share the secret of our failing marriage with her family?

Heide's sitter brought her home soon after I texted my arrival. I invited Lydia and her daughter inside for a few minutes to chat and finalize our babysitting plans for the rest of the week. While the two girls ran off to Heide's room for a few more minutes of play, I thanked Lydia for stepping in to help. I told her Allison had been called away to Maryland on a family matter. I studied my neighbor's reactions to see if she knew anything about why Allison was gone. If she was aware, she masked it well.

Afterward, I occupied myself by cooking dinner. Heide had returned home in a good mood, and I was wary of disrupting it. I kept the meal simple, but as I moved through the motions of grilling chicken and preparing a garden salad, I experienced the first bit of calm during that long day. I slowed down my pace to extend the feeling, and my guard began to come down.

The house phone rang as I was setting the table. I was inclined to ignore it, but then I remembered I hadn't heard from Allison all day. When I saw her cell phone number on the display, I answered at once.

"How are you doing?" I asked straightaway. "Are you safe?"

As I waited for Allison to respond, I heard rambunctious voices in the background. They faded away and I heard a door click into place.

"Yes," she answered. Her voice was timid, which was unlike her. "No problems at all. Just a long day."

"It's late there," I said. "I'm surprised to hear so many people on a Monday night."

"Liz decided to throw a surprise party. Almost the whole family is here."

Allison's sister was always ready to host a gathering, but I worried Liz was also in the mood to celebrate my removal from the family tree. "I see."

"It's been nice seeing everyone, but I'm going to bed soon. I'm tired."

Allison sounded as unenthused and awkward as I felt. I took no comfort in the thought.

"That's probably a good idea."

"How are you?" she asked with a tone so polite it was a social obligation. "How was your day?"

"Work was fine, but I was distracted."

"How is Heide doing?" Here, finally, there was some emotion in Allison's voice.

"Good. I'm just getting ready to put dinner on the table. You probably want to say hello to her. Let me get her on the line."

"Thanks."

"Yeah. Sure," I mumbled. "Hold on."

I kept the phone to my ear as I made my way to Heide's room, but our conversation ceased. I informed Heide that her mom was on the line and handed her the phone without fanfare. Then I left the two of them to speak in private, returning to the kitchen to finish dinner preparations.

After a while, Heide jogged into the kitchen and put the receiver back on its charger base. Apparently, Allison had said enough to me for one day and I pushed down the sharp sting of resentment. The last thing I wanted to do was put Heide in a place where she was forced to take sides. There was no need for me to campaign for my daughter's love. I already had it. There was no need to force her to choose one parent over the other, especially when our separation would only last a matter of days.

Dinner was strange, even mildly uncomfortable at the outset. Heide took her seat at the table and stared at her plateful of food.

"What's wrong?" I asked.

My daughter was staring at her food as though it was crawling with black widow spiders. She looked at me with suspicious eyes. "I didn't know you could cook dinner."

I sat back in my chair, incredulous. "I cook breakfast sometimes."

"True." Heide elongated the word as she considered my counterargument. "But that's breakfast. Not dinner."

I crossed my arms. "If I can cook breakfast, why is it so difficult to believe I can make dinner?"

Heide crossed her arms in reciprocation. "Dinner is more complicated."

I laughed despite my sour mood and shook my head. "How about this?" I challenged. "Maybe tomorrow I'll cook breakfast for dinner."

My daughter giggled and clutched her stomach. "Don't be silly, Dad."

"I promise I can cook a perfectly acceptable dinner. Please give it a try."

I gestured to her plate and watched as she picked up her fork and took an experimental taste. Satisfied, Heide dug into the meal.

"How was school today?" I asked as I took my first bite.

"Fine."

"That's it? Just fine?"

She nodded.

"How did things go when Mom dropped you off this morning?"

"Good. She gave me a hug and said she'd bring back a present."

"Oh yeah?" I did my best to sound casual. "That's nice."

From there, our conversation moved along for the next twenty minutes. We were both aware of Allison's absence, but neither of us brought it up again. Allison was coming back just as soon as she had a few days of rest and relaxation in familiar surroundings. If Heide could accept the situation, I needed to do the same.

When Heide went to bed, I read her a story and chatted with her some more. There was no sign she worried over her mother's absence. She fell asleep soon after I turned off her lights. I locked up the house and retreated to my room, grabbing a book to keep me company.

Kitty Hawk followed me to bed and curled up on Allison's empty side. I read a chapter and scratched the cat's head while keeping an ear out for anything unusual. By the second chapter, the words blurred together on the page, which surprised me. I'd expected to be restless that first night, but the week's exhaustion caught up to me. I set the book aside, turned off my bedside lamp and eased into a deep, dreamless sleep.

After dropping Heide off at school and stopping for coffee the following morning, I pulled into the parking lot at work. Kathleen exited her car and waved when we spotted one another. She waited for me to join her and we walked to the office building together.

"How's it going?" she asked.

"No complaints so far. I actually slept really good."

"You sound surprised." Her observations were always so acute.

I hesitated to answer, not wanting to steer the conversation too personal. We were getting close to the building's front door so I slowed to a stop and faced her.

"Have you ever had one of those nights when you thought you couldn't possibly sleep? But then you did?"

Surprised, her demeanor shifted. She crossed her arms over

her chest as though an arctic breeze had just struck. "I've had a few of those."

I wondered if she could hear my heart pounding in my chest, but one look at her face told me she was deep inside her own thoughts or preparing for something unpleasant. Guilt bubbled up inside me. I hadn't meant to make her uncomfortable.

"It's just a relief when you wake up in the morning and you're rested far beyond your expectations."

Her shoulders and expression relaxed. "That's a good thing," she said with a nod. "I hope the rest of your day goes as well."

"Thanks, Kathleen."

She turned, and we resumed our walk to the office. We reached the front door together and I grabbed the handle before she could.

"Please. After you."

She went inside without a word. I was surprised when she paused in the lobby.

"Are you happy?" she asked.

I froze in place.

She began to fidget in her high-heeled shoes. "I mean... are you happy you moved here?"

I was afraid to answer because I feared giving away everything I was determined to keep secret.

Yet again, Kathleen's intuition kicked in to overdrive. "I'm sorry. It's none of my business. It's just that you said you expected to get a bad night's sleep. I'd hate to think it's because you're having second thoughts about this job." She lifted her pretty green eyes to mine.

I allowed our eye contact to linger for several significant moments. "I like my job. Very much."

Kathleen blinked and nodded as a satisfied grin appeared. "I'm glad. Robert made the right decision choosing you, Jack. You're good for this place."

She went through the door to the reception area and I followed behind her.

chapter Eighteen

AS THE days marched on, I expected them to angle back toward a semblance of normalcy. I slept soundly every night, but the same uncomfortable, awkward mood filled my days. Allison booked her return flight to Eugene, but even this wasn't enough to dispel my unease. I couldn't decide if my family was moving forward or falling apart. I accepted this latest version of reality as best I could and kept my thoughts to myself. If nothing else, I wanted to protect Heide from the unpleasantness.

In the meantime, the two of us adapted to our routines. I'd drive Heide to school in the mornings and pick her up from Lydia's on my way home from work. I cooked dinner every night, finding some of the day's only enjoyment in surprising my daughter with my wide range of culinary skills. Afterward, she'd help me with the dishes and we'd talk about our plans for the next day. At bedtime, I tucked her in and read her a story. We only had each other at home and from my perspective, the warmth and love between us grew at a time when it could have been tarnished.

Many nights, Allison would call to speak to Heide. I would answer the phone and exchange a brief greeting, but Allison's focus was always on her. When her contact ceased two nights before she was to fly home, I was surprised. Heide didn't appear to notice this development, likely because she was so focused on Allison's return. In the end, I chose to dismiss it.

When my cell phone rang at noon on the Saturday we were due to pick Allison up from the airport, my nerves were raw from months of disconnection and weeks of strife. My wife's name and smiling photo flashed across the display as I answered it.

I immediately heard her crying. "Allison?" Dread pumped through my heart. She wasn't prone to hysterics. "What is it? What's the matter?"

Allison struggled to regain her composure. "I missed my flight."

I took in a deep breath and allowed my relief to conquer my fear. Her extreme reaction to such an annoyance was unusual for her. I wasn't sure how to continue, but I was grateful she had contacted me with the problem. The first step was to calm her down.

"It's okay," I told her. "Don't worry. We'll get it figured out. I'll call the airline and get you on another plane."

"No!" Allison's heightened pitch revealed her panic. "I don't want you to do that."

Confused, I made a second attempt at reassurance. "You're upset. You've been away from home for a while and had a stressful morning. It's the least I can do."

There was a heavy pause, followed by a shaky breath. "You're not understanding me, Jack." The level of irritation lacing Allison's voice sent my own blood pressure soaring.

"You're right about that," I snapped. "What don't I understand? You missed your flight. You called me upset. I'm trying to help you solve this, so you can feel better and come back home. What else am I missing here?"

On the other end of the line, there was complete silence. Allison had quelled her crying during my outburst.

"Are you still there?" I asked.

"I can't live in Oregon." Her statement was so quiet, it took a few seconds for me to understand what she'd said.

I rubbed my forehead in aggravation. "What are you talking

about?"

"I never left for the airport, Jack."

It was my turn to be silent. I waited for Allison to say something—anything that made some goddamned sense.

"Please talk to me," she pleaded. "Don't shut down now."

"Why not? You're shutting down on me. On us. Why wouldn't you go to the airport?" I asked, trying to keep my thoughts rational, but the hurt dominated my voice.

"It wasn't a choice. I just couldn't do it." She burst into a fresh round of sobs. "I can't leave here. Not even for Heide. Something's wrong with me."

Her emotions were all over the place, as were mine. I was worried and angry, but something was happening to her that neither of us had dealt with before.

"What do you mean? Something's wrong? If there's something you need to say, please tell me."

"I don't know if I can," she confessed. "I'm scared, and I know I'm upsetting you," she said.

I gathered my courage and softened my tone. "I can hear how miserable you are. I'm still your husband and you called me. Tell me what's wrong. Let me help you, Allison."

Moments drifted by, but when she spoke it was as though her mental floodgates had opened. "Everything hurts," she blurted. "I can't stop crying. I'm scared. I can't stand the thought of eating even though I know I need to. I can't sleep at night. I have no energy to walk out the door."

"Is it depression?"

"I think so. I just can't shake it. I can't relax. And the closer the time came to leave here, the stronger those feelings became. This morning, I woke up from a deep sleep and I was already crying. Tears were running down my face. My heart was pounding. I woke up afraid."

Hearing Allison's admission was painful, but her pain was far worse than my own. I understood a mere fraction of her agony, and yet it was enough to render me helpless. I could do nothing more from our home in Bend than to offer her words of comfort.

"You were right not to get on the plane." I angrily wiped the tears from my eyes.

"Okay," she breathed. "Yes. Good."

I sniffled. "You made the right decision."

"Now what do we do?"

"You should have Liz take you to the doctor. Don't put this off, have her take you to the emergency room as soon as we get off the phone. Do you need me to talk to her? What can I do to help you?"

"I can do it," she told me. She had processed my acceptance and some of her strength returned. "I'll ask her to take me, but..." Allison's voice drifted off as we both realized the inevitable.

"You'll have to explain to her what's happening," I said, finishing her thought, and allowed us both a moment to absorb the impending public revelation of our fragile marriage.

"I understand," I told her in a voice that I prayed was confident enough. "You should be honest with your family. It's the best thing for you."

"I need to stay here, in Baltimore, for a bit longer. I'm sorry. I promise I'll come back next weekend. I'll be okay by then."

She was seeking some version of control, and although I wanted to be respectful of her words, I knew she was offering a guarantee she couldn't deliver.

"Things are fine here," I said. "I have everything under control. I'm not going anywhere, so take all the time you need. Don't think about this stuff right now. Just get to the hospital and see a doctor."

"Okay."

"Can I ask something of you?"

"What?"

"Keep talking to me. Don't cut me out. Keep me updated on what's happening."

"Sure."

"I care about what happens to you. I always will." I should have told her I loved her, but she would have been suspicious of the sentiment. She needed to seek treatment, not question my motives.

"Thanks."

"Is Liz there now?"

"Yes."

"I'll let you go so you can tell her what's happening. You promise to go right to her?"

"Yes."

"I have Liz's number, so I'll call her this afternoon. She can update me on how everything's going. I just want you to focus on making yourself better. Please."

"I will. I'm sorry, Jack."

"I'm sorry, too. I really am."

Allison uttered an urgent goodbye and ended the call. I stared at my phone for a minute, feeling as though she'd deserted the conversation before one of us had a second chance to reconsider the impromptu plan.

The sound of Heide opening and closing her dresser drawers drew my attention. Here was my next impending calamity. Heide had jumped out of bed that morning, her spirits high with the excitement of welcoming her mom home. Now, I was going to have to tell her that Allison wasn't coming home yet.

I set my phone down on the counter and entered the living room from the kitchen. I paused behind the sofa and gripped it for support as I turned my head toward the hallway that led to her bedroom.

"Heide!" I winced when the barking sound of my own voice echoed down the corridor. I hadn't intended to sound cross. I waited and watched for my daughter to appear, wondering how she'd interpreted my mood.

She bolted through her doorway in a flash and ran full speed into me. She wrapped her small arms around my waist in greeting, oblivious to my tension. I reciprocated her hug with bittersweet expectations.

"Is it time to go?" Heide's beaming smile was always beautiful. I hated being the one to make it disappear. I placed a palm against her small cheek.

"Come sit with me on the sofa," I said, making a deliberate effort to rein in my harshness. "There's something I need to tell you."

Heide let go of me and dashed around the couch. She leaped onto the cushions with a cartoonish flair. As I took my seat, she bounced nonstop.

I rested my palm on her knee, hoping to capture her focus. "You're very excited," I began, "but we have to be serious right now."

Heide was always a good listener, and she ceased her movements.

Knowing I could only capture a six-year-old's attention for so long, I jumped right into the conversation. "I have some bad news."

Heide's smiled faded. "What is it?"

"Mom isn't coming home today."

Heide tilted her head as she understood the sudden shift of the day's events. "Why not?"

I didn't know what I'd say as I answered her, but I was as careful as possible.

"When Mom woke up this morning, she wasn't feeling well enough to go to the airport. She just called to let us know, and she's upset about not seeing you this afternoon."

Heide's faced registered a mixture of sadness, concern and ire.

"When I'm sick, Mom always tells me to get some sleep. She says sleep is the best cure. Why couldn't she just sleep on the plane?"

I shook my head. "If she could have, I know she'd do it for

you, but I'm afraid that wasn't possible." I took Heide's tiny hand in mine. "Aunt Liz is going to take Mom to the doctor right away, so she can start feeling better."

Heide crossed her arms as her remaining traces of sadness transformed into irritation. "She could've slept on the plane, and then she'd be home and see the doctor here."

"I know you're disappointed, Heide. I am, too, but we both need to remember something."

"What?" she asked sulkily.

"That the most important thing right now is for Mom to do whatever she needs to feel normal again."

"How long is it going to take?" She continued to pout.

"Heide..." The tone of my voice was disapproving but controlled.

Heide reacted to my change in mood, and her response was quiet and sad. "She's been gone two weeks, Dad. That's a long time."

"It is a long time, and you miss her, and she misses you just as much. Maybe more. The truth is, I don't know how much longer she'll be in Maryland, but I do know that Mom needs to rest. The more she can rest, the better she'll feel to travel again. Can you understand that?"

Heide stuck out a lower lip to go with her crossed arms. "Yes," she mumbled.

"I'm sure you want to know when Mom will be coming home, but I don't want to tell you it will be in a day or two. Or even next weekend, because the truth is we don't know what the doctor is going to tell her yet. Can you understand that I don't want to say something to make you feel better, only to disappoint you again?"

"I guess so."

"All I can do right now is promise I'll tell you what's happening as soon as I talk to Mom again."

Heide's head dipped down to stare at the floor.

"I understand you're upset. Is there anything I can do?"

Heide shook her head.

"Do you have any more questions about Mom?"

"Not right now."

"I'll call Aunt Liz later today to see if there's any news about Mom's visit to the doctor. For now, we have free time this afternoon. Is there something you want to do? Someplace you want to go?"

"I can't think of anything."

"Do you want to sit here with me or go back to your room for a little bit?"

"Go to my room."

I was helpless to turn Heide's mood around. I wanted to cheer her up, but in the end, she stomped back to her room to work through her emotions.

I left my phone sitting on the kitchen counter. I kept busy but avoided occupying my time with significant projects. I wanted to be able to walk away from a household chore at a moment's notice should Heide change her mind about sitting in her room. I checked on her several times, but she was content to keep company with her stuffed animals.

As afternoon gave way to evening in Baltimore, I decided it was time to check on Allison. I retrieved my phone, sat down at the kitchen table and called Liz. As I waited for her to answer, I glanced out the window.

"Hello, Jack." Liz's greeting was void of its usual bubbly tone, but at least she was civil.

"Hello, Liz. How is Allison doing? Were you able to take her to the ER?"

"We're still here. There was a bit of a wait to see a doctor. Can you hold on for a second?"

"Sure."

Liz pulled away from the phone and told Allison that she was stepping outside to speak with me. She promised to return within a few minutes. I strained to hear my wife's voice over the line but was disappointed when Liz walked away. She walked through a couple of doors and then the dull roar of traffic filled the line as she exited the hospital.

"All right," she finally said. "We can talk now."

"How is she?"

"She's a mess. Worked herself into a terrible migraine."

"Damn."

"She had to curl up in a corner of the waiting room for an hour or so. She was crying and puking and trying to be subtle about it."

"That's awful."

"She's in a dark exam room now. They put her on IV fluids and gave her pain medication. She's still and quiet. The meds are making her drowsy. The doctor wants her to have a CT scan, just to make sure nothing else is going on. We're waiting on the radiologist."

"Okay." I let this last syllable drift away, on the verge of telling Liz everything I could. I was willing to say anything in that moment to help Allison recover. But Liz beat me to the punch.

"Allison told me in the car that her visit isn't a vacation."

"What did she call it?" I asked.

"A separation." I heard the sisterly protectiveness in Liz's declaration and prepared for an onslaught.

"I wish that wasn't the case."

Liz's response was a slight sniffle, so I pressed on.

"I'm as worried about Allison as you are. I'm not going to be an asshole here. I want her to feel better. I want her to come home."

"Before you say something you might regret, Allison didn't give me the specifics."

I was grateful for this important revelation. Even amid severe distress, she'd kept our deepest secrets confidential.

"If I'm being honest with you," Liz continued, "I'm not surprised."

Here was an opportunity I'd never considered. "Why not?"

"You're not a bad person. It's just…" Liz's voice faded away.

"Just what?" I pressed without sarcasm or demand. I wanted to know what perception someone on the outside might have of our marriage.

"It's like you two are still dating. You're a couple, but it's like you're trying to figure one another out and trying to adjust to each other. I was at your wedding, but even after all these years, I still have to remind myself that you two are in a marriage. You've always been two individuals, rather than a whole."

"I see."

"I'm not trying to be mean. It's a deep question for me to answer in the middle of the ER, watching my sister have a breakdown. I've never seen her like this, Jack. Have you?"

"No. I haven't, but we've been in trouble for a while now."

"How long?"

"A year for sure. Maybe longer. After hearing your description of us, maybe always."

An awkward pause extended coast-to-coast, and I decided to divert our conversation. "If they're sending Allison for a CT scan, will she be admitted to the hospital?"

"Only if they find something. They're going to stabilize her and then discharge her. Once they let her go, I'll take her back to my house and put her right to bed."

"Good."

"You know how these headaches take her down. She'll need a couple of days to sleep and recover. I'll let her do that, but I'm going to call my doctor on Monday and make her an appointment. We'll take everything else from there. She misses Heide, but she told me she doesn't want Heide to see her until she feels more in control."

"How much control does she have right now?"

"Little to none. It's scary, Jack. She's not in charge of what's happening to her."

"All right. There's not much I can do from here, but if

anything comes up that is overwhelming for her, let me know. I haven't given up on our marriage. I do want her to get better. I want to do what I can for her. And for you, Liz."

There was a significant pause. When she responded, her voice was gentle and forgiving. "I understand. I'm sorry this is happening."

"Me, too, but Allison needs you. If this was inevitable, I'm glad it happened to her while you were around. This has been building up for a while. Maybe she went to Baltimore because she wanted to feel more at home."

"I'll take care of her. I promise."

"Thank you. Please tell her that I'm thinking about her nonstop. That I'm worried about her. If I'm the one upsetting her like this, I don't want her to be afraid of me. Please try to make her understand that. If she only wants to speak to Heide, I'm not going to interfere."

"How is Heide doing?"

"She's upset that Allison didn't come home today, but I think she understands there was no way around that. If Allison asks, let her know that I told Heide she wasn't feeling well and nothing more."

"I will. I don't mean to cut you off. But we're waiting for the doctor to come back and I don't want to miss him in case there's a development."

"I understand."

"I'll call you if something comes up, but if not, I'll wait until we're back home."

"Sounds good, Liz. Thanks again for everything."

"Bye, Jack."

chapter

Nineteen

KATHLEEN DIDN'T *return to the office for the rest of the week, and she kept a low profile. The likelihood of her accepting a job offer in Colorado increased with each passing day. The longer she was away, the more she was considering a future without me. My days and evenings rolled by with sluggish dread. I missed the springtime when everything had been so happy. I missed Kathleen and understood that if she moved to Denver, I would always miss her.*

I was in critical need of a good day, and Heide needed time to shine.

My brave seven-year-old daughter had survived a life-threatening accident, her parents' divorce, and the uncertainty of my rocky relationship with Kathleen. As her father, I was concerned about Heide's overall well-being. Her health was more important than mine. I wanted to tell her that life was returning to normal, but it would be premature to do so now. Having seen Robert and Kathleen, I'd come to understand what resulted when a father and daughter lost trust in one another. I needed to talk to Heide about everything without overwhelming us both.

Summer had given way to autumn, and the weather was turning cool. Heide's body was still healing, and she was adapting to the reality of living without fully operational lungs. Her injury from the backstop collapse was one she would never overcome, and I didn't want to compromise her fragile health. I had to get creative when picking a place to spend an afternoon away from the house.

I settled on the idea of taking her to the Bend Fall Festival. With Allison's thoughts focused on her upcoming return to Baltimore, a local tradition was a good place for just the two of us. As we navigated past countless vendors and their tents on our way to explore the Family Fun Street, I took my cues from Heide. When she grew tired inside a maze built of hay, I carried her in my arms. We sat and rested while watching the boxcar derby. She grew irritated when she wanted to do more than she was physically capable of, yet I refrained from pressuring her to move along to something new. All it took to reinforce my patience was the fear I'd experienced the day she'd been hurt. I'd been certain Heide was going to die. I'd been terrified we wouldn't enjoy moments like these ever again. From now on, I would never rush her through anything.

We spent the better part of an hour hand-painting a pumpkin, and when we finished, I gave her a piggyback ride to a restaurant that offered comfortable seating and a kid-friendly menu. After she ordered her macaroni and cheese, I smiled at my daughter.

"We have a lot to catch up on," I said. "There are some things I need to tell you."

She took a sip of her apple juice and nodded. "I know."

As usual, I couldn't suppress my delight over her wise reactions. "You do?"

My daughter stared at me and quirked an eyebrow. "We've had this talk before."

Although these words also took me by surprise, I didn't find any humor in them.

"That's true." I sat back in my seat and absorbed the truth of her words. "I'm glad we can have these talks. Aren't you?"

"I guess so." She appeared somewhat confused and looked over my shoulder and out the window. I tried to simplify the moment.

"At times, we have to talk about things that aren't easy. When

I say I'm glad we can talk, I mean that I'm glad we can get through the tough times together."

She returned her attention to me, her eyes searching mine.

"Heide, some daughters fear their fathers. I never want you to be afraid of me."

"You're not scary." She was trying not to find the thought funny, but she couldn't help it. My words of wisdom gave her as big a kick as hers gave me.

"Good. I was hoping you'd say something like that."

"What do we need to talk about?" she asked, the uncertainty between us forgotten.

"There are several things, really. First, your doctors think you're almost ready to go back to school."

Heide nodded.

"Do you feel ready to be away from home all day without Mom or me close by?"

She gave my question thoughtful consideration. "Recess will be hard, but sitting in class will be okay."

"What worries you about recess?"

"I shouldn't swing. Or go down the slide. What if another kid knocks me down? I don't want to get hurt again."

I took her hand and gave it a reassuring squeeze. "We'll help you figure out recess. We can talk to your principal and your teacher."

"What about PE?"

"We'll figure that out, too."

"Okay."

"Is there anything else about school you're worried about?"

She shook her head.

"All right. That's good. Are you ready to talk about something else?"

"Sure."

"Have you talked with Mom about her going back to Baltimore?"

"A little bit."

"How do you feel about that?"

Heide folded her arms on the table and rested her chin on them. *"I'll miss her."*

I was far more concerned about her mother's departure than her return to school. Although the date for Allison's return to Baltimore hadn't been finalized, we'd spoken about it during the week. We'd agreed that Allison would wait until Heide was settled at school and accustomed to spending her days away from her mother. Allison admitted she would need time to adapt as well.

"It's been good Mom could be here to help. But you understand why she's going back, right? Maryland is her home."

"And Oregon is yours." She took another sip of her juice.

"That's right." I swallowed my emotion and tried to keep a brave face. *"But both places will be home to you. We want you to have a vote, too."*

"What do you mean?"

"If you're unhappy here in Bend, if you think you'll miss Mom too much, you could go with her."

Worry flashed in my daughter's eyes. *"Do you want me to go?"*

I gave her hand another squeeze. *"No. Never. But I wouldn't stop you if that's what you want. After everything you've been through with your accident, it would be understandable if you didn't like Bend anymore."*

She answered me without too much thought. *"I like it here. I like my school and my friends. I like the mountains. I like Kathleen."*

Heide's declaration reminded me of an afternoon in Portland, when I'd held Kathleen in my arms and listened to her express similar thoughts about my daughter. My heart clenched with bittersweet intensity.

"She likes you," I replied.

Heide began to fidget a bit in her chair.

"What is it?" I asked with growing concern.

"Why doesn't she come over to see us?"

"That's difficult to explain, but I can try."

"Is it because of that fight in Portland?"

"Not completely. But I know that one of the reasons she doesn't come over is because she doesn't want anyone to fight. She wants you to be happy, and she wants you to get better. She cares about you and she knows that the fight upset you."

"I miss her," Heide replied.

"I miss her, too."

She crossed her arms in defiance. "At least you get to see her at work."

"That's true. It's not the same though."

"When Mom goes to Baltimore, will Kathleen start coming over to see us again?"

I hesitated to answer this question, but Heide watched me expectantly. I scratched my cheek as I struggled to find the right combination of words. I wanted to be truthful, but I didn't want to cause her unnecessary distress.

"Kathleen wants to see you. I'm sure of that."

"What about you? Doesn't she want to see you?"

"I don't know. I hope so."

"Is she still your girlfriend?"

"That's what we're trying to figure out."

Her face projected her deepest concern yet. There was a level of sorrow in her eyes that I hadn't been prepared for.

"Why is it so hard for grown-ups to stay friends?"

"I'm not sure. Maybe because grown-ups have more things to worry about. They get busy and they lose touch with each other."

"Did you tell her you were sorry?"

"For the fight?"

She nodded.

"I did. And to be honest, I need to tell you I'm sorry, too. It wasn't fair to put you through that. I wasn't being a good parent.

I'll always feel bad about that afternoon."

Heide stood up and walked around the table to my side. She didn't hesitate to climb onto my lap, even though she needed some help. She wrapped her arms around my neck, pulling our foreheads together.

"It's okay, Dad. We were all tired."

I wanted to squeeze her hard but needed to be mindful of her fragile ribs. I kissed her forehead instead.

"You're amazing. You know that?"

She ignored my praise and moved on to her next point.

"Did you tell Kathleen you'll always feel bad about that afternoon?"

"I've told her a lot of things, but I still have more to say."

She leveled me with a serious stare. "You need to take care of that, Dad."

"I know. But I'm trying to be careful with her, too."

"Why do you need to be careful?"

"Well, it's kind of like you and recess. She's afraid something bad is going to happen, and she'll be really hurt by it."

"You talk to me because you don't want me to be scared. If you don't want Kathleen to be scared, you need to talk to her."

I froze as I contemplated these words. Kathleen's biggest hope was that I would trust her in the same way she had trusted me. I did trust her. I'd been telling myself so all along, but I hadn't proven it. I'd convinced myself that my past wasn't important to my future. I'd decided the truth would cause more harm than good, and I didn't want to become someone else who'd hurt her. But where had that logic gotten us? Kathleen was frightened of where our relationship was headed and was preparing to uproot her entire life as a result. We'd never been farther apart, emotionally or physically.

"You're right. You're such a smart person. How did you get to be so wise?"

"I don't know. It just came to me."

Our server returned with Heide's lunch and she carefully climbed off my lap and reclaimed her seat. Then she began eating her meal with enthusiasm while I gathered my thoughts and my courage.

chapter Twenty

ANOTHER WEEK passed before Allison called us again, but Liz had been updating me via text messages. The results of Allison's medical tests were negative, and she returned to her sister's home for further rest and recovery. The news came as a tremendous relief. Uncertain of how much Allison wanted me to know, I accepted Liz's updates with gratitude without pushing for more information.

Several days after her visit to the emergency room, Liz informed me that Allison was diagnosed with severe depression and anxiety. This news struck me like a punch to the gut, but Allison embraced it. She'd spent many years battling a downward spiral of pain and suffering, but there was no more hiding her condition. The action of acknowledging her symptoms and sharing them with her family liberated Allison from her emotional prison.

On the night when Allison finally called, she sounded strong. I handed Heide the phone and left her alone in the living room to reconnect with her mother. Forty minutes later, Heide found me in the bedroom and extended her arm, offering the phone back to me and letting me know that Allison wanted to talk.

I accepted the proffered cell phone with a sense of melancholy. I listened without interruption as Allison explained that her isolation in Oregon—far away from family, friends and familiar routines—had only exacerbated her stress. When Allison told me that she wasn't coming back, that our marriage could not survive, I experienced both sorrow for the loss and sympathy for her predicament. The only element of surprise was when I realized I was romantically indifferent toward my wife. Allison's physical and emotional recovery were far more important to me than holding on to an unhappy marriage.

Our primary concern was for Heide's well-being. Allison was full of guilt where she was concerned. She hadn't gone to Maryland believing she was leaving for good. She'd only left thinking she needed some distance from me and our problems. She'd wanted to figure out the best path forward, but she never intended to leave Heide for the long-term.

With an emotional confession, Allison explained to me that as soon as she'd arrived in Baltimore, the reality that she didn't want to continue with our marriage overcame her. Our family was irreparably altered. I'd failed both Allison and Heide with my many mistakes, and so I resolved never to do so again. I shoved aside the temptation to indulge my selfish pride and offered Allison my unconditional support.

Allison didn't want Heide to be a firsthand witness to her depression and grief, and so we made the difficult decision together to leave Heide with me in Bend. Child custody was not a battle to be won or lost. We each had to accept a painful challenge. Allison would have to endure an extended time separated from our daughter, while I would be the parent who would navigate Heide through the difficult process of our divorce.

Allison also had other things to figure out. She needed a job to support herself and a place to live. Settled into my new home and job in Oregon, I offered up our savings to allow Allison to do what she needed. She was surprised. After everything we'd been through during our marriage, the last thing I wanted was to fight with her. What good would that do? How could animosity between us be of any value to Heide's health?

We ended the call with an agreement. We would take the

weekend to mull over how to inform Heide of our decision. When the time came, we would tell her together.

We also promised to keep talking to one another.

Five days later, I was sitting in the conference room at work. I had no idea what the meeting was about. Thinking about Heide and Allison had me distracted and upset.

The previous night, we had broken the news to Heide via FaceTime. Heide had been sitting on my lap while Allison led the conversation. I supported every one of Allison's statements and held Heide close as she absorbed what our divorce meant to her. She was sad and worried, so we spent most of our time reassuring her that we both loved her. We tried our best to help her understand that the decision was the right one for our family. We let her ask her questions and express her emotions and encouraged her to talk whenever she needed to. After we ended the call, Heide clung to my neck and cried. I held her tight and offered what comfort I could. I didn't move us from the chair until she was ready. She spent the rest of the night tucked into my side on the living room sofa, eventually falling asleep when weariness overtook her. I carried her to her room and placed her in the bed. I watched over her for several minutes, leaving only when I was sure she was down for the night.

The next morning, we both awoke in somber moods, but stuck to the usual routine. When I dropped her off at school, she strolled into the building with her head up but without a wave goodbye. She didn't look at me once after exiting the car, and that image had been looping nonstop in my mind ever since.

I snapped back to reality when Robert impatiently called Kathleen's name. Twice. Robert aimed his seething glare at Kathleen, and her attention was centered on me. I froze as a mixture of wonder, apprehension and an odd dose of longing bolted through me.

The third time Robert called on Kathleen, she registered his command. "S-sorry," she stammered, dropping her gaze. "I was working on an idea."

"Work on it later," he responded, returning to the agenda.

Robert stayed moody for the rest of the meeting. He had his sights set on Kathleen. When the meeting concluded, and the others began to filter out of the conference room, he narrowed his eyes at her and opened his mouth to speak. But I interjected before he could utter a syllable.

"Do you have a minute to speak?" I asked him. "In private?"

Robert took more than a few seconds to look in my direction and answer. When he did, his response was devoid of emotion. "Sure."

Robert gestured for me to leave the room and he followed close behind, but just as I stepped into the hallway, he turned to Kathleen.

"Wait here," he grumbled, closing her inside the room. Robert strode past me, moving toward his office. I followed him, relieved to put some distance between father and daughter. I looked back over my shoulder at the closed door. As I passed by the reception desk, Tracie caught my eye and frantically twirled her fingers, telling me to turn back around and follow the boss. I complied, but it wasn't easy.

When I entered Robert's office, I shut his door and took my preferred seat in front of his desk. He settled in his executive chair and stared at me with expectation. Knowing that Robert was not one interested in entertaining intricate setups, I got right to the point.

"I need to take some time off over the next few afternoons."

Robert was moody, and my announcement wasn't improving the situation.

"For how long?" His voice was gruff and annoyed.

"This week for sure. Possibly next week as well."

"May I ask why?"

I'd been nervous about posing this request even before the debacle in the conference room. I'd been warned during my first week that Robert did not look kindly on new employees asking for time off. I was risking Robert's wrath, but I was willing to deal with the consequences. I'd do anything for my daughter.

"My wife has returned to Baltimore," I said. "We're getting a divorce."

On the other side of the desk, Robert's expression was stoic but engaged.

"Our daughter is here with me and struggling with the news. I want to pick her up after school over the next few days and spend time with her. I need to watch how she's taking things and, I don't know, just be there in case she needs me."

Robert kept his silence, and I shifted underneath his unrelenting gaze.

"I'll work through lunch and make up the rest of the time when things settle down."

Robert raised a hand to quiet me and derailed my train of thought.

"Is she still speaking to you?" he asked me.

I blinked as I processed my confusion. "Who? My wife or my daughter?"

Robert hesitated. "Both, I suppose, although I was thinking of your daughter." A new expression overtook his features—the look of chagrin.

I shifted in my seat yet again, trying to decide how much personal information I should reveal to my new boss.

"She was as of last night," I managed. "They both were, actually."

He offered a nod of satisfaction. "Good."

An awkward silence ensued while I waited for his decision. He drummed his fingers on his desk. One large sigh preceded his announcement.

147

"You're new, but you work hard. Take the time you need this week, and we can revisit the matter again on Monday. See where things are at then."

"Thank you, Robert. If I could, I'd like to say one more thing."

"What is that?"

"I want to reassure you that I am where I want to be. My decision to stay in Bend isn't going to change because of my divorce. I may have found Aurora by luck, but I want to make a career here. I still want to build my new life in Oregon."

Robert studied me. "Do you mean that?"

"I wouldn't say it otherwise."

Robert sat back in his chair and tented his fingers. He watched me and then he nodded. "I have a special project in mind. One I've been considering you for." Robert scratched his chin. "Do you have a minute?"

"Sure."

"Let me pitch it to you. If it sounds good, perhaps we can consider this whole thing even."

"What's the project?"

"As you know, the firm has its roots in Portland and we like to honor that. Each spring, we hold a luncheon up there. It's a long-standing tradition and a signature moment. It was my father's project, and when I took over Aurora and moved headquarters here, the continuation of that luncheon was one of the conditions I agreed to. Although these kinds of things aren't my area of expertise, I've come to recognize its importance to both the company and the family."

I nodded.

"A few years ago, I passed the project along to Kathleen, and I tasked her to find ways to make it more innovative. She's done a good job, but I'm curious to see what a fresh perspective could add to the event. There's seven months to develop new ideas, so I'd like you to co-manage this year's luncheon with her."

"I see. How does Kathleen feel about the idea?"

It was now Robert's turn to blink in confusion. "I haven't spoken to her about it, but the idea has been on my mind for a bit now. If you're on board, I'll tell her today."

It wasn't my place to question Robert's management style, but my instincts were more than a bit wary. There was a distinct possibility that Kathleen wouldn't welcome my assignment. But, given the options, I believed it would be easier to find ways to assuage Kathleen than to refuse Robert. I didn't know her well, but she was more reasonable than her father. I took care with my reply, however, offering up what I hoped was a diplomatic response.

"I'm happy to be of any service for the event."

"Great." Robert grinned for the first time since the conference room. "You should plan on scheduling a meeting with Kathleen about how to move forward, but let's talk again on Monday. Use this week to catch up on your current projects and to take care of your daughter."

When Robert rose from his chair, so did I and turned to open the door. "Good luck with your family, Jack," he said in a voice quiet full of trepidation.

I wasn't used to hearing that tone from Robert Brighton, and I turned back around to face him. Although he didn't say so directly, Robert's tone conveyed his understanding.

I knew enough of the Brighton family history to realize that Robert had some difficult days raising his own daughter. I took some comfort in the thought that his daughter had stayed by her father's side professionally, despite what appeared to be some personal difficulties in their relationship.

My thoughts returned to the woman who was waiting alone in the conference room to contend with her irritated father, because of my own personal distractions. She was loyal, hardworking, and a gentle soul. I decided to remind him of her goodness.

"I'm looking forward to working with Kathleen on the luncheon. She impresses me and represents your firm and your family with elegance. She's the perfect choice to lead this event. Thank you for the opportunity, and please pass along my thanks to her as well."

Robert offered a curt nod and a quick dismissal from his office.

chapter Twenty-One

I SPENT the rest of my work day inside my office. I had no idea what happened between Robert and Kathleen, but I was certain I was the reason she'd stayed in the conference room after the meeting. My guilt grew with each passing hour. From behind my desk, I caught glimpses of those who wandered by my doorway and gauged what I could, but I wasn't prepared to face anyone. Even so, thinking about what may be happening on the other side of the office was a distraction from my personal troubles.

Barricaded away from the rest of my colleagues, I had some level of control over the unfolding events of the workday. I was grateful when it was time to leave the office to pick Heide up from school. I gathered my things and made a straight shot for the door to the building. I got no more than four steps outside when I ran into Kathleen.

We made eye contact with each other and halted. She was carrying something, and my nosiness got the best of me. She was holding a Chinese takeout box.

I gestured toward the box. "Late lunch?"

She looked down at the takeout. "I suppose, but at least dinner will be taken care of, too. Win-win." She lifted her head, smiling at me.

While her lightness relieved me, I couldn't express my gratitude in that moment, so I gave her a polite nod. I wasn't feeling as carefree as she appeared to, and my anxiety grew as

Kathleen's mood turned serious.

"Is everything all right, Jack?"

"Why do you ask?" My response wasn't defensive. At least I didn't think so. I was simply curious about how she knew.

"It's unusual for you to leave work so early." Kathleen gestured to my messenger bag and the blazer draped over my arm. "And, you were upset in the meeting this morning."

I stared at her, unsure how to reply.

As the seconds ticked by, Kathleen became nervous under my scrutiny. "Forget I said anything." She took a step forward to move past me, and I took one step to the side, effectively cutting off her retreat. She paused.

"It's fine. Actually, I've been feeling guilty about what happened this morning," I said, making an extra effort to keep my voice gentle.

All traces of Kathleen's nervousness evaporated, only to be replaced with concern. "Why would you feel guilty about anything?" she asked.

"If I got you into hot water with Robert, I'm sorry."

"It doesn't matter." Her response was robotic. The mention of her father's name was enough to flip her emotional switch.

"It matters to me," I replied.

The silence grew between us as Kathleen's mood shifted yet again, this time into confusion. She shook her head. "It's finished."

Not knowing what else to say to her, I waited for a change of subject. I wanted to see if Kathleen would mention our new assignment to me. She didn't. If anything, she appeared to be waiting for me to say something.

"I hope I didn't cause you any trouble," I reiterated, holding her gaze and hoping she understood how much I meant it.

Kathleen was the first to blink, and when she did, she dropped her shoulders, letting go of all her tension.

"Robert was irritated with me," she told me. "But it's not the first time and it won't be the last."

Kathleen took another step forward and moved past me. Her declaration bothered me, but it was clear she wanted the last word on a difficult topic.

Regardless, she had shared something intimate with me, and so I turned and said to her retreating back, "My wife and I have separated."

Kathleen stopped just as she reached for the handle on the large glass door. Her hand dropped down to her side, and she turned to face me with surprise and concern.

"That's why I'm upset," I explained. "We've decided to divorce."

"I'm sorry." The sadness in her tone was genuine emotion.

"I told Robert about it after the meeting. You're the only other person here who knows."

Kathleen tilted her head. "Why tell me?"

"Because you deserve to know why I was distracted this morning."

As uncomfortable as the prospect was, I would have to make my divorce known at the office, but I resolved to keep the details private. I was more determined than ever not to jeopardize my career at Aurora. There was more at stake than ever before.

Kathleen waited for details that wouldn't be forthcoming. When I didn't elaborate on the situation, she nodded. "I understand. I won't say anything. Neither will he."

I returned Kathleen's nod.

"Where are you going now?" she asked me.

"To pick up my daughter from school. I want to spend some time with her. Make sure she's doing all right."

Kathleen's gaze settled somewhere on the horizon decorated with mountain peaks bright with fresh snowfall. Her eyes glistened in the autumn sunshine. "That's so good of you, Jack." She blinked several times. She looked at me once again and offered her bashful smile. "I'll let you go. You shouldn't be late."

My heart stammered in response to her mysterious

vulnerability. "Thank you."

Without another word, she turned and entered the building. I watched until her silhouetted frame disappeared.

Late last night I'd ruminated on an idea for a finicky client. When I'd arrived at work, I'd gone straight to my office, started in on the task and hadn't come up for air for hours. I paused my work on the new project with an air of satisfaction. I sat back in my chair and stretched.

Although the work was progressing, I stepped away for a few minutes. I'd brought some leftovers from home to heat up in the break room. I'd intended to eat at my desk and work through the lunch hour, but decided it was best to come out from isolation and interact with other adults, as I'd secluded myself away from my colleagues for a second straight day.

When I arrived in the break room, Kathleen was there, preparing a cup of tea. I ate lunch earlier than most, and always broke away from the office to do so. We'd never crossed paths like this. She looked over her shoulder but returned her attention to her beverage without a greeting or smile.

Her coolness was unusual and unmistakable. I went to the refrigerator, retrieving my lunch and placing it in the microwave. Having worked with her for a few months now, it had become easier to gauge her moods, but this lack of reception was a new experience.

I was tempted to say something but settled for watching the green digital timer as it counted down. When the oven beeped, I pulled out my food and took a seat at a nearby table. I pulled a discarded newspaper close enough to glance over the day's headlines.

"Jack?" Kathleen called.

I looked up just as she pulled out the chair across from mine.

She sat down with both hands wrapped around her mug. "May I speak to you for a minute?"

"Sure," I replied. "What's up?"

"I think you know the answer to that." There was a slight tremor in her voice. She was worked up and I held my tongue, afraid to trigger her further.

"After you left the office yesterday, Robert spoke to me about the Portland event."

She sounded annoyed, and I needed to figure out why. Or at least, who she was upset with.

I pushed the newspaper aside. "What did he say to you?" I asked without preamble.

"He made it clear to me that we're both project managers."

I nodded. "That's exactly how he presented it to me."

"You're telling me this was his suggestion?" Kathleen was incredulous, and her attitude made me self-conscious. I hadn't done anything wrong, but her reaction made me question my own actions from the day before.

"It was," I responded with a grim tone that matched my internal turbulence.

She leaned forward and fixed me with a hard stare. "You didn't campaign for the assignment?"

I shook my head. "I didn't even know about the luncheon until Robert brought it up yesterday morning."

She rocked back in her seat. "He assigned this to you yesterday?"

"Yes."

"Before or after the meeting?"

I hesitated. Robert had offered the assignment after she had upset him in the conference room.

"It was after," I admitted. "But he mentioned he'd been considering the idea for a while."

"I see." She lifted her tea and took a thoughtful sip.

She had blindsided me with her accusatory assumptions, and

there was a part of me that wanted to be angry with her. But at the same time, I saw her point of view. If Robert hadn't insisted on such a condition in earlier years, she was right to wonder about what had spurred the change now. I watched as she ruminated and found the need to help her process this unexpected development.

"I asked him how you felt about the idea," I offered.

"What did he say?"

"He admitted he hadn't spoken to you about it yet." It was now my turn to lean forward. "Do you mind if I ask a question?"

"Go ahead."

"Did Robert pass along my thanks for the opportunity to work with you on the luncheon?"

She angled her head. "No, he didn't."

"I have no interest in taking anything away from you. If it's important to Robert for us to be perceived as co-managers, then let him. But from what I understand from Robert himself, you've done a great job with this event, and I have no intention of fixing something that isn't broken. Consider me your backup, nothing more. Use me wherever you think best. I trust your judgment."

I sat back and returned to my lunch, hoping what I'd said was enough to soothe things between us. I stirred my food with more force than necessary. I was irritated, but not with her. Robert had mishandled the opportunity to strengthen my working relationship with Kathleen, and I didn't appreciate seeing our progress erased.

"I apologize," she said. "He gave the luncheon to me five years ago. He's never insisted on something like this before. I assumed you'd approached him with the idea."

I couldn't bring myself to make eye contact with her. "I promise you, I didn't."

"I guess he doesn't believe in me enough to manage it on my own."

Her admission pierced me right through the heart. If Heide had ever said such a thing about my confidence in her, it would shatter me. I set my fork down with care, pondering how to make

Kathleen feel better about the whole thing.

"I didn't get that impression at all. And if he had said something like that to me, I would have strongly disagreed with him."

Kathleen nodded, but didn't elaborate further. In the end, she accepted the situation with a lukewarm reserve and left me to finish my meal alone. Her lack of enthusiasm made me uneasy. Her opinion was important.

Despite a few warm exchanges over the months, we didn't know one another outside the confines of our careers. It was clear I was navigating some turbulent emotional territory when it came to the Brighton family dynamic. Until I was on more solid ground with Kathleen, I decided it was best to be brief in our exchanges and focused on the task at hand.

After all, I had my own personal problems to deal with. I didn't have the capability to take on hers, too. I just wanted to get through the event without any major fuckups.

chapter Twenty-Two

ROBERT BRIGHTON lived in Awbrey Butte, one of Bend's most exclusive neighborhoods. The luxury homes sat high above the downtown skyline and had unobstructed views of the nearby mountains. The area also offered complete access to more than one golf course. Although I hadn't yet seen it in action, Robert's love of the game was the stuff of office legend. There was no doubt why he'd bought a home in this part of town.

It was difficult to tell how old the homes in Awbrey Butte were. To my East Coast eyes, everything in Oregon was new compared to the architecture in Baltimore. As I drove my car on the circular drive of the Brighton home and took in the sight of their six-car garage, I wondered if Kathleen had been raised in this mansion. Everything about her was so unassuming, I had a tough time imagining the well-manicured and ornate property as her childhood home.

I pulled to a stop next to the main entrance of the house, and a young valet greeted me. I exited my new BMW and allowed the young man to park the car at a nearby, albeit undisclosed, location. I stood underneath the outdoor chandelier and peered between two column pillars as my only means of escape disappeared into the darkness.

Behind me, the festivities inside the Brighton home were well underway. It sounded as though most of my coworkers were already inside. Truth be told, I was waiting for the first opportunity to summon for my car and go back home. The days since I'd begun divorce proceedings with Allison had been difficult and drained my energy. Heide missed her mother a great deal but was beginning to accept our new way of life, partially because I had gone out of my way to make her as comfortable as I could. Spending all my social energy on her meant I had no reserves left for anyone else.

Tonight, Heide was enjoying a sleepover at a friend's house. I'd dropped her off on my way to the Brighton house and just before she dashed away for the evening, she'd startled me by asking if I was taking a date to the party. When I told her no, she wasn't disappointed.

It was a rare night off, and I was trying to talk myself into enjoying it. But I was having trouble relating to others at the office. Everyone was polite and respectful, but the only person I'd gotten a chance to know was Kathleen. To my dismay, her guard had gone up as soon as Robert had assigned us to work the Portland event together. I had responded in kind, halting our more casual interactions. Our brief exchanges at work were now only about our mutual project.

I buttoned my suit jacket and gave myself an uninspiring pep talk as I passed into the foyer of the Brighton mansion. I wandered the first floor of the home, exchanging a few simple greetings with my colleagues until I spotted the bar. The hosts of the party were nowhere to be found, so I was content to nurse my first beer on my own.

I sought out a quiet corner and let my eyes roam the groups of other guests throughout the large room. They were animated and gathered in even-numbered packs. I appeared to be the only person without a date and grumbled to myself upon the realization.

Thirty minutes later, I traded an empty bottle for my second beer and decided it was time to explore other parts of the house. I strolled into the living room, which was less populated than the room with the bar. The large stone fireplace on the far end caught my attention, but it was the woman sitting on the hearth who captivated me. I halted midstep when I saw her.

Kathleen was dazzling. I'd never seen her in evening wear and I was unprepared for the appearance of this goddess. The merest glimpse of her at the party was enough to make me forget my unease. Her midnight-blue dress was gorgeous against her pale skin. I couldn't take my eyes away from her.

The soft firelight caressed her perfect face, but something wasn't right. She held a champagne flute in her left hand, the bubbling liquid untouched. She was alone. Her eyes were distant and unblinking. Lost within her own thoughts, she was unaware of everything around her.

Her sadness pulled me to her with gravitational force. I closed half the distance between us until I reached the side of a large, brown leather sofa. She hadn't noticed my approach, but my eyes never left her. I sat down on the arm of the couch, beer in hand and one foot set on the floor. I was prepared to move either forward or backward, just as soon as I made up my mind.

I waited for a couple of minutes, convincing myself that her foolish date must have walked away. She must have been waiting for him, waiting for someone to celebrate a toast with. Whoever the prick was, he made me furious. I was angry he would date her. I was mad he would leave her. I was livid he would make her look as sad as I felt.

Time passed and no one else appeared. I waited with anticipation for Kathleen to notice my presence and considered my options. If she was at the party with a date, even a selfish one, I would retreat. But if she was alone, like me, perhaps we could salvage the night together.

Kathleen's beauty was undeniable. I'd noticed it from the moment we met. She'd always been attractive, but now I was free to indulge my sweltering curiosity. I allowed the idea to swirl around my brain, absorbing the permission to look at her anew. Once comfortable with the thought, my eyes moved over her body with intense deliberation.

Her long hair was pinned up in a style never worn at the office. Her neck was exposed, leaving me to wonder how many minutes I could spend brushing my lips over every inch of her creamy skin. My nomadic gaze rested on the bustline of her cocktail dress that made viewing the tops of her breasts easy. Kathleen was tall and slender with a fine figure highlighted by an attractive curve of her hips.

Her naked body would no doubt be ample and soft.

The hemline of her dress was shorter than the skirts she wore at the office, allowing me to glimpse her stunning legs to mid-thigh. She'd always been beautiful, but now I allowed myself to admit how sexy she was, too. I sat a few feet away from her, undetected, watching her sit by the fire on a lonely winter's night.

A woman had never aroused me this much.

I began to rise from the arm of the sofa, prepared to take that next step toward her, but then my eyes returned to her face, and I was reminded of her sadness. Whatever was on her mind was profound, and I'd been mere seconds away from adding to her complications. I wasn't a happy-go-lucky man. I was in the middle of a divorce with a young daughter who needed me. My marriage to Allison was over, but I wasn't free to explore the possibilities with Kathleen.

The weight of reality pushed me back down on the couch, but I didn't stay for long. Just long enough to memorize the fine details of Kathleen's profile. Here was someone else like me in this universe. Someone battling her own set of demons, but she never blamed others for whatever ailed her. She was graceful and strong, and I yearned for an ounce of her wisdom to help me navigate my upcoming challenges. This magnificent woman had me entranced.

I wanted to rise and ravish her body. Instead, I sat and allowed her goodness to fill my spirit before walking away.

She left my sight, but she never left my mind. I tried to mingle with others at the party, but I found the small talk annoying. Their proximity was stifling. I wanted to be left alone. I wanted to think about Kathleen and nothing else for the few peaceful hours I had that evening. When I was sure I couldn't fake my way through another minute of conversation, I wandered upstairs, seeking total privacy. I ducked into one of the bedrooms and discovered a door that opened to the outside.

Fresh air was a great idea, so I strolled over and unlocked the bolt. I stepped onto the upper balcony of the immense home. The upper tier was a fair distance from the ground and ran the full length of the west side of the house. It was well past sunset, so I couldn't see the mountains, but I knew Bend well enough to distinguish I was staring in their direction.

With everyone else enjoying the party on the main floor of the house, I found some welcome solitude. The air was chilly, but not unlike other winter evenings I'd experienced throughout my lifetime. I placed my hands on the railing and let my head drop, exposing the back of my neck to the December breeze. It was too warm indoors and the brisk air felt good on my skin. I brought my thoughts back to the gorgeous, sad woman sitting by the fireplace. I started thinking about Kathleen, and this time I allowed my thoughts to wander. Within moments, they were drifting into a vivid fantasy.

I recalled the flattering bustline of her party dress. The outfit pushed her breasts together in a delightful fashion, lifting them high and forward. I found myself focusing on that image. Seeing more of her feminine shape than she'd ever allowed at the office was an exceptional thrill.

If only she were here with me now. Just the two of us.

I wanted to unzip her dress and expose her pert breasts to the night sky, right there in the middle of the party. The prospect was exciting. I wanted to place her in front of me, holding her back to my chest. From behind, I could wrap my arms around her to caress her naked skin. Given the opportunity, my touch would linger on her nipples, so I could watch them harden against the winter air.

The reverie was so strong, I could almost feel her hands reach back to grip my thighs, a signal that she wanted more than just my fingertips on her breasts.

I imagined stepping out from behind her, kissing her roughly and pushing my tongue inside her mouth before backing her up against the wall of the house. I wanted to feel her naked body press against my chest. I wanted her to experience the passion trapped inside me. With the two of us enveloped in dark shadows, I would kneel in front of her, hike up her skirt and tug her lacy, black underwear to the side.

I wondered if she would be bare. I hoped that she wasn't. I wanted to enjoy myself as I explored the hidden desires of her most intimate beauty. Tasting her. Licking her. Pressing my face in between those beautiful legs of hers would assuredly drive me into a frenzy. I'd make sure neither of us would be concerned about the guests milling inside the house. I'd make her forget everything but my tongue on her body. I'd whisper against her thigh, begging for her fingers to grasp my head, holding me tight against her. I'd vocalize my pleasure against her soft skin, and I'd ensure her legs would tremble around my face as I offered her a large orgasm.

When I'd feel her come, I'd raise my eyes to watch her. I visualized Kathleen with complete clarity, picturing her lovely face as she tilted it up to the stars. Her heated breath would be visible in the chilled nighttime air. Her bliss would only enhance her exquisiteness.

I returned from the intense fantasy, gripping the balcony railing with white knuckles. I'd been swept away by the moment. My heart was pounding, and I exhaled the air I'd been holding. As the indulgence of our imaginary sexual encounter consumed me, I'd developed a massive erection. I adjusted myself and paced the balcony, forced to endure my newfound desire for Kathleen without satisfaction.

When I was able to return to the party, I couldn't stop myself. I went looking for her, determined to punish myself. I couldn't make Kathleen mine for many reasons. Reasons that added up inside my head as I descended the main staircase inside her father's house. But none of these reasons were enough, either on their own or collectively, to dissuade my mission. I'd been lost for months, even years, wandering in a loveless desert. Only Kathleen could quench my thirst. She was my long-sought-after oasis. Even if all I could do was sit in the same room with her and drink in the sight of her, it was more than enough.

I returned to the living room, ready for anything. Prepared for everything, except for what I found—an abandoned champagne flute, the bubbly still untouched.

chapter
Twenty-Three

NOT LONG after Kathleen disappeared from the holiday party, I sought out Robert. He was holding court with a small crowd, so I waited my turn. I rehearsed my greeting in my head and when the time came, I stuck to the script word for word. I thanked him for his hospitality and wished him a happy holiday. We engaged in small talk for a few moments, and it took everything I had not to ask for the whereabouts of his daughter.

Kathleen's abrupt departure had rattled me, and my unease compounded when it became clear that her father was undisturbed. He was in a festive mood with no cares in the world. When Robert clapped me on the shoulder and broke away to speak with another colleague, I made my quiet exit from the Brighton mansion. As I waited for my car, I searched the visible grounds of the property in vain. It was foolish to think she would be standing anywhere outside the house, but I looked for her just the same.

When I pulled into my driveway, it wasn't even ten o'clock on a Friday. I had the night to myself, and it was the first time I'd been alone in the house since moving to Bend. Although I hadn't made any elaborate plans beyond attending the company party, it was disappointing to be back home so early on my night off from parenting. I shook my head and grinned as I emptied the contents of my pockets onto the coffee table, wondering what had happened to the days when I'd stay out until dawn. Even so, I was glad to have some time to myself.

Kitty Hawk greeted me with a happy chirp and followed me to the bedroom when I called her name. She ran past me, leaping up to take her usual spot on the corner of the bed. Now that winter was here, she always chose the spot of the bed closest to the wall heater. She was getting older and slept better with an extra bit of nearby warmth. She stretched out all four legs on the mattress and settled in for what was probably her tenth nap of the day. I gave her a quick scratch underneath her chin before undressing for bed.

With Allison's persistence over the years, I'd grown accustomed to sleeping in my boxer briefs. Now, as the only parent Heide could rely on in the middle of the night, I accepted the responsibility of doing so without a grudge. But this evening, the gesture wasn't a necessity. Seeking to claim some wildness in my resurrected life as a single man, I stripped away my underwear, turned down the lights and slid underneath the covers.

My body temperature was running warm, and the cool sheets felt good against my skin. I settled on my back and pulled one leg out from underneath the blankets. My eyes closed as I allowed my mind to wander. Within seconds, all thoughts returned to Kathleen. As I pictured her lovely face, every part of my body tingled with anticipation. I didn't want to stop thinking about her and the effect she was having on me, which was a good thing because I simply couldn't stop myself.

Although my arousal lingered from my earlier fantasy, I was also concerned. Our working relationship had started out warm. But in the weeks since Allison had left me, Kathleen had also become moody and guarded. I wasn't arrogant enough to believe the turmoil of my personal life was now harming hers, but I found the alignment of our individual turbulences a fascinating coincidence.

My observations of her at the party bothered me. I didn't have to know her well to see she was intensely sad. I'd seen many of her moods in the short time I'd known her, but this was different. Something must have happened, but whatever it is was unique to her. It hadn't touched her father. Or upset anyone else at the party other than me.

I was worried. I wanted to seek her out, but I didn't know where she lived. I wanted to look into her eyes, hear her voice and look for any clues about her emotional state. I wanted to tell her I would listen to anything she wanted to share. I wanted to offer words of comfort and be someone she could count on for support.

I rolled onto my side with a sigh and found myself facing the empty side of my large bed. I imagined Kathleen lying next to me. I was naked and wasn't ashamed to be. But I pictured her wearing one of my Orioles jerseys. The black one with orange lettering would be an alluring contrast against her pale skin. I wanted her clothed in this fantasy, and my favorite piece of Baltimore would look fantastic on her.

I held on to the image, waiting for awkwardness to overtake me while my eyes adjusted to the darkness. Thinking about Kathleen Brighton in my bed was dangerous for multiple reasons, but it didn't feel that way. On the contrary, the idea wasn't just appealing, it was inspired. The more I enhanced my vision, the happier and calmer I became.

Soft and intimate words danced though my imagination, but no matter how hard I tried to figure out why she was so upset, or how much I offered my advice, our conversation was limited to the few things I knew about her. The imaginary discussion stalled, but I wasn't ready to let the moment go. Instead, I changed tactics and pictured myself reaching out to move my fingers through her bangs, smoothing them away from her forehead. How nice it would be to touch her hair, her skin, and not have her question my reasons for doing so. I basked in the warmth of that promise.

As my own mood improved, I pictured her bashful smile replacing her despair earlier that evening. I saw that lovely grin of hers and couldn't stop my own from answering. It had been quite a while since I'd seen that smile at the office, and I wanted it to return.

Earlier in the evening, I'd thought about Kathleen with an insatiable lust. Hours later, I was still aroused—erect once more and alone. I could reach down and satisfy my physical urges without the possibility of interruption. I wouldn't have to lock myself away or rush. I could just lie there, thinking of Kathleen clad only in my baseball jersey, and take as much time as I wanted. The thought was tempting, but then my concern for her returned to the forefront of my thoughts. I yearned to offer her emotional pleasure, and just like that my sexual gratification became secondary.

What could I do for Kathleen that would make a difference?

When she had communicated her offense at Robert's decision to have me co-lead one of her signature projects, I'd experienced my own knee-jerk reaction. Stunned by her resentment and later withdrawal, I'd since reacted in a similar manner, convincing myself that I had enough going on in my life without taking on her issues.

I sat up, drawing my knees to my chest and running my hand through my hair. I glanced at the other side of the bed, unsurprised to see Kathleen's mirage had faded away. I'd allowed my blossoming friendship with her to wilt just like I'd neglected my relationship with Allison. It was premature in more ways than not to compare the two, but at the same time I could see that I was falling back into old habits. The realization was disturbing.

I'd offered words to Kathleen that day in the break room, assuring her of my support on the upcoming event, but I hadn't done much to back up that statement. I couldn't articulate it at the time, but I needed things to be different. Going forward, I needed to be more respectful. I wanted this for myself as well as for my daughter. I didn't know what the future held for me, but it began by making sure I followed through on this first promise.

It wouldn't be easy though. I would have to move forward with care, considering my actions in advance. I didn't have the luxury of acting on impulse. My attraction to Kathleen Brighton could easily be unrequited, but I had to accept that I was past the point of no return. I needed to be careful with her, but that didn't mean I shouldn't offer my absolute support.

I would do what I could to alleviate her misery. I never wanted to see that look of sadness on her face again.

chapter Twenty-Four

I ARRIVED at work and hastily dropped my belongings on my desk. My first task was to make sure Kathleen was all right. I strode to her office but stopped short of barging in when I saw her door open and the light on.

This had become a habit starting with the Monday after the holiday party. I'd made a point to check on Kathleen each weekday. I abhorred the idea that Kathleen, Robert or anyone else might find my actions creepy. I always moved ahead with extreme care. I didn't need to spy on her. I wasn't trying to eavesdrop on her conversations or interfere with her life. I just needed the reassurance that she wasn't in harm's way.

I slowed my pace when I noticed papers spread over her desk. She was deep in thought, scribbling on a legal pad at a furious pace. Nothing appeared out of the ordinary. I wasn't sure whether to be relieved or troubled.

I knew better than to interrupt anyone's creative flow. I took one last look around her surroundings, spotting a coffee cup with a windmill and a plate of apple slices on the back corner of her desk. Everything was good enough for now. Her basic needs were met, so I moved on with my day.

Later in the morning, Kathleen arrived at my office door unannounced.

"Do you have a minute?" she asked.

I stared back in complete surprise.

She blinked and wrung her hands. "I'm sorry. You're working. I can come back later." She began to back out of the room, but I turned away from my computer and gave her my full attention. She halted her retreat, and I pushed my paperwork aside.

I gestured to the chair on the other side of my desk. "Please. Come in." I rose as she approached to take her seat. A heightened nervousness I'd not experienced since my college days overtook me. I adjusted my necktie as I moved from behind my desk to sit in the chair next to hers.

She crossed her legs. My mouth went dry.

"H-how are you?" I posed the question before I could stop to think about what I was asking her. I swallowed a lump as I chastised myself. I needed to watch my impulses.

Kathleen took a moment. It didn't matter if she took all day just so long as she continued to sit within a few inches of me.

"I'm fine." She wrung her hands again. She was nervous, too. My hand moved of its own accord, intent on soothing hers. I managed to navigate it to my knee instead, but I had to grip my own leg to keep it under control.

"You?" she reciprocated. "How are you?"

"Good," I replied with a quiet sincerity, so happy she had sought me out on a day when I wanted to reconnect with her. My next instinct was to ask her about her weekend, but I refrained.

"Things have been busy," she began. "We haven't talked in a while."

I offered her a restrained grin. "I was just thinking the same thing. What can I do for you?"

"I wanted to chat with you about the Portland event. We haven't gotten off to the best start."

"You don't think so?"

"Don't misunderstand me. I'm responsible for that."

I opened my mouth to object, but Kathleen raised her hand.

"I'm here because I want us to start working together. As a team."

She gave me the smallest smile, so full of charm that it dismantled my anxiety.

"Whatever you need," I said.

"I want your full input," she clarified. "Not just your help."

"I'd like that."

Kathleen straightened her posture. Her professional confidence on full and glorious display.

"I'm taking a field trip this afternoon, and I'd like you to join me. I realize it's short notice. That's my fault. I'll understand if I didn't give you enough time. If you need to pick up Heide from school."

"She's taken care of today but thank you for thinking of her. Where are we going?"

"To see Christopher Moffitt, owner of The Orchard. I..." Kathleen paused and brought her hand up to cover her face. When her fingers settled back into her lap, I couldn't help but follow their downward journey. Fortunately, I brought my eyes to her face before her gaze returned to me. "I'm sorry. I meant *we*."

I shook my head and grinned once again. "Think nothing of it."

"We are going to pitch a sponsorship. See if he'll sign on to cater the luncheon. It's a bit of a long shot."

"Why?"

"Hosting an event, more than a hundred miles from home, to a clientele that isn't from the local neighborhood can be a difficult sell. It could be a logistical nightmare."

"That is a big commitment," I agreed.

"Exactly, but I've always relied on Portland-based restaurants. I'd like to give Bend an opportunity to shine at this year's event. I think..." Kathleen's voice drifted away along with her gaze. She tilted her head away from me and glanced toward my door. I wanted to twist in my chair to see what she was looking out for, but I held my place until she turned back to me. "Robert would appreciate it."

"What do you need from me?" I asked.

"You're good at securing new deals. I want you to close this one."

I nodded.

"I'll make the introduction. We'll pitch together, and you can lead the negotiation."

"What are we willing to give in exchange for their services?"

"I'll leave that up to you. You know this part of the business much better than I do. Whatever it is, I'll have your back."

"I'll need a little bit of time to study the restaurant."

"How much time?"

"Give me an hour," I told her. "I'll take a crash course and then you can give me a local's perspective on our way over there."

"Sounds good. The appointment is at one o'clock."

"I better get started."

We both rose, and when she didn't step away from me, I was quite pleased. "Thank you."

Our eyes met, but we each held our professional composure. I stood as still as possible, inhaling the sweet scent of her rose petal perfume.

"Stop by my office when you're ready to go. Christopher's home is a bit out of the way. I'll drive."

Kathleen stepped away from me toward my office door.

My forehead furrowed as the meaning of her words sank in. "Kathleen? Wait."

She placed her hand on the doorframe and turned back to me. "Yes?"

"Why is the meeting at Christopher Moffitt's house?"

"He sometimes works from his home office." Kathleen shrugged her shoulders. "Today just happens to be one of those days."

I'll bet.

"Is something wrong?" she pressed.

One of the many skills honed during marriage was the ability to recognize a woman's warning tone. Kathleen's question was thick with it.

"No," I breathed out with care. "It's just... I don't know this man from Adam. How well do you know him?"

I gave her a pleading look, one I hoped would convey a level of care. I hated that she had agreed to a work appointment at another man's home. I really hated it.

She held my stare as her shoulders relaxed. When she responded, her voice was softer. "I've known him for a long time. Since we were kids."

"I don't mean to offend you," I said. "But I'm glad you're taking me along." I flashed an apologetic smile that was returned.

"I'm glad you're going with me." She waved and disappeared into the corridor.

I sat in the passenger seat of Kathleen's white, sporty Lexus sedan. I'd never been inside her car and hadn't given the vehicle much thought whenever I'd spotted it in the parking lot at work. I studied the immaculate interior and soft leather seats and wondered how I'd never noticed what a high-end automobile she drove. The car was a perfect extension of the woman—classic, effortless and sexy.

Kathleen drove along the high-desert winter roads with ease. I was safe with her, but the experience was also a bit odd for me. I wasn't opposed to being driven around by a woman. I considered myself a modern, progressive man, but I was usually the one who drove in any given situation.

It was a mild day with plenty of sunshine and clear skies. The arrival of spring was still weeks away, but we were enjoying a taste of what was to come. It was a perfect afternoon for breaking away from the confines of the office. Kathleen was wearing a tailored skirt that rested just above her knees. I learned to appreciate my time in the passenger seat as soon as I secured my seatbelt.

I relished sitting next to her, watching her bare legs as she drove us back into town. I also paid close attention to her hand as it held the gear shift knob in the middle console. Her car was an automatic, but she preferred to rest her hand on the knob as she drove. She even traced her fingertips along it from time to time. My wandering and sex-deprived thoughts imagined how beautiful her hands would look surrounding my cock. I couldn't help it. The mental image was so intense and alluring that I embarrassed myself with the salacious thought. Just not enough to peel my eyes away from her.

Conversation between us was intermittent. Kathleen appeared comfortable enough to enjoy our small talk, but she was careful to avoid asking me any questions of a personal nature. She stayed clear of my divorce. Everyone at the office did, and I was grateful for that. I considered that she wasn't interested in me, but I wasn't fully convinced of the notion. It seemed more likely that she was being respectful and minding her own business. I tried my best to act the perfect gentleman even though my imagination was anything but.

Our meeting with Christopher Moffitt had gone well. Kathleen's friend and potential client had listened with unwavering interest to our pitch. Afterward, he'd expressed his appreciation to us for thinking of him first. He viewed the prospect of catering the luncheon in Portland as a challenging opportunity, not a burdensome request. He'd smiled at Kathleen, met her warm gaze with his own and offered her a strong maybe. He was eager to help, but he explained that he needed to consult with his head chef and double-check their business calendar. Kathleen was happy on the return trip to the office, so I was happy, too.

I took advantage of one break in the conversation to refocus. I looked out the windshield and glimpsed the nearby mountains. They always reminded me of Heide. She'd become quite proud of the many local peaks during our brief time in Bend. She talked about them as much as she spoke about her new favorite game.

"Do you mind if I play some music?" Kathleen asked.

"Go ahead," I replied, anxious to see where her musical tastes would fall.

She wasn't the type of woman who demanded attention. She was the type who could be comfortable with a lull in the conversation. She activated a playlist on her stereo and started playing a pop song. I was fascinated when she began to sing along. Within a few notes, I recognized the musician's voice.

"Is this George Michael?" I asked.

"Yes." She risked a quick glance away from the road to offer an exuberant grin.

"I don't know this song."

"It's called 'Amazing.' I first heard it back in college."

"It's catchy."

"It always makes me happy."

I stretched in my seat, turning my attention back to the song so that I could concentrate on the lyrics. The tune was upbeat, one that would fit right in at any celebration. It was a song about discovering new love in the wake of loss. It described how heartbreak had the ability to mislead you into believing that all happiness could disappear from life, but by some miracle you go on to find the best thing that's ever happened to you.

It was an inspiring song, made more enjoyable when Kathleen began to sing along. Her voice wasn't a professionally trained one, but she had enough of an ear to match the right notes. I'd always found her speaking voice pleasant; however, her singing was even more attractive. The display showed me a side of her personality I'd never experienced at the office. By singing, Kathleen showed that she had a certain amount of comfort in my presence.

I couldn't help but feel flattered, but not because I believed she was singing to me. I understood that she wasn't. But she was singing next to me, and she wasn't self-conscious about it. I decided to listen to her without interruption and looked out the passenger window to hide my broad grin.

My attraction to Kathleen was growing. Every moment I spent with her elevated my fascination. As we drove through town, I considered whether she might agree to a date with me. I didn't know her age, just that she was younger than me, but not so much younger that dating her seemed ridiculous. My divorce was still in progress, and that fact alone was enough to keep me from asking her out. But the lightness emanating from her was irresistible.

It was time to investigate her a bit. I'd never seen her with a boyfriend, serious or otherwise, but I also had a tough time believing she was available. I couldn't press her for too much information. I was nowhere near ready to reveal my feelings to her or to anyone else at the office. Or anyone outside the office, for that matter.

"Let me take a guess," I ventured. "This song is dedicated to you. By someone special."

Even though I'd started the conversation, the moment she turned down the volume on the happy music was bittersweet.

Kathleen kept her eyes on the road, but her voice was light. Playful. "No."

"Dedicated to someone special by you?" That consideration was even worse. I picked at the knee of my lint-free trousers as I braced for her answer.

"Maybe someday," she said. "I haven't found him yet."

Had I heard right? Kathleen Brighton was indeed single?

"Valentine's Day is coming up." Kathleen was skewing the conversation in another direction. Mine. "Do you have any plans?" she asked shyly.

"I've been planning something fun for my daughter," I said. "But I might be in over my head."

"How so?" she pressed.

"I'm hosting a party for Heide and some of her new friends at our house. Giving the girls a chance to create some memories outside of school."

"And giving some other parents an opportunity to enjoy their own celebrations." She smirked.

"I hadn't considered that, but I guess you're right."

"What kind of things do you have planned for the party?"

"I'm still figuring some of that out. I want to surprise her, so I've been trying to ask questions without telling her what I'm up to. But we'll make some good treats and watch a movie. I've been trying to think of some crafts the girls could make. Maybe a few other things they enjoy doing." I shrugged and looked over at Kathleen. "What do you think of the idea? Am I going overboard?"

She shook her head. "She's going to love it. You're giving her something special. Something she'll always remember what you did for her. It's a lovely gesture."

"Good. That's what I'm going for."

When we pulled back into the parking lot, I was disappointed our field trip was at an end. This was the most personal Kathleen had ever been with me. It was the most relaxed I'd ever seen her. Those minutes in her car taught me just how often her serious nature shrouded her. She'd finally let her guard down around me, and what I'd experienced was exquisite.

I made up my mind that I was going to see this side of her more often.

chapter

Twenty-Five

I WAS running late to pick up Heide from school. I prided myself on my promptness and hated being overdue for any appointment. My blood pressure spiked at the thought of her standing outside, wondering where I was. I'd fought like hell to keep everything on track for today. I'd fought, and I'd lost.

Heide was waiting for me to drive her to spring soccer tryouts. Trying out for the new team was all she'd talked about for days. Things were going well for Heide at school. After an initial bout of shyness, she'd made new friends. Now she was happy and excited to join them on the playing field. She'd turned the corner and had put the stress behind her, and while disappointments in life were inevitable, I didn't want to be the one to let her down on such an important day in her young life.

It was early March, and even though a hint of winter still hovered in the air, the locals in Bend were ready for springtime activities. I was dashing to my car when my cell phone chimed with an incoming call. Irritated, I glanced at the screen long enough to register the Baltimore area code. I answered the call out of nothing more than sheer habit.

It wasn't Allison. I'd stored her photo in my contacts and it flashed on my display screen whenever she called. Not that it mattered because she never contacted me when she knew that Heide and I weren't together. Still, the call could be about Allison, so I accepted it. Months after her return to Maryland, I was still worried about her health. I was also having trouble letting go of my marital duties.

"Hello," I answered as I fished a hand inside my suit jacket pocket for my key fob.

"Hello, Jack," the woman said in a haughty voice, distracting me. I tripped over the curb next to my parking space and almost fell into the side-view mirror.

"Shit!" I uttered the expletive forgetting I had an audience. I wasn't as concerned about the woman on the phone as I was about another golden-haired beauty who was somewhere nearby. I looked around the parking lot. Thankfully, Kathleen was nowhere to be seen.

When the woman on the phone laughed at my exclamation, the recognition hit home. My stomach lurched as I regained my posture.

"Did I call at a bad time?" she asked me.

My voice was cool. "Kind of."

She faltered a bit. "Maybe I should have texted you first."

I wasn't in the mood for banter. "How did you get this number, Elyse?"

"From the woman who answers the phones at your new office. Should she not be giving it out?" Elyse played innocent, but only to the extent that she thought it playful. "Perhaps that firm of yours needs to rethink their privacy policy."

I verbally ignored Elyse's jab at Aurora Advertising. Elyse was quick to move on to another subject. "Allison has returned to Baltimore."

I narrowed my eyes in suspicion but opted not to deny the truth. "Yeah."

"Rumor has it, she's staying here. I wondered if you'd be returning, too. You know, to make it easier on your daughter."

"No."

Ignoring my answer, Elyse surged ahead. "I can work some magic. All I would have to tell Cal is that you're considering moving back here. You'll have your old job back within a few days. You could even get a raise out of the deal."

"Not interested."

Elyse was undeterred by my frigid reception. She simply altered course. "I have unused vacation time I need to burn this year. Spring break is coming up. I also heard your daughter is coming out here to spend time with Allison. I could fly out to Oregon if you can't break away. Or, better yet, we can meet up somewhere for the week. You can choose where. That part doesn't matter much to me."

"I'm married, Elyse," I responded through gritted teeth.

"Not for much longer," she reminded me. "And only by word. Certainly not by deed."

I peered around the parking lot, searching for the words to shut Elyse down for good. Just then, Kathleen and Tracie exited the office. They were headed to the coffee place a few doors down from the office. I was always happy to see her, but Kathleen was exactly what I needed in that tenuous moment. Elyse was still talking, but I'd tuned her out as soon as Kathleen came into view.

She was in a happy mood, modeling a brilliant smile and laughing good-naturedly at something Tracie said. She even waved to me as they passed by. I waved back and turned just enough to watch her retreat, my eyes transfixed on her sublime figure. She was wearing dark leggings paired with a light gray, cowl-neck sweater. The outfit was a treat, for she mostly wore skirts to the office. She only dressed casually when she wouldn't be called away to represent the firm outside its office walls. Even so, her fashion choices were contemporary and a perfect complement to her natural beauty. My eyes drifted to her curvy backside, and my face heated up despite the crisp, mountain air.

I watched Kathleen until she disappeared inside the café. Then I picked up the frequency of Elyse's voice. She'd continued talking, without realizing she'd lost my attention. I allowed her to keep rattling on, if only to figure out what she was proposing. As it turned out, Elyse had been pleading her case for us to get together.

"...I just need to blow off a ton of steam. You're always so great helping with that."

Elyse's timing was terrible. Her last, best chance with me would have been last fall, right after Allison left, when I was most vulnerable to such offers. Instead, Elyse had made the mistake of holding off too long.

Everything had changed the night I discovered Kathleen sitting alone by the fireplace. I wanted to be worthy of her. I wanted to become the man my father would want me to be. I couldn't explain the personal changes that were underway since I'd acknowledged my attraction to Kathleen. Doubts lingered about my ability to be the kind of lover she deserved, but there were no doubts about what it meant for Elyse and her overtures of casual sex.

"The answer is no," I said in a tone intended to leave no room for negotiation. Regardless, I elaborated my point. "The answer has been no for years. Don't ruin good memories by trying to force something that will never happen again. Goodbye, Elyse."

chapter Twenty-Six

THE DISPLAY on my office phone showed the name of Aurora's receptionist, but there was no guarantee it was her on the other end of the line. I answered the call with a formal greeting.

"Jack Evans." I was on edge but made every attempt to disguise this. Ever since Elyse's call, I cringed a bit whenever I picked up the phone. She hadn't tried to contact me since I turned her down, but I hadn't shaken the fear that she would make another attempt to seduce me.

"Relax," the familiar voice teased. "It's just Tracie."

I grinned in response to the chipper voice. "What's up?"

"Robert is in the conference room. He wants you to join him."

"I thought you told me to relax."

"Stay loose. Just get over here."

"On my way." I stood up from my desk before I even hung up the phone. I was so surprised by the impromptu summoning from Robert that I left my office without bothering to grab my blazer.

I made my way to the conference room, wondering what he would throw my way. The entire scenario left me rattled. I wasn't good at dodging curveballs, and I'd been ducking one after another for a while now. I was weary of the unexpected.

Everything about this new life in the Pacific Northwest was the definition of chaos. My new job had cost me dearly but had also given me a necessary dose of routine and serenity. My budding attraction to Kathleen threatened the brittle tranquility I clung to. I'd never been one to believe in signs. I'd never bothered looking for messages in the stars, but I was entertaining the idea that there was something meant to be between us.

Kathleen simply wasn't aware of the admiration of the soon-to-be divorced man sitting across from her, and it enhanced her beauty. She was intelligent, professional, polished and cautious. She moved through every workday with a humble nature, but also with the full understanding that her actions were being watched. Her words were always being listened to, so she was careful not to open herself up to controversy.

I respected her professional choices. With the breakdown of my marriage still fresh, I was wary of office scandal, and so my attraction to Kathleen stayed a treasured secret. But as our work projects became more intertwined and we spent more of our time together, it was difficult to resist my impulses.

There was something unique about the way I was falling for her. Something I recognized and was determined to honor. I wanted to protect her from the weaknesses that ruined my marriage. I had known love with Allison and had, in fact, created a most perfect daughter from that love. But we'd made mistakes throughout our relationship. Over time, these mistakes took an irrevocable toll on our family.

There would be no screwing up with Kathleen. My heart and my sanity weren't up to another loss. She made my days at work enjoyable. She made the nights spent alone in my bed endurable. She was worth every second of the wait. My patience was bolstered even as I searched for the courage to confide in her.

All these thoughts invaded my mind as I made the short walk from my office to the conference room. I scrubbed my face as I rounded the corner in a poor attempt to redirect my concentration back to professional concerns. When Tracie's desk came into view, I was hopeful she'd offer a small bit of insight about the matter at hand. Unfortunately, she was busy with a phone call. Robert's booming voice was nearby, so I took a preparatory deep breath and stepped into the meeting room. I stopped just inside the doorway when I saw I hadn't been the only one called to the conference room.

Kathleen was standing next to the floor-to-ceiling windows with her arms crossed and her mind a million miles away from her father's demanding presence. The incoming sunlight kissed her soft hair, evoking my envy. She was wearing a navy minidress and the cut of her neckline left her shoulders partially bare. I allowed myself the luxury of gazing upon her exposed skin. She paid no attention to my entrance, however, until I closed the door behind me.

When the door clicked into place, she jumped and turned to face me. Her glowing smile only appeared after her green gaze drifted across my powder-blue dress shirt. She wasn't used to seeing me without a blazer, and I made a mental note to leave my suit jacket behind more often. I returned her smile in greeting.

"Good afternoon, Kathleen." I nodded toward our boss. "Robert."

"Now that you're both here, take a seat." As always, Robert surged straight ahead. Together, we pulled out our chairs and sat down at the conference table. Robert rarely wore a suit to the office, usually opting for slacks and a polo shirt. Whenever he could escape the confines of the firm's four walls to conduct business outdoors, he did.

"I have good news," he began without any emotion. "The *Portland Business Journal* will be running a cover article about the firm, spotlighting our luncheon up there. They're sending a journalist here for the interview. Kathleen, I want that local freelance photographer there, too. Let's get some good shots of the both of you." Robert waggled a finger between Kathleen and me for emphasis.

I blinked in surprise. "Me? Are you sure about that?"

"Yes. Hiring you away from one of Baltimore's biggest firms is a significant step forward for the company. I want this article to be about the future of Aurora. The two of you are heading up this luncheon for that very reason."

This was indeed exceptional news, so I was perplexed when Kathleen bristled and shifted in her seat.

"When will this reporter be coming?" she asked.

"Thursday," Robert answered.

"In two days?" She narrowed her eyes but kept her voice even. "Why are we just now hearing about this?"

"What do you mean by that?" There was no misunderstanding Robert's tone. He was insulted.

"A publication like that just doesn't make a last-minute decision to feature us in a cover article," she challenged. "That takes planning and negotiation. Why keep us in the dark until now?"

Robert exhaled, his nostrils flaring. "What exactly are you saying, Kathleen?"

She raised an interesting point, but in a way that her father had taken offense to. The negativity between them was escalating.

"This is a fabulous surprise, Robert," I chimed in. Kathleen turned toward me, her expression impassive. I nodded in the hopes she would understand my logic. "Although I do appreciate Kathleen's concern. We already have a lot going on with the luncheon and we'll need to use some of that time to strategize our angle on the story. We'll have to hope Chad is available for the photo shoot and not booked for another job. Can you provide us with any other details?"

Kathleen kept her attention on me, avoiding the scrutiny of her father. Robert watched her before shaking his head and addressing me.

"You're right. It is short notice. I only found out about it this morning." Robert turned to face his daughter again and waited until she made eye contact. This time his voice was less brusque. "Theresa heard the event was evolving this year and called in a favor with the editor. She sold him on the idea. You know how she is when she decides to go after something."

Kathleen's demeanor shifted from guarded to acceptance. "Yeah. No one says no to Theresa Mayfair."

"Not even me," Robert joked.

Now it was my turn to be confused. "Who's Theresa Mayfair?"

"A friend of the family from our days in Portland," Robert explained. "She has more connections than just about anyone in the state."

"That's a good friend to have," I replied, glancing at Kathleen. I wanted to draw her back into the conversation, but she sat quietly. She appeared tense, but I had no idea why. She had a streak of moodiness inside her. I'd grown accustomed to her sudden changes in demeanor over the months, but she kept too many things to herself and it frustrated me. I wanted her to trust me, yet I also understood why she continued to withhold a part of herself. Given the dynamics involved with working with family, I had to admit she handled it far better than I ever could.

"What is the reporter's name?"

"Josh Baldwin."

She nodded, jotting down the name on a small notepad. "I'll read some of his other articles and get a feel for his interviewing style. You mentioned the future of the company. Is there anything else you'd like us to mention?"

"No. Just don't fall into any traps. Keep control of the conversation."

"All right," she agreed. Robert stood up, a signal that the meeting was over.

Upon his exit, I returned my attention to Kathleen. "While it's just the two of us, can I ask you a question?"

She deliberated my request and nodded. I stood up and closed the conference room door Robert had left open. There was a nervous knot in my stomach, and no easy way to continue. I waited to speak until I sat back down in my chair.

"I understand the need to keep control of the conversation, but I have to ask. What did Robert mean about falling into traps? Is there something I should be made aware of before a journalist asks about it?"

Kathleen dropped her gaze to exam the polished shine of the table. "That's a fair question, but I honestly don't think so."

This reaction wasn't what I'd expected. Her demeanor projected worry and her tone revealed doubt. I was now compelled to see this awkward conversation through to its conclusion.

"We don't know one another outside of this office. We're partners on this event, and I want to honor that. The last thing I want to do is violate your trust."

"I trust you, Jack." I wanted to believe her words, but her answer was robotic and unnerving. On a certain, necessary level she did trust me, but I also understood she was either unwilling or incapable of offering that trust in full. I sat back in my chair and forced myself to look away from her distressed posture. I needed a few moments to interpret her mixed messaging.

"I wouldn't say or do anything during an interview that would place Aurora in a bad light. Please don't misunderstand me. I don't mean to sound accusatory. I just like to be prepared."

I watched for Kathleen's reaction but saw no discerning motion. Her chest rose and fell with controlled breathing while I waited for her to speak. Still looking down at the conference room table, Kathleen offered a small but important piece of information. "What Robert was referring to is personal. There will be no traps as far as the business is concerned."

Her face stayed hidden from my view, but the sudden bashfulness in her voice was full of heartache, taking me even more by surprise. "Please don't ask me anything more about it," she requested. "If the question comes up, it will be directed at me and I'll deal with it."

Kathleen had said her piece, but when she continued to avoid eye contact, I became more concerned.

"What is your schedule like tomorrow?" I asked her.

She looked up, her eyes inquisitive but vigilant. "I'm open in the morning. Why?"

"On my first day on the job, you told me you don't like being blindsided in front of an audience. Let's meet and prepare as best we can for the interview. You don't have to share anything you don't want to. I'm not going to pry. Let's just talk about ways we can keep the focus on the firm and away from anything too personal."

"That would be great. I'm used to Robert handling that part of the business. These things make me nervous. You?"

I shook my head. "I'm used to it."

"Oh. Good." Kathleen's voice still had an obvious level of anxiety.

"Are you all right?"

She squared her shoulders and recovered her professional posture. "I have to be."

"You'll do great. You have nothing to worry about."

"Are you sure?"

There was an abundance of compliments I could lavish on her. There were so many wonderful things I'd noticed about her over the brief time we'd worked together. I wanted to make her happy but had to choose my next words with the right mixture of precision and positivity.

"You're articulate and thoughtful. And, if you don't mind my saying so, you're very photogenic. You're perfect for an article like this."

Kathleen's unexpected blush was an alluring shade of pink. "Thanks, Jack. That makes me feel better."

I smiled, content to end our talk on a good note. "You're welcome. Ten o'clock okay for you?"

"Sure. I'll meet you in your office."

"Sounds good."

chapter Twenty-Seven

ON THURSDAY afternoon, Kathleen and I were sitting on padded chairs at a small table. We were inside a modest photo studio located on the lower level of the office building. While the photographer, Chad, occupied himself with setting up his shots, the two of us settled in for our interview with Josh Baldwin.

The journalist also sat at the table with a digital recorder. He was younger than I'd anticipated and was the quintessential twentysomething hipster Portland was famous for nurturing. Josh's look was complete with tall hair, bushy beard, multiple tattoos and black-rimmed glasses. He was the trendiest business reporter I'd ever seen and while he did his best to charm Kathleen, he avoided eye contact with me.

I disliked him at once.

I risked a quick glance at Kathleen and winked when she smiled sweetly. We'd enjoyed a productive meeting, and it showed as Kathleen's moment in the spotlight began. She'd arrived at the office a few hours earlier, wearing a designer leopard-print skirt and a long-sleeved black blouse that plunged in a dramatic V without managing to expose her cleavage. She looked refreshed and ready to take on the world.

To Josh's obvious delight, she listened as he explained how he conducted interviews. She didn't hesitate to say yes when he asked if we were ready to go ahead.

"Tell me about the name of the firm," Josh began by

addressing Kathleen. He flashed her a smile, displaying perfect teeth. It was nauseating. "What was the genesis for Aurora Advertising?"

"My grandfather chose the name. All on his own. He made up his mind about it and never looked back."

"You're referring to Stanley Brighton?"

Kathleen beamed at the mention of her grandfather's name. "Yes."

"What is the significance of Aurora? What does the name symbolize?"

"It's nothing complicated. My grandfather is a no-nonsense man who dearly loves my grandmother. Aurora is her name."

"Stanley Brighton named his company after his wife?"

Either Josh Baldwin was the most unprepared reporter in Oregon or he was feigning surprise at Kathleen's answer. I shifted in my seat and rubbed the back of my neck to keep from rolling my eyes.

She nodded. "Her theory has always been that he did it to keep her from becoming jealous of the other love of his life."

Josh paused to type a quick note on his tablet. "How long have they been married?"

"Sixty-four years and counting."

"That's amazing." Josh was impressed, as was I.

"It's a family record and, unfortunately for the rest of us, they're both very competitive."

My ensuing laughter boomed in the room, managing to draw a shy grin from Kathleen.

Josh narrowed his gaze, studied us both and made another quick note before moving forward. "Your grandfather built an advertising empire in the Pacific Northwest. How does one go from high school to the navy to becoming one of the region's most successful businessmen?"

"To me, he's my grandfather. He can do anything."

Josh entered a few more impressions to his growing

document, and she fell quiet for several moments, giving his question more thoughtful consideration. As she spoke again, she shrugged. "Seriously. The older I get, the more in awe I am of his achievements. I suppose he learned a lot about discipline from his military service, but my grandfather is also a natural leader. He always knows what do in any given situation. He takes advantage of opportunities without sacrificing others in the process. If anything, he puts family and community before his own self-interests. He's been able to serve both his clients and the city to everyone's benefit. Portland has been as good to him as he has been to Portland."

"Many would agree, and then many would go on to say that your father is more of a risk-taker," Josh responded earnestly, pleased to have broken the ice with Kathleen. She straightened up in her chair. "Many do say that."

"Yet he took Stanley Brighton's company to the next level. Has Robert Brighton been as good to Oregon as Oregon has been to him?"

"Without question."

The reporter and I both looked at Kathleen. My expectation was for her to elaborate on her answer, but she didn't. Maybe she'd decided nothing more needed to be said about Robert's professional success.

"There is anticipation that Kathleen Brighton will take Robert Brighton's company even higher," Josh added, exploring another angle.

She blinked in genuine surprise. "I don't know about that, but it is kind of people to say so."

"You'd be the first woman to head Aurora Advertising. What does your grandmother think about Kathleen Brighton's potential?"

"I grew up admiring my grandmother. I've always considered her a woman ahead of her time. She's feisty, funny and loving. She's also cultured and intelligent. Above all else, she's confident, and she's never missed an opportunity to teach me how to embrace life the way she does. When the day comes, and my father retires, she will be right there, urging me to be the strongest leader the firm has ever seen."

"Your grandparents are in their eighties now. Do you think they will live to see you fulfill that dream?"

"They damn well insist on it. They aren't going anywhere until I take the reins."

Josh laughed while I kept my own considerable admiration of this woman to myself.

"When your time comes, will you keep the company headquarters in Bend? Or will you bring Aurora Advertising back to Portland?"

This was the first question that gave her pause. She stared at her interviewer, assessing her response. I'd coached her to think before answering any question that raised her suspicions. I held my expression in check but was anticipating her response with great interest. I'd been on the receiving end of her sharp intuition and wasn't surprised when the young reporter fidgeted under her speculation.

"I feel at home in either city, and it will always be important to me to maintain strong connections with both." She leaned forward, clasping her hands together on the table's surface. "But I think what you're really asking me is who do I take after. Stanley or Robert?"

Josh nodded, impressed with her observation, while my heart quickened with a surge of pride. "Perhaps. Are you a natural leader? Or more of a risk-taker?"

"As far as who I am? I'm still figuring that one out myself, but I do know that I would never make a move like that on pure whim. Our employees and their families depend on Aurora for stability. I'm committed to doing what's best for everyone."

As I absorbed her statement, Josh typed furiously on his tablet, recording the biggest impression of the interview so far. As soon as he finished, he returned to the conversation.

"I'd like to circle back to Robert for a minute. His decision to move Aurora's headquarters to Bend would make a certain amount of sense today, but thirty years ago Oregon's business community found it perplexing. What has he explained to you about that decision?"

"At the time, I was a child, so I understood very little. All I knew was that we were leaving Portland to live in Bend. We'd been here a few times and something about the area just connected with Robert."

At this, she turned to face me. "Jack is a newcomer here. As I remember from his recruitment, one of the things he and Robert had in common was a desire to make a meaningful change in their lives. Both men saw pursuing careers in Bend as the opportunity of a lifetime. In this regard, Jack has a better understanding of Robert's motivations than I would."

The young journalist's attention reluctantly refocused on me. "Is that so?"

"I suppose so."

She had deferred to me and I understood why. She was allowing me the opportunity to praise Robert. I'd watched her since Christmas and knew she hid her frustrations with her father well from curious eyes. Josh was no exception. He hadn't homed in on her hesitancy to share details of her relationship with Robert, and I was doing my best to respect her privacy.

As my attraction to her grew, however, it became more difficult to ignore the cool relationship between the two. I wanted to understand more about why father and daughter had such trouble connecting despite the fact they'd both committed their own lives to continuing Stanley Brighton's legacy.

"When did you join the Aurora family?" Josh said, moving on to me, and I complied so that Kathleen could collect her thoughts.

"Just a few months ago. I moved here from Baltimore."

"How does a professional from the East Coast decide to move

out to Bend?"

I tapped my fingers on the table as I began talking. I needed to proceed carefully. "I'd accomplished everything I could in Maryland, and I'd always heard remarkable things about Oregon."

Josh narrowed his eyes. "So, you'd never been out here?"

"No, but the opportunity opened up at Aurora. The job was a great fit for me and when I flew out here for my first interview, I saw for myself how incredible Bend is."

"What do you like best?"

"I'm still discovering new things every day. The open spaces are refreshing. Living in the high desert is an experience unlike any other. The people are welcoming, and the mountains fascinate my daughter."

Josh's eyes darted to my left hand where my wedding ring was. Although my divorce from Allison was well underway, it wasn't final. I was still married and would wear the ring for the time being. I was extracting myself from the marriage with as much care as possible. Despite our inability to reconcile, Allison and I were united in making this transition as easy as we could for Heide.

Josh opted not to ask anything about my family. I watched with considerable scrutiny as his posture relaxed.

"Has Robert given you any advice about making the change from urban to rural?"

"I hardly think of Bend as rural. It's Oregon's largest city outside of the Willamette Valley. For the most part, I have the same comforts here as I did back east. I see myself making a very good life here."

"How does your experience working at Aurora Advertising compare with your experience on the East Coast?"

"It agrees with me. Robert has hired a tremendous pool of talent, and the atmosphere lends itself to more creativity. The employees are encouraged to spend time with their families and be active in the community. The Brighton family understands that

Aurora's success relies on far more than keeping expenses in check. It's also about the relationships the firm has with their clients and Oregon's consumers. I'm proud Robert and Kathleen have brought me onboard and I intend to give them my all while I'm here."

"Kathleen says she's still figuring out who she is. What are your thoughts about her?"

My heart stuttered once again at the question. Without thinking, I turned my head in her direction and smiled. "The Portland event is the first project we've worked on together, and it's been a real joy. She's bright, level-headed and has a vast knowledge of the Oregon market. She may feel like she still has things to figure out, but from my perspective, Kathleen will be ready to take over when Robert decides to play golf full time."

chapter Twenty-Eight

JOSH LINGERED after the interview concluded, taking time to add more notes into his tablet. Kathleen and I rose from the table to give him space and to check our phones. I was in the middle of answering an e-mail message from Allison when Josh stood up from the table and approached Kathleen, his hands tucked into the pockets of his designer jeans.

"Are you heading back up to Portland now?" she asked. "Or do you get to spend the night in town?"

"I'm staying the night. I thought I'd go to Bend Brewing Company. I wondered if you'd join me for dinner."

My fingers froze over my phone. It was impossible not to be within earshot of their conversation, but I was doing my best not to stare daggers at the young man. I'd never been in the position of having to size up any potential competition when it came to Kathleen. I didn't know what type of man she'd dated, but Josh wasn't right for her.

I was right for her.

"I'm so sorry, but I can't." She smiled at Josh and I turned my back to hide my own grin. "Did you get a chance to meet Tracie upstairs? She's the one who introduced me to that place. She's always looking for a reason to go. She's a lot of fun, and she knows everyone down there. You should ask her."

"Great." Josh was disappointed, but his recovery was quick. "She's the one with spiky hair, right? Yeah. I think I will."

"Please do," I encouraged him, unable to resist. "You'll have a fun time with Tracie."

Josh returned to the table to gather his things. Afterward, he said his goodbyes and went upstairs to speak with his Plan B.

"Who wants to go first?" Chad brought us back to the matter at hand.

Kathleen stepped back to the table and picked up her purse. "I'd like a few minutes to check my makeup. Why don't you go first, Jack?"

"Sure."

Over the years, I'd gotten used to having my photograph taken for work, even to the point of adopting a trademark pose. I wandered across the studio and took my place in front of a dark blue backdrop. I took the familiar stance, but the photographer shook his head.

"Too formal. You need to relax."

The smile slid off my face. "Um. All right?"

I heard Kathleen's light laughter from across the room and dared to look her way. She was watching this awkward moment and my face warmed. Kathleen took one last glance into the mirror of her compact before snapping it shut and setting it down. She rose from the chair and began a slow, thoughtful approach. I couldn't take my eyes off her. Her figure was hypnotic.

"He's right," she told me. "You just need to relax."

"How?"

"Pace the room a little bit and then come back to your mark. Don't think about anything, just come back and stand like you normally would."

I followed Kathleen's instructions and when I returned to my spot she was standing right behind Chad's shoulder.

"What's Heide up to at school right now?" she asked.

My self-consciousness evaporated the moment I thought of my daughter. I grinned with pride and love. The photographer began taking his shots, one right after the other. I did my best to ignore him and instead focused on Kathleen and her question. I told her about Heide's latest progress report and as I did I noticed a perceptible shift in Kathleen's regard of me.

"You have a great smile. These pictures are going to be amazing, Jack."

At first, I was embarrassed. She was watching me, but as the moments passed I grew more confident. I was flattered by her attention. Chad instructed me to reposition my stance and as I did, I asked, "You think so?"

Kathleen nodded and smiled. "You're always so well put together. You're a good dresser. This backdrop is going to show that off."

She was complimenting the photographer as much as me, but she'd never spoken to me so personally and her words caught me off guard. I still wasn't one to believe in signs, but this was an admission that she'd been noticing me.

"Thanks," I said, my voice deep with sincerity. I wanted to say something more, yet I couldn't find the words. What would be the right response in this scenario? I recognized this rare moment of emotional vulnerability and made eye contact with her. It wasn't just the lingering sting of my divorce that ruled me at this moment, it was also her. She was the one woman in Bend who had captured my interest, and I was experiencing her deliberate consideration for the first time.

"I shouldn't say this at work, but you've raised the bar around here," she admitted with total honesty and a tender expression. "You're one of those whole-package types. I have a feeling many women are going to develop a sudden interest in the business side of advertising when they see your photo on that cover."

"She's right." The photographer's interjection jolted us both, severing our connection. We both glanced at him as he scrolled through the digital images on his camera. "I have what I need here. Why don't you two switch places?"

I stepped away from my mark and the backdrop with a bit of

disappointment.

"Should I go?"

"Not yet," Chad answered. "I want to take a few shots of you two together. It makes the most sense for the cover shot, but I may want to play around with the backdrops a bit. Let me take some pictures of Kathleen and then we'll figure it out."

"Right. Of course."

I watched Kathleen as she took her place and saw a new and unexpected confidence appear. She needed no pep talk and Chad began taking photos right away. She was smiling appropriately and doing an excellent job of modeling for the camera. She came across as a natural, not mugging too much for the photographer or acting too bashful as she took her turn in the spotlight. Spending time at her side this afternoon, listening to her talk about her family and watching her watch me during my own photo session left a deep impact. My attraction to Kathleen had been growing, but this was the first time my guard was coming down in her presence.

I was drawing closer and closer to asking her out on a date. I'd waded through a long mental list of pros and cons. We worked together, and not only that, her father was my boss. I was older, not quite divorced and a single parent. She was young, but not immature. Kathleen was someone I could introduce to Heide, but I was still contemplating how to approach my seven-year-old with the prospect. Dating Kathleen was not a carefree consideration but watching her date anyone else was unacceptable.

The biggest barrier, however, was my own past. If I was going to pursue Kathleen, I was going to do so in a way far different from my past relationships. I was in my forties, but I had yet to successfully manage my love life. I had always approached romance with far less care than I should have. I was tired of losing at love and, more importantly, I had my daughter's welfare to consider. I needed Heide to learn how a man should treat a woman.

"Okay, Jack. Time for you to jump back in." Chad had caused

another interruption, but this time I wasn't upset.

I strolled over to Kathleen's side, and Chad followed close behind. As she held her place, Chad instructed me where to stand behind her. He posed us close to one another and I detected a lovely, floral scent on her skin. In her high heels, Kathleen was nearly as tall as me. Chad retreated to pick up his camera while I racked my brain for something to say.

"Sixty-four years of marriage?" I began. "I'll never make that milestone."

Kathleen angled her head even closer to me. "If it makes you feel better, neither will I."

"He's out there somewhere," I told her, hoping I didn't sound as wistful as I felt. "Probably closer than you think."

Kathleen looked over her shoulder and arched a playful brow. "Actually, I've decided to break the family record for remaining single."

"Oh? Well. Then I guess my proposal is out the window."

"No! No!" she protested even as she returned to her original stance. "Propose all you want. Just remember I'll have to say no."

We both laughed, and I noticed a slight shiver move through her when my warm breath brushed the back of her neck. We were both doing our best to hold our pose for Chad, but I just couldn't help myself.

As the photographer brought the camera up to his eye and prepared to take the shot, I gave in to temptation, leaning forward. "Maybe I shouldn't say this at work," I repeated her words in a low cadence intended solely for her, "but the scent of roses on you is perfection."

I stretched an experimental finger forward, running it across the exposed palm of Kathleen's hand. "And your skin is as soft as a petal."

Her reaction was beyond my expectations. She smiled with luminosity at my touch, her own happiness encompassing me. I grinned broadly at my successful flirtation. We were both relaxed and radiant as Chad took our first picture together.

My fingertip lingered on her wrist for the rest of our photo shoot, undetected by the photographer. Our first secret.

The pleasure of this simple touch electrified me.

Her acceptance of my admiration was flattering.

My body surged with passion as though we were experiencing our first kiss.

All too soon, the session ended. Chad told us we were free to go, and we no longer had a reason to stand so close together. With regret, I pulled my hand back from hers and held my breath as Kathleen turned to face me. She didn't step back an inch, her full breasts so close to my own body I could feel their warmth. Chad was busy putting his equipment away, and I was thankful for the added seconds of privacy.

"You surprise me, Mr. Evans."

I chuckled at Kathleen's unusual formality. "Please. Don't call me that."

Her eyes sparkled with an emotion I could only describe as pleading warmth. "You surprise me, Jack. You do."

"In a good way, I hope." Recalling the moment I first touched her skin, I became nervous. I glanced at the backdrop we'd just posed in front of. "I know that was forward of me."

Kathleen's face lit up with a blushing smile. I hoped the kindness in my stare was clear to her. She was also nervous and fidgeting in place, but not in a way that communicated unease or distress.

She was the one to break the silence. "Thank you for everything you did over the past couple of days. You really helped me."

"Give yourself some credit." I waved a hand around the studio. "This comes naturally to you. I doubt you needed my help at all."

"I absolutely did," she disagreed, shaking her head. "Um... I like working with you."

"The feeling is mutual."

Kathleen brought her hands together over her stomach and began twisting her fingers. "I've handled this event alone for a few years now, so when Robert said he wanted to raise the bar and have you work with me, I wasn't sure how that was going to go. I can be a bit territorial." Her expression morphed, and she was now looking at me with concern.

I nodded at her predicament. "That's understandable, but you hide it well."

The alarm on Kathleen's face deepened. "I didn't mean to say that I resent you. Or that I didn't like you. I just have trouble sometimes."

"Trouble with what?"

"Allowing others to get close, I guess. What I mean to say is, working with you puts me at ease. If you think interviews and photo shoots come naturally to me, I think it's only because you make things like this worth looking forward to."

I hadn't received a compliment like this in a long while, and the pleasure Kathleen's words gave me was a boost to my ego. The urge to ask her on a date damn near overtook me, but I swallowed it whole. She deserved the best version of me I could muster. I didn't ask her out in that moment, but I would soon.

I chose my next words with joy. "I want nothing more than for us to succeed."

Kathleen nodded. "I'd like that, too."

chapter

Twenty-Nine

ON A cloudy, unassuming Friday morning six weeks later, I gave Heide some added instructions along with an extra hug. I'd be working late that night and arranged for a babysitter to welcome my daughter home in the afternoon. Heide would be in bed by the time my day was over, so she humored me.

The drive to the office was uneventful. I pulled into my usual parking space and made my way inside. There was an unusual gathering of employees in the break room. The chatter from the group was boisterous and caught my attention. Wondering what it was about, I popped into the break room rather than dropping off my things in my office.

"And there's the man of the hour!" Robert bellowed from across the room. He was staring right at me, but I looked over my shoulder, convinced he was addressing someone else. He wasn't. I turned back to look at him, perplexed.

"Over here, Jack!" Robert beckoned me with an enthusiastic wave.

As I made my way to him, our colleagues stepped aside, creating a path. They were smiling along with Robert, and I couldn't figure out why. It wasn't my birthday, and I wasn't up for a promotion. Then I figured out why and stopped in the middle of the room.

On an easel in a back corner was an enlarged copy of a magazine cover. One brilliant word dominated the headline:

Aurora. Right below it, Kathleen and I were prominently displayed, standing close together with magnificent smiles on our faces. I had to admit it was a decent picture of me, but Kathleen's splendor consumed my attention.

I'd never seen her smile like the one captured in our photo shoot. I stood there, recalling every time I'd found her attractive and it was nothing compared to this photo of her, my finger secretly touching her porcelain skin. She was joyful. She was gorgeous.

I'd known the picture would turn out well, but this was beyond anything I'd imagined. We were a professional match made in heaven. Transfixed by the enlarged photo of us, I saw something new.

We were good together. Really fucking great.

"Where is Kathleen?" I asked her father. "Has she seen this?"

Robert lifted one side of his mouth in a half smile. "She saw it. Took a quick glance and turned around. She's in her office."

"This is great, but it's a bit surreal, and she's been nervous about the article. Are you going to keep it in here long?"

"Nervous? Why?" Robert fixed me with a penetrating stare.

I realized I had information he considered valuable, but I wasn't going to breach Kathleen's trust.

"She didn't want to let the family down. She knows how important this type of coverage is for the firm. Perhaps a less central location would put her more at ease." I was nervous about my suggestion and willed myself to hold Robert's gaze while he considered it.

"What would be a better place for it?"

I grinned in relief. "Your office seems good."

"Very well. I'll have it moved this morning."

"Thanks, Robert."

"Thank you, Jack." Kathleen's father turned back to the picture and an unfamiliar expression transformed his rugged features. He clenched his jaw as he sought to withhold his emotion.

"What is it?" I asked, wondering what could affect Robert Brighton so strongly.

"She has her mother's smile. It's just been a very long time since I've seen it," he said in a thick voice. He cleared his throat as he stared at Kathleen's picture.

I searched for a question to move the conversation forward. "Have you read the interview yet?"

At this, Robert's eyes returned to mine. "No. Is there something I need to be aware of?"

I smiled. "You'll be proud. She was fabulous. Have a good day, Robert."

After a quick handshake with my boss, I left the break room. I pondered checking in with Kathleen to say hello and congratulations, but her office door was closed. I decided to respect her privacy.

Instead, I entered my own office and went about my normal routine. I unpacked and stored my messenger bag before sitting down at my desk. As I reached out to turn on my computer and answer my morning e-mails, a glimmering reflection in the monitor caught my eye.

I swiveled around in my chair and spotted a silver gift bag on top of my file cabinet. There was a small envelope nestled in white tissue paper. My name was written in feminine handwriting, and I opened the card.

Jack,

Thank you for all you've done to help me.
You are a soothing presence in a life often brimming with irritation.

Your Friend,
Kathleen

Delighted by the unexpected gesture, I read the card several times. Happiness from her declaration of friendship washed over me. After setting the note down, I removed the tissue paper and pulled out a large picture frame with our magazine cover.

In combination with her handwritten card, the present overwhelmed me. I carried the frame to my desk and sat down in my chair. Now that I could study the cover shot in private, I traced the outline of Kathleen's face with my finger. I'd never been one to believe in signs.

Until this moment.

I considered my options while staring at my naked ring finger. My divorce from Allison had finalized two weeks earlier and my wedding band was now tucked away in a desk drawer in my home office. My intentions had been to wait out the summer before asking Kathleen out on a date, but the events of the morning had changed everything.

I didn't rush to her office, although the temptation was strong. Instead, I happily went about my work with my mind made up about Kathleen. The importance of the Portland event was paramount. I wanted her to succeed in every way she could. I was going to see to it. I'd committed to a long work day and I wanted to reach my goals. Frequent glimpses at Kathleen's precious gift energized my mood. When my cell phone alarm jarred me out of the zone at seven, I stood up from my desk and stretched. It was Friday night, and many had cleared out of the office as early as they could, but I heard a distant noise elsewhere on the floor.

I stepped outside my office to investigate the source. It didn't take long. Kathleen's door was halfway open, light shining from within. I heard the distinct noise of her fingers on the keyboard. We were the only two people in the office.

It was now or never.

I approached Kathleen's door with care. I didn't want to scare her, even though it was inevitable, and did my best to make my presence known in a gentle way. I closed my fist and knocked softly on her office door.

Kathleen's chair squeaked as she whipped around.

I pushed the door open and stayed on the threshold, hoping to calm her. "Hey," I said.

She looked relieved. "Hey, yourself."

"I saw you were still here and just wanted you to know it was me here with you."

"Thanks, but late night on a Friday, huh? You must be working on some big event." Kathleen grinned.

I waved a hand and stepped inside the office. "I worked on that all day. I'm catching up on a few other things tonight."

"Is everything going all right? I hope this luncheon isn't taking too much time away from other projects."

"It's fine. I'll be leaving for the weekend with a clean slate."

Kathleen nodded and turned back to face her computer screen. "I shouldn't keep you waiting. I'm sure you want to get home to your daughter."

"My stuff is done, but what about you? Can I help you with anything?"

Kathleen shook her head and kept her eyes on her monitor. "Thanks, but I promise I won't stay much longer. Maybe another hour or so. I came in early, too, so I'm losing my focus. Head on home. I'll see you Monday."

"No."

Now I had her full attention. She leveled me with a serious expression. "No?"

"I don't like the idea of leaving you here alone. You shouldn't walk out to your car by yourself."

Her look of bafflement was adorable. "I've been doing it for years."

"That doesn't make it right." I leaned against the wall and rested my hands on my hips. I wasn't going home until she did.

Kathleen watched me, and her eyes slid over my frame in the way I ached for every single day. Something about her attention this evening was different. Significant. Her green eyes lingered on my left hand and she stilled.

"Give me ten more minutes?" she finally asked.

"Very good." I moved back to her doorway when another thought occurred to me. "Thank you for the gift this morning. And thank you for the card. I like them both very much."

She leaned forward, placed an elbow on her desk and scratched her shoulder absentmindedly. "Really? Are you sure?"

"I'm a part of the Aurora team now. It means a lot to me."

Kathleen's bashful nature took over and she avoided eye contact. "I was on the fence about it."

"Why?"

"I don't know. I worried it might be vain. I just… I enjoyed our time together that afternoon. I thought it would be a nice keepsake for your office."

I glanced around Kathleen's workspace. "Did you have one made for yourself?"

She blushed and let out a quiet laugh. "How about I just come over to visit yours?"

I dropped my voice to a serious, honest tone. "Of course. Anytime."

Not knowing what else to say about the matter, I shifted topics on her. "You came in early this morning?"

"Yeah."

"When was the last time you ate something?"

She pointed to a desk drawer. "I brought my lunch in with me."

"Lunch was over seven hours ago, Kathleen."

She had no response to that, and she glanced at a decent stack of files sitting on her desk.

"Why don't we go get some dinner?"

Kathleen's sharp gaze landed on me, and I almost flinched. I'd spent weeks training myself to take things slow with her, but I'd lost my willpower. It was impossible for me to break old habits.

On impulse I'd just asked my future boss out on a date in the middle of the office. She was going to turn me down, and I wouldn't blame her one bit.

Idiot.

"Do you have somewhere in mind? Or should we just pick at random?"

Now, it was my turn to be surprised. "How about someplace… grown-up?"

Kathleen raised a playful brow. "Getting tired of Red Robin?"

"Please don't tell Heide."

We both laughed, and Kathleen crossed her heart, her slender fingers gliding along her chest.

Damn.

"Have you been to The Blacksmith?" she asked.

"Not yet. Will we need a reservation?"

"Probably not this time of year. Either way, I know the manager. I'll let him know you're a dutiful father on a rare night out."

"You know everyone," I teased.

"Some better than others," she shot right back.

"The Blacksmith it is. I'll go get my things and make a quick phone call, if that's all right?"

"Sounds good."

"I'll be back in a few minutes."

Kathleen waved with another friendly smile and turned her attention back to her computer.

A few minutes later, we were headed to the parking lot.

"I'd like to drive you, but maybe it makes more sense for me to follow you to the restaurant?" I didn't want her to worry about anything, including how to break away once our dinner was over. It was supreme luck that she had accepted my invitation, and I wanted her to lead the rest of the night.

"I suppose you're right," she told me, although I registered a hint of disappointment in her tone. I walked with her to her car, even though my own was nearby. She opened the door and turned to me. Her eyes sparkled with the light from a nearby street lamp.

"Do you know where we're headed?"

My anticipation spiked. "I think so."

She reached out boldly and smoothed my necktie. "Someplace grown-up."

Kathleen began to pull her hand away from me, but I wasn't ready for that yet. Without thinking, I closed my left hand over hers and pressed it against my chest. I couldn't think of a thing to say, but my heartbeat was strong as it pulsed against her palm. We stood in comfortable silence for a good minute before I stepped back from her. I smiled at Kathleen while she took her seat behind the wheel of her sedan, and then pushed the door closed.

The night had only just begun, and it was already memorable.

chapter  Thirty

AS WE waited to be seated at The Blacksmith, anticipation swirled in the air, rendering us both silent. I studied our surroundings. The dining area was accented with brick walls, black leather furniture and low, romantic light. Kathleen could have taken me anywhere for a quick bite, but instead she'd chosen a steakhouse that guaranteed a leisurely meal.

I stayed one close step behind her as we walked to our table. I paused to pull out Kathleen's chair and placed a light hand on the small of her back, guiding her into the seat. I removed my fingers from her body and opted to sit on her left rather than across the table. We both settled in and when our eyes met, she pulled me right back in. I reached over and covered Kathleen's hand with my own.

"This is on me," I said.

"Thank you so much," she returned, gracious enough not to argue.

"Consider it my thanks for a night at the grown-up table."

We both laughed, and the movement of our bodies reminded me that my hand was still over hers. She hadn't pulled away and didn't appear to be in a hurry to do so. I ran my thumb along her skin, slowly. I took my time to withdraw from her and only did so with great hesitation. The moment gone, we picked up our menus and regarded our choice of items until our server approached the table.

"Can I interest you both in a starter and something to drink?"

I deferred to Kathleen and was thrilled with her next question. "Will you share one with me?"

"I'd love to. Your choice."

She glanced back at her menu and made her decision. "Tuna poke, please."

"And to drink?"

"How about the German Riesling?" I suggested.

"That's perfect."

"Two glasses or a bottle?" the server asked.

"Just the glasses for now," I replied, looking up from the menu. "We may want to select something different for the entrée."

"Very good." The server retreated, giving us our privacy, so I started a new conversation. "You mentioned that tonight wouldn't have been your first time walking out to your car alone. Do you work late often?"

Kathleen shook her head. "It's not a habit. If anything, I prefer to set things aside and come in on the weekend."

"So why did you stay tonight?"

She shrugged. "It's been one of those weeks."

"What kind of week is that?" I prodded with a smile.

"The kind where you work like a fiend but can't seem to make any headway. Quitting time came, and I still had good focus. I figured I could get things squared away and guarantee myself a normal weekend. So, I stayed."

I nodded. "I remember pulling a lot of nights like that in Baltimore. I can't say I miss it much."

Kathleen took a thoughtful sip of her water. "It has to be trickier for you because of your daughter," she said, setting her glass down on the table. "You must have to plan ahead for those kinds of things."

"I do."

"Where is she right now?"

"I have a sitter at home. She also has a friend over, so it's a treat."

Kathleen rested her hands on the menu and leaned forward. I mirrored her movement, bringing our faces close together. Her green eyes twinkled with mischief and candlelight.

"Can I ask you a personal question?" she asked. "I'm curious about something."

"Uh-oh," I teased.

"How did the Valentine's Day party go? You never told me."

I leaned back in my seat as a rush of heat surged through my cheeks. "Oh. That."

"I've been dying to know," she confessed with a dazzling grin.

"Well, I guess I'd have to call it a success, although I feared for my masculinity at one point."

"How so?" Kathleen giggled.

I raised one hand. "Let's just say I was lucky to get out of the living room without getting my fingernails painted."

"What color?" Kathleen didn't miss a beat.

I squirmed and scratched my chin, but not because I needed to search my memory. "Dandelion yellow," I mumbled with a smirk.

Kathleen laughed heartily, and my heart pounded in response to her giddiness. "Oh my," she exclaimed, placing her hand right between her breasts. "That's a bold one."

Her jubilation emboldened me. "It was Crayola."

"Really?"

"I'm serious. One of the girls brought over an entire box with eight colors."

"You could have had a mosaic. And you, the creative advertising executive, wouldn't let those sweet little girls express their artistic whims?" she said in a teasing tone.

"No, I do have my pride. Although the girls were impressed with the potential canvas, I possess more real estate than they're used to working with."

Kathleen reached for my hand. "Let me see."

I raised an eyebrow in her direction. The current topic of conversation wasn't one that would solidify my manliness on our impromptu dinner date. But, it was my fault for telling her the story in the first place. I wasn't comfortable talking to my love interest about the possibility of having my nails done, but it was an undeniable excuse to touch her again, so I extended my hand. Thankfully, Kathleen didn't linger on the subject. Instead, she rubbed my fingers as she studied them. The sensation was electric.

"I see what all the fuss is about," she said in a distinctly sexy tone.

"Yeah?" My reply was husky.

She grinned but didn't release my hand. I allowed her to explore me for just a few moments before twisting my wrist to claim her hand with my own. We both fell quiet as I began to explore her petite fingers. Her grip relaxed, and I resisted the urge to lift her hand up to my mouth for a gentle kiss.

We only parted when our first course arrived. Our server requested our entrée order, and I looked to Kathleen yet again.

"Are you willing to share again?" she asked me.

"Yes."

"Is the Tomahawk For Two still available?" she asked our server.

"It is. What sides would you like?"

Kathleen perused our choices. "Sautéed mushrooms and green bean sauté, please."

Not spotting a zinfandel on the menu, I settled for ordering us a bottle of cabernet. As soon as the server retreated, I dished up the tuna. After the first bite, we returned to our conversational bubble.

"You know," she said, "I've never asked you where you live."

"In Northwest Crossing."

She nodded. "That's a nice neighborhood. It suits you."

"I considered some larger homes, but comfortable simplicity has always worked well for me."

"How many stories?"

"Just one. It's a bungalow but there's more than enough room for us."

"Which street are you on?" she asked.

I answered and mentioned some of the nearby landmarks. Kathleen was able to narrow her mental search down to a couple of homes.

"It's the brown one," I offered, "with the brick columns and white trim."

"I've always been curious about that house."

This was a pleasant surprise. "How so?"

"I wondered if it's bigger than it looks from the front."

"It is. When I first pulled up to it, I wondered what the Realtor was thinking. But it has a unique layout, not your typical cookie cutter suburban home. "You should come over for a tour." My words tumbled out without any thought.

Kathleen's fork paused midway between her plate and her delectable mouth. She smiled but didn't respond.

"I apologize. I didn't think about how that sounded."

"It sounds fine to me." Her fork resumed its upward journey.

Now, it was my turn to smile and go mute. I cleared my throat in a poor attempt to regain my senses.

"It doesn't have to be tonight," I clarified. "I mean. I don't want you to think this is a now or never invitation. You're welcome to stop by whenever it suits you."

She enjoyed her next bite of tuna, swallowed and met my waiting gaze. "I could come over after dinner."

I blinked. "Are you sure?"

"The way I see it, I have three options tonight. I can go home, go with you, or meet up with Tracie at some club over on Bond Street."

"Club?" I didn't like the sound of that.

"We look out for each other. It's our unspoken rule. If one of us is going out, the other will check in at some point during the night."

"I won't keep you up late."

She shrugged casually. "Doesn't matter."

"You don't have any plans tomorrow?"

Kathleen grimaced. "Nothing I'm looking forward to."

I laughed. At the time, I thought she was making a joke.

"I keep bouncing back and forth about the table layout in Portland. Something as simple as changing the perspective can liven up the luncheon."

Kathleen leaned back in her seat, her arms crossed. She focused on imaginary table settings at the future event and not on the present.

I shook my head. We'd dismissed our dinner plates, and I was enjoying the relaxing effects of food and fine wine. "No talk about work."

Kathleen's attention returned to me, razor sharp. "What should we talk about?"

As we contemplated potential subjects, the moments stretched out between us. It was Kathleen who broke the extended silence.

"Was moving to Oregon worth it?" Her question was laced with concern.

I looked away, tapping my fingers on the stem of my wine glass. "I'm still figuring that one out, I suppose." I'd been so careful to guard my personal struggles from everyone at the office. It was a difficult habit to break. I lifted my glass and took another taste of the cabernet. "But you've always lived here, so it must be someplace special. Right?"

Kathleen shrugged and didn't answer my question. I watched her carefully. She didn't look back up right away. Dread wafted through me as the sadness from the Aurora holiday party resurfaced in the middle of our dinner date.

"Do you remember when I first interviewed for this job?" I asked, intent on distracting Kathleen from her inner turmoil.

She appeared confused. "More or less."

"You grilled me about why I would choose Bend instead of one of the larger cities. You didn't believe I'd be happy here."

She nodded.

"Why did you ask me that?"

"It was nothing personal," she replied with confidence. "It's just been my experience that outsiders think they know what they're taking on when they settle here. Most don't have a clue what they're committing to."

"You think of me as an outsider?"

She looked sheepish. "On that day, I did."

"You told me Bend would be very different from Baltimore. And you're right, it is. Everything still feels new."

"You've done well," she told me. "I've never heard you say a disparaging thing about life in the Wild West."

I chuckled. "At the time, I rattled off some answer that showed off what little I knew about this place. But I was holding back."

"What were you holding back?"

I was straddling a line. I took a few moments to reconsider my answer, to come up with something less intimate. I dismissed each possibility, knowing that Kathleen was too intelligent to be fooled with anything less than the truth.

"You told me I was too polished to fit in here. That stung."

I wanted to look at her, to gauge her reaction, but I couldn't. Instead, she slid her hand across the table to cover mine.

"I'm sorry," she said. "What did I know?"

I slid my fingers between hers and gently squeezed. "I'm not sorry you said it. As it turns out, I needed to be taken down a peg or two."

Somehow, I found the courage to look back up. Kathleen's beautiful face was full of concern and tinged with confusion. She waited for me to explain myself.

"I'm happy to be here now," I confessed. "I like Bend and Heide likes it, too. But there's a lot I did wrong to get here."

Kathleen opened her mouth to speak but stopped short. I assumed she was about to ask about my wrongs, but something changed her mind. It was a relief. I was glad she wasn't ready to hear about my sins, because I wasn't going to share them with her.

chapter  Thirty-One

WE LINGERED at the restaurant after our meal with the excuse of allowing the physical effects of our wine to subside. We sipped sparkling water and spoke about current events, avoiding talk that revolved around work or anything too personal. The time was fleeting, and eventually I conceded that I needed to return home. I'd assumed that Kathleen would change her mind about moving our spontaneous date over to my house, but to my surprise she was still committed to the idea.

I paid the bill and asked Kathleen to give me a ten-minute head start. I apologized for the request. I was hesitant to leave her alone at The Blacksmith, but I needed to square things away with Heide and her sitter. I wanted to welcome Kathleen into my home without any unnecessary complications. She was understanding, reassured me she would be all right and would see me again soon.

When I opened the front door, I discovered two sleeping girls on the living room floor. Lydia had spread out a soft blanket and pillows for them to lie on. One of Heide's favorite channels ran on the television, but the volume was low. Lydia was curled up on the sofa, engrossed in an e-book. We greeted each other in whispers.

"How was the date?" she asked.

"Um. Good." I stepped closer to the sofa and slid my hands into my pant pockets. "Still going, I suppose."

Lydia peered over at the closed front door, and a wicked grin appeared. "Oh?"

"She's coming over. Just for a little bit."

Lydia stood up and gathered her things to leave. She moved as though to wake up her daughter, but I waved her off.

"I hate to wake Ava," I admitted. "She's welcome to stay the night here."

Lydia shook her head. "That's sweet, but you have plans. It's no big deal."

"At least, let me carry Ava to the car," I insisted. "Give her a few more minutes of undisturbed sleep. If that's helpful."

I removed my blazer and set it on the back of the sofa. "I'll put Heide in her bed first."

I approached the sleeping children and leaned down to scoop up my daughter. Heide stayed mostly undisturbed by the jostling and only stirred long enough to wrap her arms around my neck. She leaned her head against my chest, and I carried her with ease down the hall. I entered the bedroom, placed Heide in her bed and tucked her in with minimal fuss.

When I returned to the living room, Lydia was waiting by the front door, car keys in hand. I went to Ava and wrapped the blanket around her before lifting her into my arms. I offered Lydia a bashful grin as she reached for the doorknob.

"I hope you don't feel rushed."

"Nonsense. Maybe someday soon you can return the favor for me." She flashed another broad grin heavy with meaning. I followed Lydia to the car and placed Ava inside.

"Thank you," she said, after closing the passenger door. "I'll get your blanket back to you next week."

"No worries. Whenever." I leveled her with a serious expression. "Will you be all right from here?"

"Oh yeah." She waved at me as she opened the driver's side door. "I'll pull the car into the garage and we'll be fine. Don't worry about us. Enjoy the rest of your date."

"Thanks, Lydia. For everything."

"Anytime," she replied while closing the door. The car's

engine roared to life, and I stepped away from the vehicle. As Lydia pulled away, I waved and returned inside.

I made a quick attempt to tidy up the living room in preparation for Kathleen's arrival. The girls had marked their territory throughout the evening with toys and dishes but hadn't made any significant messes. I heard Kathleen's car pull into the driveway just as I finished the task.

I took a deep breath, opened the front door and stepped outside. I strolled to the car to greet her. When Kathleen came out, she was quiet but wore a friendly expression.

"You're right on time," I said. "You knew where to go."

I turned and made my way toward the house. She followed me.

"When it comes to Bend?" she replied, "I know the back roads to the back roads."

On the front porch, I opened the door while she stepped past me. I inhaled her floral perfume. I was nervous and stayed on the threshold as she stepped inside. The last thing I wanted was for her to change her mind, but I also wanted her to feel safe. I wouldn't close the front door until she offered me a signal that it was all right to do so.

I watched Kathleen's slender back as she paused to look around my living room. She studied her new surroundings with consideration. When she finished her inspection, she looked over her shoulder. In that moment, I was hyperaware that we barely knew each other. She smiled at me, eyes sparkling and lovely cheekbones on full display. She looked very much at home. I returned her grin and stepped inside the entryway, closing the door behind me.

I moved, closing the distance between us without drawing too close.

"Welcome," I said.

"Thank you." Kathleen extended her arm toward the living room. "This is cozy."

"Heide helped me put it all together."

"Maybe she'll become an interior decorator someday."

I laughed. "You haven't seen her bedroom."

I didn't have a clue what to do next, except for one thing.

"Speaking of Heide, if you'll excuse me for just a moment, I'd like to check on her."

Kathleen blinked and shifted her weight from one foot to the other, drawing my gaze right to her hips. "Yes, of course."

"I'll be right back," I managed to utter, pointing to the living room. "Please. Feel free to take a seat."

There wasn't much reason to look in on my daughter. Heide was a sound sleeper. If she hadn't woken up during the commotion of the past fifteen minutes, she wouldn't now. But I was anxious and felt my composure slipping away. I stepped into Heide's room and stood over her as I processed the unfolding scenario. As thrilling as the evening was, having Kathleen in my home was an unexpected turn of events. I hadn't had enough time to think about where the night would go, but obviously it couldn't go too far.

I glanced at Heide's peaceful face, seeking a fraction of her tranquility. I'd invited Kathleen over for a tour of the house. Nothing more. More than anything else, I needed to remember this. She was my coworker and she had extended her trust at the office. I'd hold my professional guard in place, and she would let me know when she was ready to leave. It needed to be as simple as that. Things would only become complicated if I allowed them to. Kathleen's opinion of me mattered. She appeared to see me as someone better than I was. I wouldn't let her down by moving our budding friendship faster than it should.

After I committed to a plan, a weight lifted from my shoulders. I returned to the living room and found Kathleen sitting in the center of the sofa, one bare leg crossed over the other. Her purse was resting nearby, and she wasn't alone. Kitty Hawk was standing on the cushion next to her, sniffing her extended fingers.

Kathleen looked my way when I approached. "You have a

cat."

"She's not bothering you, I hope. I can put her in the laundry room."

"She's fine. We're just introducing ourselves."

Kathleen scratched Kitty Hawk's chin with an experimental finger. I waited to see how the cat would react. She allowed it—but only for a few seconds. The cat jumped down from the sofa and stretched out to bathe herself on the floor.

Kathleen rose and offered me her full attention. "Is everything okay with Heide?"

"Yes. She's sound asleep."

"That's good." Kathleen paused and took in a quick breath. "It's been a long week. I shouldn't keep you up late. Shall we take that tour?"

"Uh. Yeah." I swiveled. "We can start here, I guess. Most of the house is the other way."

"Okay."

Kathleen followed me throughout the house. I wasn't inclined to make a fuss over anything, but she had an eye for detail and asked questions about items and features that caught her attention. She didn't rush through rooms but always offered a clear signal when she was ready to move along. We stopped outside the door to my bedroom, which I intended to leave shut. That was until Kathleen inquired about my home office space, which was part of the en suite space.

"So, you keep your office in your bedroom?" She appeared confused by the concept. "How can you ever just relax in there?"

I glanced at the closed door and then back to her, my calm eradicated.

"Do you want to see it?" I asked, unable to disguise the uncertainty in my voice.

"Only if you're comfortable. I don't mean to intrude."

"There's no intrusion. A quick look around should be fine."

I opened the door and waited outside as she entered the space.

I only reached into the room long enough to flick on the light switch.

Kathleen stood right next to the corner of the mattress in what appeared to be an ordinary master bedroom.

"I don't understand," she murmured.

I stayed in the hallway but pointed to the left. "The office is in the next room. There's a light switch on the wall to the right."

Kathleen followed my directions and discovered the hidden office. "Oh! I see! What a great use of space. It's removed from the rest of the house. That's clever."

Kathleen's steps paused for a moment, and then her high-heeled shoes clicked on the hardwood floor, moving back in my direction. She leaned out from the office doorway but didn't step back into the bedroom. She examined me from head to toe.

"Are you nervous?" she asked me with a playful expression.

"Kind of," I admitted.

Kathleen beckoned me with a tantalizing finger. "It's all right, Jack. This is your house, remember? If I'm not anxious, there's no reason for you to be."

I considered her words and then nodded. When she turned her back to me, I quickly went through my bedroom to the office. Once inside the room, I noticed Kathleen examining one of the bookshelves against the eastern wall.

"Are you a reader?" I asked.

"I was. Once. I miss it sometimes. I've been thinking about it more lately."

"What do you like to read?"

Kathleen gave her answer some thought. "I'm not sure. It's been so long. I'd like to read something that offers a bit of everything—good, evil, laughter, sadness, comfort, fear, love and hate. I'd like to be able to feel those things in one story."

I moved to stand next to her and peered up at the shelf closest to us. I spotted one book and reached for it. I held the novel in my hands and showed the cover to Kathleen.

"*The Girl Who Loved Tom Gordon*," she read the title aloud and crossed her arms over her body. "What's it about?"

"It's about a young girl who gets lost in the woods."

"How young?"

"Nine or ten. She has to rely on her own wits to survive, and she uses her Walkman to keep her company. She can listen to baseball games on the radio. Her hero, Tom Gordon, is a pitcher."

"How did she get lost?"

"She was with her mother and her brother on a hike. The mother and brother argued a lot, and the girl got tired of listening to them. She wandered away and couldn't get back to her family."

A shadow of apprehension flickered across Kathleen's face.

"It's a good book," I insisted. "It's also a short read. You could borrow it if you like."

Kathleen didn't reach for the book, but she studied the cover again. "I'm not sure I'm brave enough for this one, but you have such great taste. I promise to think about it." She offered a quick grin and placed her hand on the back of my shoulder. She massaged it for a few brief moments before retreating from the library. I registered Kathleen wandering back into my bedroom as I pondered the book in my hands.

Something about Kathleen's demeanor had changed when I told her about the novel's plot. She'd gone from being curious about a new read to feeling unsure. But even so, she'd offered me a kind compliment and a reassuring smile along with her delicate touch.

I hadn't struck out. Yet.

chapter

I SET the book back on the shelf with a definitive and satisfied feeling. I'd taken bigger risks with Kathleen since our photo shoot, and she had been receptive to every one of my exploratory advances. This night was the first one we'd spent together outside the boundaries of the job, and it had been enjoyable. There was a trust and a chemistry between us and the more time I spent with her, the more confident I was of our mutual attraction. Now was as good a time as any to tell her I was interested in seeing her outside of work. And again. I was ready to move forward.

"Kathleen?" I called her name as I began to stroll back toward the bedroom door. "If it's not too late, how about a glass of wine on the patio? I can light the fire pit and we can talk…"

My voice drifted away when she came back into view. Kathleen was sitting on my side of the mattress, her back to me. She was staring at the picture in a silver frame on my bedside table of Heide and me. Kathleen's hands rested at her sides but clenched the edge of the bed.

It was odd to see her sitting on the very spot where I slept, and I couldn't bring myself to disturb her. I wanted her to stay there for as long as possible, knowing I would think about this moment long after our impromptu date ended. As I continued to watch, I noticed her rigid posture—a sign that something wasn't quite right. She also hadn't responded to my offer to sit outside underneath the stars.

I didn't understand what had gone wrong so quickly, and I struggled with my decision to approach her. As my uncertainty amplified, my heartbeat grew stronger. Despite my decisiveness, I'd had my fill of doubt for months. Maybe I was being overconfident. Maybe I had misread the evening. Maybe she was sitting on my bed, wondering how in the hell she had let things between us get to this point. With care, I walked around the mattress and stood beside her, albeit at a respectful distance.

Kathleen's chest rose and fell as I approached, and she refused to move her eyes away from the picture. I looked at it as well. The photo was from Heide's first birthday party, and I'd kept it nearby since the day my own mother had given it to me. Although the picture was a father's priceless treasure, it was a surprise to see Kathleen so affected by it.

I wasn't sure what to do. Or what to say. I looked from the photo to her. And then, a tear ran down her cheek.

Her emotion spurred me into action. I sat next to Kathleen on the mattress and brushed the pale skin underneath her chin with a single finger. She turned toward me in response, facing me and revealing that her tear was not a solitary one. I watched in mounting worry as another fell from her shiny, green gaze.

"Kathleen?" I spoke her beautiful name again, my concerned gaze holding her weepy one. "What is it?"

She didn't answer me. Her breathing was shaky as though she was struggling to rein in her sadness. I watched as a third tear dropped from the corner of her eye. As it ran down her cheek, I lost all ability to resist her.

I leaned forward with determination and rested my mouth against her cheekbone, capturing the tear. Once it was secured, I ran my lips slowly with gentle accuracy along her skin, following the salty trail to the corner of her eye. I pulled back just long enough to move over to the corner of her other eye, where I caught another drop of moisture just as it slipped from her eye. With that tear smothered, I moved my lips down her other cheek, doing my best to remove any traces of her crying with tender kisses. As I approached the corner of her mouth, I halted my chase but did not pull back from her.

Instead of retreating from my touch, Kathleen's warm breath caressed my own. She tilted her head in a way that brought our lips together. I didn't question her decision and rejoiced as the tip of her tongue slid from her mouth. She licked my lips with a delicate but deliberate stroke. I opened my mouth to her. She pushed forward, twisting her tongue around mine without fear.

The gentleman in me wanted to pull back and ask if she was all right. I didn't want to take advantage of her emotional state while still trying to process what had set her off. Kathleen was a composed woman, not prone to submitting to her emotions and desires. She'd never let her guard down enough to expose them. Logic told me I should slow things down and check on her well-being, but curiosity was in control tonight.

Kathleen rested her palm in the center of my chest, establishing more intimate contact between us. I lifted my hand to cover hers, and she pushed forward, deepening the kiss. We knew so little about one another, but in this moment, she was seeking comfort. After months of admiring her from a respectful distance, I was more than eager to give myself over to her. Whatever she wanted from me, she would get.

I cupped her cheek, stroking my thumb along her high cheekbone. Her skin was soft, and her hair tickled my fingers whenever a stray lock brushed against them. The intoxicating scent of her floral perfume drifted around us. Her lips were full and so warm. Her tongue moved in a glorious and erotic dance with mine.

Our first kiss was a perfection I'd never known.

Kathleen should have felt like a stranger within my arms, but that wasn't the case. Everything about this moment was new, but it also felt like fate. I'd spent a considerable amount of time second-guessing many of my decisions when it came to my relationship with Allison. With Kathleen's mouth against mine, I experienced an awakening.

I had blindly pursued a profound life change and insisted upon it at the expense of my own marriage. Perhaps Allison had been right all along. Perhaps Kathleen was the reason I'd opted to stay in Oregon rather than cutting my losses and returning to Maryland. Perhaps I'd known it from the moment I first met her in the conference room, and I just hadn't acknowledged it.

The intensity of the kiss eased only when we paused to catch our breath. Kathleen didn't pull away from me. She lowered her head to my shoulder with her mouth close to my throat. I yearned for her tongue to taste my neck, but she held still. We had reached a crossroads. We would either break apart for the evening or we would keep going. After months of celibacy, I craved her body, but I would follow her wishes.

My hands drifted to her upper arms where I took gentle hold of her, while she cradled the back of my head with both hands. Her fingers weaved through my hair, offering me an unexpected bit of pleasure during our intermission.

"Tell me what you want." No sooner had the words left my mouth than she lifted her head and covered my lips again.

I'd allowed Kathleen to control our first kiss, but now it was my turn. I thrust my tongue into her mouth with resolve and she moaned in response. Her grip on my hair tightened and I pushed my weight forward. Our chests pressed together but even this new and magical contact wasn't enough to satisfy me. I leaned forward, and her body relaxed as she fell back on the mattress. I rolled on top of her and delighted in the feel of her body pressed against mine. With Kathleen snugly positioned underneath me, I pulled back from her mouth and dropped my lips to her neck.

"Are you all right?" I asked between kisses.

"Yes," she whispered the word laden with desire, and just like that, I knew how she would sound when I made her come.

I returned my devotion to her neck but brought my lips up to her ear when I felt her hands drift over my ass.

"You're making it impossible for me to quit."

"I don't want you to quit."

I rose up enough to look into her glistening eyes. We stared at one another, each accepting the weight of what was happening between us. She smiled at me with a bit of amusement.

"What is it?" I asked, grinning back.

"You're an amazing kisser." She said this with no small amount of wonder.

I absorbed her awe while offering a quick retort. "Don't act so surprised."

Kathleen laughed, and I relished in the sound. Her tears were concerning, and it wasn't lost on me that her emotions had swung back to happiness. I didn't know if I'd been responsible for making her cry, but I was responsible for keeping her happy for the rest of the evening.

"It isn't the only thing I'm good at," I said, kissing her more aggressively. She squeezed my ass with delightful pressure, and I responded by pushing my body against hers. Even through our clothes, the intimate contact caused us both to moan.

I slid my hand down to Kathleen's chest and massaged her breast over her blouse, causing her to tighten her hold on me. Perhaps it was selfish, but I feared breaking our kiss would mean the other touches would end as well. I pressed my mouth to hers as hard as I dared, and my excitement multiplied when she swirled her tongue around mine with equal tenacity.

Our grinding movements along one another persisted. I was very aware of how rock hard I was and wondered if she would allow me to discover just how wet she might be.

The clunk of one of Kathleen's high heels reverberating on the bedroom floor, followed quickly by the other, was an answer to my inner thoughts. She pulled her legs up on either side of me, adding pressure against my hips in tandem with her strengthening hold on my ass. She seemed to be making her intentions clear, but I had to be sure. I slowed our kiss, removing my hand from Kathleen's breast. I rose above her again and brushed my thumb over her swollen lips.

"I'm not hurting you, am I?"

Kathleen smiled and shook her head.

"It's been quite a while for me," I confessed. "I may be overeager."

"I like what you're doing."

"Have I gone too far at all?"

"No."

"How far is too far?"

She lifted her head and kissed me gently as she guided us back to a sitting position. Perhaps we had reached our limits for the evening, but I didn't experience rejection from her as I would have from Allison. As turned on as I was, these moments in Kathleen's arms were some of the most satisfying I'd ever experienced.

When Kathleen ended the kiss, I ran my fingers through her hair. I couldn't stop myself from touching her while I racked my brain for a few adequate words.

"What do you want?" I asked more out of tenderness than fear. "Anything that happens tonight is up to you. Let me give you anything you need. Let me do whatever I can to make you happy, even if you need to go home."

"What about you?" Her eyes focused on my lips. "What do you need, Jack?"

I couldn't stop myself from smiling over her sweetness. She leaned forward and rested her soft mouth against mine. This time her kiss was chaste, her closed lips drifting lovingly over my own. I sat still, savoring what I believed would be our last contact during this magical evening. When she pulled away from me, she rose from the bed without a word, but her eyes never left mine.

She stepped backward until she found the corner of the mattress. I'd just told her how paramount her happiness was, but I experienced a flicker of fear when she withdrew. I couldn't blame her if she wanted to stop. We'd gone from pleasant talk in my home office to kissing and groping one another on my bed in a dizzying succession of mutual impulses.

She didn't keep me waiting long. She began undoing the buttons of her blouse, one at a time. She slid the material down her back, dropping her shirt to the floor and revealing an elegant lace bra. The undergarment covered the most beautiful breasts I'd ever seen. I'd felt her nipples harden as we'd groped each other, and now I could see them straining against the fabric.

I recalled the plump weight of them in the palm of my hand. She had fit perfectly in my grasp and I hungered to take hold of her again. I was so entranced with her breasts I missed the moment when she reached behind her back and unzipped her skirt. When it fell to the floor, I took in the sight of her garter, stockings and panties.

I undid my trousers, and Kathleen's eyes darted to my unrestrained response. I'd been fighting the urge to adjust myself even before she revealed her sexy underwear. The sight of her gorgeous body in lingerie erased any remnant of social politeness. I reached inside my slacks and straightened myself in much-needed relief. As I did, she stripped away each piece of her underwear, one item at a time. Convinced that I was being rewarded for sitting patiently in front of her, I watched in awestruck calm. Once Kathleen was naked, she lifted her head and locked her heated gaze with mine. To my astonishment, every trace of shyness in Kathleen disappeared along with her clothes. She reclaimed the distance between us, and when she was close enough to take my hand, she guided me to stand in front of her. I obeyed her unspoken command, and she unbuttoned my dress shirt and discarded it. She slid her hand over my exposed boxer briefs. When her fingers settled over me, I found the ability to speak.

"Condoms." I glanced at the bathroom over my shoulder. "Should I get one?" Secretly, I hoped she'd tell me to go and retrieve the entire box.

"You can if you want," she murmured as she moved her other

hand along my bare chest, "but we don't need one if you'd rather not."

"Why?" I furrowed my brow.

"We don't need a condom for birth control, but I'll leave it up to you." She rose up on her toes and kissed me.

My logic battled my lust as her naked breasts touched my body for the first time. "Maybe I should," I offered without breaking our newfound connection. "Nothing is one hundred percent."

Kathleen stilled and fell quiet. I wasn't interested in explaining to Kathleen that I'd been down that road. As delightful as my daughter was, Heide was an unplanned surprise.

"Sorry, I'm just trying to be responsible. I don't want you to worry about anything unexpected."

She looked surprised but recovered and offered me a smile. "It's your choice," she reiterated, tapping the skin above my heart with a gentle finger, "but I promise you that birth control is covered."

She pushed the remaining clothes down my legs.

The anticipation began to burn inside. "I'm clean," I rambled. "I promise you that."

"You look very healthy," she said as she wrapped her hand around me.

I gasped from the contact of a woman's touch after such a long time. Kathleen began moving her hand up and down as she pulled me forward for a searing kiss. I allowed a few teasing strokes before resting my hand over hers.

She looked at me curiously, and I smiled at her.

"Let's lie down. I want to take our time." Yet again, she had initiated the moment, but I was now intent on controlling the pace. "I want you to be comfortable," I confessed. "I want you to know how much I desire you."

I wanted to do far more with Kathleen than service one another, and I wanted to do it without a barrier between our bodies.

It had been such a long time since I made love to a woman who was as turned on as I was. I wondered how long I would last once I was inside her. With this on the forefront of my mind, I found no reason to rush the act. We weren't in a hurry. There were no pressing appointments, my daughter was asleep in her own room and there wasn't work for either of us the next morning. The whole night was ahead of us.

chapter Thirty-Three

ONCE WE were in bed, I explored Kathleen, holding her close and gauging her responses to my touch. She scratched my back whenever our mouths met, and she welcomed every kiss, every caress, everywhere. I soon discovered my favorite spot was her breasts. Whenever my mouth closed over her nipple, her fingers slid into my hair, pulling me closer to her soft, agile body. I made no effort to guide her hands, but eventually she pushed me onto my back and rolled onto her side, facing me.

She took her time, resting her lips against mine before moving them along my neck and down to my chest. When she placed a kiss over my heart, her hand closed around me again. She began pumping with confident strokes, demanding my full attention.

"Feels so good," I murmured.

The tickle of her hair dropped farther down my stomach. Knowing I would erupt the second her delicious lips wrapped around me, I made a split-second decision. I pulled Kathleen back up my body and rolled her onto her back.

"You first," I said. Kathleen lay still, and I reached between her legs. My fingers began to circle eagerly, and she reacted to my movements at once, opening her legs wider, grasping my forearm and angling her body closer to mine. Watching her come undone beneath my hand was addictive. Her breathing grew louder, her body tensed, the air between us filled with her scent, and then in one glorious moment, her pleasure overtook her.

"Ah! Jack! Yes!"

I kept moving my fingers until her orgasm subsided. When she guided my hand back over her, I obliged her for a second time. Afterward, I kissed her breasts again, tenderly, giving them both equal amounts of attention as her heart pounded.

As her heart settled down, her body relaxed. It was possible her needs were satisfied, but I hoped for more. She had come twice, and I couldn't stand another moment without indulging my own desires. I grabbed her by the waist and slid her body to the center of the bed. I rested my body on top of hers, delivering a deep and sensual kiss. Our lower bodies came into their most intimate contact yet. I moved myself along the length of her in a teasing manner, and my tongue lingered inside her mouth.

It would take just one simple twist of my hips to slide inside. I was desperate to have her, but I paid careful attention for any signs of hesitation.

"Are you sure?" I asked one final time.

She lifted her hips and wrapped her gorgeous legs around me. Her thighs encircled my hips while her calves drifted along my back. The heels of her feet pressed into my backside and her hands covered my ass, urging me forward.

Her eyes locked onto mine with carnal determination. "Show me what else you're good at, Jack."

I moved above her, taking my time, inching into her slowly and enjoying every bit of her I could. She threw her head back as her body-hugging warmth surrounded me. Having brought her to orgasm, she was wet and ready, but experiencing that feeling of her around me for the first time was beyond my wildest expectations.

I pushed forward until I was fully seated inside her, and then I paused. The rest of the world fell away. There was only Kathleen beneath me. Only her around me. I was as deep inside her as I could ever be and I hadn't had more than a few minutes to prepare for that reality. I'd stilled above her just to absorb this new and intimate version of us. A crisp serenity overtook me even as I experienced a surge of powerful masculinity. I wasn't simply bedding this magnificent woman, I was offering myself to her. I stretched taut, preparing for the onslaught of pleasure I was about to unleash on us both.

I was eager to make love to her, but I had two all-important words to say to her first. "Thank you."

Kathleen's hold on my body tightened. I pulled back and pushed into her with an enthusiastic swivel of my hips. She gasped and arched, so I did this again, offering her the same mind-altering power of my first entry. I concentrated and repeated the movements unabated, one right after another. I lost myself as I listened to her cries of passion. The intensity of our physical connection was strong, so much so that at times we were both struggling with overstimulation. And yet, I couldn't slow down. I wouldn't give us rest. I couldn't go one second without hearing Kathleen pant her ecstasy underneath my body. The more excited she became, the more I was compelled to elevate her bliss.

Our lovemaking became louder and soon she was bucking her hips to meet each one of my thrusts. Her exhilaration was increasing along with my own. I pushed deep inside her and dropped down to kiss her luscious mouth. When our tongues met again, I lost control. I increased my speed, surprising myself with the ability to do so. Kathleen's body shuddered around me, her hold on me strengthening. She detached from our kiss to release a series of erotic praises into my ear. I listened to them with pride. Spurred on by her affirmations, I pulled her lower body tighter against my own, squeezing her backside and delighting in the softness of her bare bottom underneath my fingertips.

"Let me give you everything you need," I said.

"Please," she cried as she came yet again.

"Let me make you happy," I pleaded.

"Jack!"

Kathleen lifted up from the mattress and wrapped an arm

around my neck, drawing me back into another heated and wild kiss. Our bodies began gliding against one another in new and thrilling ways. I was keenly aware of the friction of Kathleen's breasts as they swayed and flattened against my chest. I pounded into her as hard as I could with little consideration for either of us.

Having lost my ability to form a coherent sentence, I thought about the first time I'd allowed myself to think about her naked body. How much I'd wanted to take her outside in the mountain air and ravage her. At the time, the fantastical image was an unattainable wish, but now she was here, in my bed, and allowing it. She was as frenzied and willing as I was, and I realized I'd never get enough of Kathleen. There wouldn't just be this one time between us. I'd take her again, as many times as I could, for as long as she would have me.

I unleashed months of want into this incredible woman. I squeezed my eyes shut and pushed my body beyond all limits. I grunted and groaned, my only concern that I was about to explode inside of her. I wasn't ready for this to be over. Not even close, but I couldn't stop myself. I was consumed.

Kathleen was the one who broke our kiss. Her eyes were on me, watching me as I lost control of my body and my mind. Her wanton words penetrated my lustful haze.

"I don't want this to end either," she panted.

I answered her with a forceful lunge that shook the entire bed.

"Let me be on top," she begged.

I didn't argue. I obeyed.

We shifted positions and I found myself sitting up with my back against the headboard. I grabbed her by the waist and reveled in watching her body control mine. She grabbed the headboard, her hands on either side of me, and brought herself down upon me. Soon, we were moving in near-perfect synchronization as though we were longtime lovers who had perfected our connection. I tried to regain some focus to calm the frenzy between us so that I could extend our time.

I watched her in awe, having never experienced a first-time encounter as idyllic and flawless as this. I'd admired her beauty for months, but nothing had prepared me for this moment. She was confident in her ability and performance. She wasn't shy about being naked with me or taking what she wanted. She not only enjoyed sex immensely, she was outstanding at knowing how to please me. She was as focused on giving me pleasure as she was on receiving it. I'd watched her come multiple times, her orgasms inspiring more enthusiasm in me.

I watched her face as her pleasure overtook her. I watched her chest as her breasts swayed with our movements. I watched my hands as they dug into her slender waistline, holding her as close to me as I could get. And then, finally, I watched without shame as I disappeared into this beautiful woman over and over again. It was the sight of our connection that unraveled my determination to carry on.

"I'm close," I grunted without interrupting our rhythm. "What should we do?"

"Just keep moving," she breathed. "I promise… I won't get pregnant. Please. Come inside of me."

In my blind lust, I made a snap judgment to trust her. I came just as she asked with her astride me, and I was proud when my own release triggered her to enjoy yet another of her own. Together, we slowed and then ceased our movements. As we focused on catching our breaths, my thoughts began to race.

After months of being fascinated by her, I could barely comprehend the events of the evening. I never could have predicted this. I had fantasized about having sex with Kathleen, but I'd never imagined anything like what had just happened. I was impatient to take her again. I wanted to watch her come apart once more, next time beneath me. Hell, I wanted to make her come as many times as she would allow, knowing that I was the one serving her with unrelenting lust.

As I watched Kathleen and considered making love to her

again, her shoulders began to tremble. Concerned, I slid my hands from her waist to her back and pulled her closer to me. Our bodies were both glistening from our efforts and although the tangible sight and the tickle of her breasts against my chest turned me on, I worried about her.

"You're shaking like a leaf. Are you cold?" I asked. I reached over to the nearby covers and began to reluctantly cover this naked beauty straddling me, but she covered my hand with her hand, stopping me.

"No." Kathleen's voice was full of wonder.

Her emotion drew me in. "Did I hurt you?" I asked and dropped the sheet.

She scratched my thighs with soothing languid sensuality. "No," she repeated, this time with a sated smile. However, she continued to quiver underneath my touch.

"What is it, then? Please tell me."

"I don't know what happens next," she confessed. "What do I do now? Do you want me to leave?"

I tightened my hold on her and did my best not to growl in response. "I want you to stay."

"Are you sure?" she asked.

"Yes. We're not done yet. I want you here all night."

At this, Kathleen's trembling began to ease. I was flaccid now, but our bodies still felt united. She was hesitant to move off my lap, and I was unwilling to let her go just yet. She looked into my eyes, and even in the dim moonlight I could see how overcome she was. Desire still lingered in her expression, but also something else. I was quiet but watchful as she processed her own emotions. She tried to guard her feelings from me, but I saw the tinge of fear in her eyes as she searched my own, as though she was waiting for something bad to happen.

I couldn't stop myself. I broke eye contact and kissed her neck, eager to offer her reassurance and impatient to taste her skin. She tilted her head back to allow me access. I shifted my hips and withdrew from her body in the process, but we clung to one another as I repositioned our bodies on the bed. We lay haphazardly diagonal on top of the covers, and she opened her legs to allow me total access to her. I settled in between her thighs, and we lost minutes to our kissing. At times, we explored one another's mouths with restraint and care, and at others we surrendered to the frenzy and passion of our mutual attraction.

As soon as I grew hard again, Kathleen smiled.

I pulled back and brushed a stray lock of hair from her forehead. "I've never seen you more beautiful."

I covered her breast with my hand and began to gently massage her. She moaned and arched her back. Her breast pressed against my palm in the process and I rolled her nipple between my fingertips, causing it to grow taut from my attention.

"I want you," I said. "I can't get enough of you."

She relaxed her legs and her knees touched the mattress. She arched her body against me even more and I slid my other arm around her slender waist.

Her dreamy eyes met my own. "You can have me, Jack. All night. In any way you want to take me."

I needed no further encouragement and pushed back inside her with careless intensity. She cried out in surprise and pleasure, but then stilled underneath me. I paused, sensing her sudden tension.

"I'm sorry." She chewed the side of her mouth. "I need to remember to be quiet."

She'd remembered we were not alone in the house, and I wanted to offer her reassurance. I pulled back and thrust forward again with intentional strength. She cried out once more, although softer this time, and I reveled in her abandon.

"Don't be too quiet," I said with a playful grin. "I like hearing you come."

She offered a lively smile of her own, looking so sexy lying underneath me. I hardened even more inside her and felt dizzy from craving her body so much. She moaned and dug her hands into my ass.

"That's it," I encouraged her. "Show me how much you like this."

"It's you I like," she corrected me between pants. "I like everything you're doing, and I like watching you."

Moments passed as Kathleen's sentiments filtered into my consciousness, but as soon as they did, I shifted back into tenderness. We didn't halt our movements. I kept pushing and pulling over her, but my palm cupped her cheek as we looked deep into one another's eyes. As I stared down at her, I was awestruck by her beauty in an entirely new way.

"I've waited so long to hear that," I confessed. "You have no idea how long."

I spoke the truth. I'd forgotten how incredible, powerful and emotional it could be to make love to someone who felt as strongly about me as I did for her. My breathing increased, almost erratic. Not because of my arousal or my exertion, but simply because she was so happy to be here, in this very moment. With me.

I brought my face closer to hers while I kept our celestial rhythm. Our eyes stayed locked as I struggled to say more to her.

"To hear you say this. To watch us move together. To feel your heart pounding. To let you reach into my soul. I'm not…"

Kathleen interrupted my unfiltered thoughts with a kiss so pure and sweet that I forgot everything else I had intended to say. Yet again, I was reduced to declaring my emotions with my body. My hands tangled in her hair as I sought to lengthen our kiss.

I heard the noises we made, along with those of the bed. There was no disguising our activity from anyone, but neither of us had a care in the universe beyond each other. Although our initial frenzy had eased, Kathleen's pleasure built up once more. She moaned against my mouth before dropping her head back. Her eyes stayed closed and her expression reflected her total concentration on her approaching orgasm.

"I'm coming again, Jack." The words tumbled away from her

lips and settled on my heart.

"So strong," I marveled aloud.

Kathleen's fingers dug deep into my shoulders, holding me as though her life depended on it.

"I have you," I promised her.

"Never..." she breathed.

"Never what?" I asked.

"Never this much with anyone," she breathed. "Never so good."

Kathleen was overcome just as she finished her declaration. She called my name repeatedly, and this was my own undoing. As Kathleen's orgasm subsided my own followed, somehow more powerful than the first. Now it was my turn to call out to her while reciprocating her grip. I was lightheaded. Out of breath. Sweating. And happier than I could ever remember being with any woman.

When my senses returned, I discovered Kathleen was pulling me down to rest against her. She stroked my hair as she encouraged me to relax. My eyes drifted shut as I welcomed her loving gestures. My fingers found her hip and I couldn't resist sweeping them up and down the irresistible soft flare of her figure.

We lay like that for some time, both of us quiet and showing our affection with our fingertips. I expected we'd both drift into sleep, but our soft touches lingered. My mind was relaxed but overflowing with reminiscences of what had taken place. I could feel Kathleen's body with my touch. Her warm, even breaths floated along my chest. Yet I was in disbelief that she'd chosen me.

I opened my eyes and my glance first landed on her hip and thigh. I pulled my gaze upwards, along the length of her body, pausing to take in her splendid full breasts before reaching her face. Kathleen was smiling, and I knew she'd been watching my eyes drift along her body. I smiled back.

"Tell me what you're thinking," she whispered.

"I'm trying very hard not to think about anything. Right now, I just want to experience lying here with you."

I dropped my hand from her hip, and she parted her thighs just enough to allow my touch. My palm came to rest between her legs. Here, she was soft and wet. My skin absorbed her heat. Kathleen didn't retreat and neither did I.

"How are you feeling?" I asked with an experimental pat.

"Happy."

"Do you need anything? Water? A warm bath?"

Kathleen's hand moved down to my own and her fingers encircled my wrist. "Just this."

I leaned forward and kissed her softly. Kathleen's hand left my arm and wrapped around my neck, pulling our bodies together. My wandering hand found her backside next as our kiss deepened.

When I pulled back, I hesitated. "Let's get more comfortable. I want you to rest."

I pulled on Kathleen's hand and, together, we repositioned ourselves on the bed. Our heads rested against the pillows and I draped the sheets over our legs. The room was warm, and I couldn't quite bring myself to cover Kathleen's stunning breasts. She rolled onto her side and I snuggled up behind her.

"Is this all right?" I asked, punctuating my question with a kiss to her shoulder.

She hummed her approval. Moments later, with my palm caressing her chest, I fell into a satisfying and deep slumber.

chapter Thirty-Four

WHEN I opened my eyes again, the bedroom was much darker. We'd both been asleep for some time, but I hadn't rolled away from Kathleen and she hadn't pulled away from me. Our bodies were slick with perspiration, and my hand was still possessively covering her breast. I inhaled when an ache, only experienced after a round of passionate sex, distracted me from my quiet observations.

I was hard once again, my immense and throbbing erection nestled against Kathleen's backside. I stirred, only intending to get a bit of necessary relief. To my delighted surprise, she pushed back against my body and reached back, settling her hand on my ass and pulling me back against her own.

"Hi," I said.

Kathleen answered by lifting her leg, opening herself to me yet again. I slid down the mattress to bring our bodies into alignment, squeezed her breast and pushed myself back into her body for a third time. She moaned her pleasure. I concentrated on my own sensitivities as I seated myself as far inside her as possible.

"Are you all right?" I asked her. "Should I stop?"

"A little sore. Not bad enough to send you away."

"If it makes you feel better, I'm a little sore, too."

We both laughed lightly, careful not to disrupt our precious connection.

I began to thrust, intent on drawing out every bit of pleasure from her that she would allow.

I kissed the curve of her shoulder and along her neck, placing my lips next to her ear. "Earlier, you asked me what I was thinking. Do you want me to tell you now?"

"Yes," she breathed.

"You are a dream." I continued to slide up and down inside her. "When you touched my chest outside the office tonight, it was everything. Our night could have ended then, and it would have been glorious. I could have come home and climbed into this bed without you, but I wouldn't have been lonely because remembering the heat of your hand over my heart would have kept me happy."

Her body stretched beside me, her head tilting up and back, allowing me to watch her face while she panted. She opened her sparkling eyes and looked into mine, her beautiful features enhanced by the pleasure I was giving her. I pushed into her with enthusiasm, rejoicing in her vocal reactions each time I did so. After a while, I slowed my tempo, allowing her a brief respite and returning my mouth to her ear.

"When you kissed me on this bed, it was like nothing I'd ever experienced. When your lips touched mine, all I could think about was how I'd give you anything in return."

I removed my hand from her breast and brought my fingers up to her jaw. Gently, I guided her face toward mine. When she was within reach, I covered her mouth with my own and delivered an ardent kiss while pumping hard into her body. She cried out against my lips while she stretched tight in response to my insistent thrusts. I offered her every ounce of physical strength I had until her orgasm subsided. When her body returned to a relaxed state, I shared one more secret with her.

"When you stripped away your clothes and offered this gorgeous body to me, I rejoiced. As long as you stay in my arms, I will give you anything you desire. And when this night fades to morning, I promise you my eternal gratitude."

As soon as the words left my mouth, the honesty of this sentiment seized my heart. I withdrew from her and she gasped in surprise. Before she could question my action, I rolled her onto her back. I pulled her legs far apart, plunging back into her body with fierce devotion. She cried out when I entered her roughly but when her legs wrapped around my waist, the matter of her tenderness was no longer a concern.

Our lips met again as we moved together on top of the covers, blanketed only by the darkness and warmth of a fragrant springtime night. Our endurance for one another was invigorating. After innumerable nights spent yearning for such passion and attention, I was enthusiastic to become Kathleen's lover. No other woman in the universe held my heart the way she did. No other woman in the cosmos quenched my thirst.

I lost count of the number of times she came, but I watched in utter fascination when her last orgasm took her, body and spirit. She began to shake in my arms as I pushed her damp hair away from her forehead. My own body climaxed as I watched her intimate vulnerability on display. I eased my movements, then slowly withdrew from her. We were both breathless, our eyes locked onto one another as we both accepted that we'd reached our physical limits for the time being.

It occurred to me to tell Kathleen I loved her. I was certain I'd fallen in love with her months earlier, but despite this magical night, I wasn't certain she returned my love.

Unable to contain my emotion, nervous laughter rumbled through my chest.

"What is it?" she asked.

"Look at us. We should stop, but I swear I could do this with you all night. I don't need sleep. I don't need water. I just need you."

"Why me?" she asked in a sweet voice filled with amazement.

I leaned forward and kissed her forehead. "You are beautiful in every way that matters."

She placed her soft palm against my cheek. Her eyes grew watery and danced in the moonlight. She looked like she was going to tell me something, so I waited. Lying in my arms, she was content. Her muscles were relaxed, and she gave no hint that she wanted to move. We stayed like that for a while, watching and holding one another without speaking. Her blinks grew longer, until her eyes drifted shut. It was only then I moved her back toward the pillows. She allowed me to guide her into place and I pulled the blankets up to cover us. She rolled onto her side, facing me.

I kissed her mouth before moving my lips to her ear. "Sleep now. Rest as long as you need. I'll be right here when you wake up."

She smiled with swollen lips and then drifted off.

chapter
Thirty-Five

"HI, JACK."

I looked up with a start. I was unaccustomed to hearing this woman's voice inside my office.

"Tracie." I stood to greet her.

"Do you have a couple of minutes?"

"For you, always." I smiled and gestured to the chair in front of my desk.

"Can I close the door?"

"Please."

I didn't retake my seat until she sat down.

"What brings you by?" I asked.

Tracie looked down at her lap and clasped her fingers. "It's quiet here this week. I don't have my break buddy."

The acknowledgement of Kathleen's absence had been an uncomfortable subject all week. I never knew when it was going to be brought up, only that I could expect it to be. Mostly, I withdrew from the gossip, but Tracie was an exception to the rule. I struggled to come up with the right response, so she continued without me.

"I can fake it for a day or two, but I miss her."

"So do I," I admitted with unexpected relief. It was nice to let my guard down a bit with someone outside of our families. "How did you handle it when she was away in Portland?" I asked.

Tracie shrugged. "She still had to work, so we e-mailed a lot.

And we chatted on the phone enough. It felt like she was still down the hall."

"This is different," I added.

"I suppose so."

We both fell silent and I contemplated the situation.

"I don't want to think about Kathleen leaving here," she continued. "People come and go. It's part of the office routine. But Robert and Kathleen are the constants."

She lifted her head and leaned back in her chair. "She especially. I mean, Robert has been here for decades, but we expect him to retire soon. She's supposed to be the future of this company."

I tilted my head and made eye contact with her. "I'm sure she's taking that into consideration. She cares about everyone here."

Tracie appeared unconvinced but didn't argue with my assessment.

"How long have you been at Aurora?" I asked her.

"Eight years," she answered. "It's a good job. There's just enough responsibility to keep me interested, but not so much that I can't walk away from it at the end of the day."

"And you're excellent at what you do."

She laughed self-consciously. "Thanks."

"I should have seen this coming, but I didn't." This was not an easy confession for me. I shifted in my seat just as soon as I said the words.

"I know what you mean."

"Yeah?" I'd expected Tracie to rebuke me.

"Kathleen's great at the job. She always knows what to do. But she hasn't found happiness like most do."

I had no response to this, because I was ashamed to have contributed to Kathleen's sorrow.

"Something was changing in her, though," Tracie went on. "She wasn't so cautious anymore. She was more open to just...

feeling things."

"How so?" I pressed.

"She was soaking up some of the awesome sunshine for once. She was taking more risks and they seemed like the right ones."

Tracie looked at me pointedly. "She told me about you two when your daughter was hurt. It was the first time she uttered a word to me about something so personal."

"I'm surprised to hear you say that. You're good friends."

"We are, but there are just certain things she won't share. She had boyfriends here and there," she said. "I met a couple of them, only just because I bumped into her when she was on a date or something. But she never spoke of any guy with me. Until you, she wouldn't have dropped everything to go be at someone else's side for weeks on end."

Yet another silence took hold as I processed this information. Her declaration was significant, and I owed her a great deal for sharing her thoughts.

"Between you and me?" I ventured.

Tracie nodded. Her gaze was razor sharp.

I held eye contact as I said, "I never wanted to make her sad."

Tracie's scrutiny was undeniable.

"I want her to stay at Aurora," I elaborated.

She continued to watch me without speaking. Or blinking.

"I want to earn her trust back."

Tracie didn't respond to this. Instead, she stared at me with dubious eyes. "I love her." The emotion I always experienced when I spoke of my love for Kathleen broke through. Tracie won the staring contest when I looked down and brushed a tear from the corner of my eye.

"I nearly forgot," Tracie announced with her usual bubbly voice. "I came in here for a reason."

I lifted my head and furrowed my brow in confusion. "What?"

"Have you heard from Kathleen?"

"Not really," I admitted. "The last time we spoke was when

she got on the plane to Denver."

"She told me you called her. She didn't share the details, but whatever you said had a lasting impact." Tracie crossed her legs and leveled another stare at me. And it occurred to me that she was waiting for me to ask her a question.

"When did you hear from her?" I prompted.

Tracie grinned. "Yesterday morning, she texted me and asked me to go into the conference room to call her from my cell phone. She wanted total privacy."

What Tracie said resonated with me in an unexpected way. "You disappeared yesterday after lunch."

"I told Robert I was having bad cramps and wanted to go home. That kept him from asking too many questions."

I nodded at her ingenuity. "That's a good one."

Tracie's expression grew playful. "It was, but that's not the point."

She leaned forward with a knowing grin. "Kathleen was getting on a plane to Eugene. She asked me to pick her up at the airport, but she didn't want Robert to know she was coming back. She said she still needed some time before she saw him."

I was speechless.

"I drove her home last night," she said. "She'll be at her place for the rest of the day. She's not coming in to work until tomorrow morning." With that, Tracie rose from her chair and walked to the door.

"Did she say anything about me?" I blurted.

"She was pretty tired. She didn't say much."

I made no effort to hide my disappointment.

"She also didn't tell me not to tell you she was back in town." Tracie opened the door and raised her voice as she stepped into the corridor. "I don't know. You look a little peaked to me, Jack. If you want, I can reschedule your appointments this afternoon? You should take the afternoon off. Go and get some... rest."

chapter Thirty-Six

I'D LOST track of the number of times I'd worried about Kathleen. It had been terrible enough when she left to spend a weekend interviewing for another job in Colorado. I'd almost succumbed to a public meltdown when she didn't reappear at work after three days. With only a single text message between us, another four days had drifted by in agonizing slowness. That one conversation wasn't enough.

Now, Tracie had stunned me by mentioning Kathleen's return to Bend. After Tracie's departure, I locked myself in my office and leaned against the door. I was upset. Kathleen had come back to Oregon and hadn't let me know. No call. No text. No e-mail. I was distraught because she had made her decision about what direction her life was going to take. The possibility that she could choose a life without me in it hovered like an oppressive cloud.

I was frustrated. Things between us were so uncertain. I was afraid to speak to her, but I missed her more with each passing hour. I wandered back to my chair, unsure about how to carry on. Soon, I found myself staring at the framed magazine cover she had given me.

The day we'd sat down together for an interview and posed for that cover shot was so far removed from recent experience. The sharpness of the moment had faded to a dreamlike quality. It was even difficult to understand that the photograph had been taken less than a year ago. So much had happened between us since that magical afternoon when I discovered her attraction to me.

I stared at that extraordinary portrait of us and sought a way to dredge back the euphoria of that day. During that photo shoot, I'd found the courage to share my affection with her. I'd shown her what was in my heart and she had accepted me.

What would have been different had I kept my admiration a secret? We would have denied ourselves a passionate and emotionally intimate springtime. It was reasonable to assume that Heide's accident would have still taken place with or without my involvement with Kathleen. What would I have done without Kathleen's love and attention to see me through that awful summer? She had brought me peace no one else could have. Her love had kept me strong during the biggest crisis of my life. She had done everything right to earn my respect and my trust. My shame burned inside because she hadn't been able to rely on me for the same.

No sooner had this thought drifted through my head than I knew what to do.

I reached for my phone and dialed her number. I didn't have a plan in mind. I just wanted to hear her voice and know that, no matter what the fuck was going on between us, she was all right. I just needed her to consent to my call.

"Hello?" She sounded surprised, even though she would have recognized my number on her display.

"Hi, Kathleen."

There was a slight pause. "Hi, Jack."

"I know you're back in Bend," I said, stumbling over my next thought. "Tracie may have told me."

"That's all right," she replied. "I may have wanted her to tell you."

Her words were a revelation that unleashed a necessary surge of confidence.

"We need to talk," I said. "Can we? I want to come over to your place, but I understand if you don't want to see me. I'll settle

for this phone call as long as you'll talk to me."

"I want to see you. But I'm nervous to say yes."

I shook my head. "You should never be anxious to see me."

Kathleen sighed into the phone. It wasn't a sound of exasperation. It was more like sadness. "I want to see you, and I want to hold you." Kathleen sniffled. "If I wrap my arms around you, I don't know if I'll be able to let you go."

I grinned. We were making progress in our negotiation. I looked out my window, making sure something mysterious hadn't happened to my car. "I'd like that. Very much."

"Leave work now," Kathleen instructed with determination. "I'll unlock the door. Just come in."

"You'll wait for me?"

I needed her to say the word.

"Yes."

"I'm on my way."

When I entered Kathleen's condo, it took a Herculean effort not to burst through the door.

My patience was rewarded, however, when I discovered her standing in the small foyer. She was waiting for me just as she'd promised.

My eyes dropped to her rosy lips as I pushed the door shut behind me. Two steps into her apartment, and we wrapped our arms around one another in frantic reunion.

"Jack—" she began but I interrupted her.

"Wait," I pleaded as my hands tangled in her hair. "Just wait. Forget logic and forget heartache and let me kiss you."

She pulled me in. When our lips met, our mouths opened, and she whimpered. I didn't break our contact. I was incapable of doing any such thing.

With my mouth drifting along hers, I said, "Don't pull away."

I thrust my tongue between her lips before drawing it back just enough to say, "Be strong. Stay right here. Like this."

We were kissing for the first time since that god-awful fight in her father's apartment in Portland, and I basked in the glory of this triumph.

"I think about you all the time," I confessed. I dropped my hands from her hair and ran them up and down her sides, delighting in the familiar territory of her soft and curvy body. "I dream about you at night and fantasize about you during the day."

She slowed her agitated movements but didn't pull away. She opened her eyes and watched me. Her look of concern was enough to end the kiss, but I didn't let her go and I didn't pull back. I pressed my forehead to hers and held her in my embrace.

"What is it?" I asked. "What are you afraid of?"

"I don't want you to hate me," she admitted. "I can't stand the thought. I need you, even if we can't be together anymore. I can't let you go." She made a valiant attempt to hide her emotions, but her eyes conveyed her fear.

I ran a gentle hand through her hair, trying to soothe her anxieties. "I don't know why I matter so much to you," I said as my eyes scanned her dear face.

"Why would you ever say that?"

"Because I have a terrible record and not just with you. I've never been able to keep a woman happy."

At this, she dropped her gaze, and distress began to take hold.

I placed a finger underneath her chin and lifted it, so she would see my determination. "You're more precious to me than anyone other than Heide."

"Even though I went to Colorado?"

The pain in her voice tangled around my heart like a persistent vine. A dull ache filled my chest. "Yes, and you mean so much to me, and yet I've still managed to hurt you terribly. Look at where we are. You're willing to leave everything you've ever known to put space between us. To shield yourself from the pain

I've caused you. I hate that, but I could never hate you."

She brought a shaking but gentle hand to my cheek. I hadn't been mindful of my professional appearance since she'd been out of town, and my face had more stubble than she was used to. I reveled in her temporary fascination with the roughness.

"You know this is more complicated than that," she said even as she continued to stroke my face.

"I do. That's why I'm here. I'm going to give you what you need to make the right decisions for you and your future." I leaned in for one quick peck on the lips, seeking some of her bravery. "I've spent my entire life thinking I know how to fix things, but the truth is I'm awful at it. I'm not going to do that this time. But I won't lie. I'm scared, and I want to keep kissing you because your touch gives me the strength to move forward."

And here was the essence of my being. Without Kathleen's loving heart and body to nourish me, I was wilting. Kissing her was dangerous, for while our physical connection fueled my hope, I also knew this could be the last time she opened herself to me. I moved in one last time, savoring her mouth, lips and tongue just as I was mourning their inevitable retreat. When we broke apart, I took her hand and sought a place to talk.

Avoiding the sofa where we'd had sex, we sat down at her small dining room table. She sat across from me, not next to me. One quick look at the table's surface confirmed something important. It was set in a way that was pristine. Although well-designed, it was clear that she never ate a meal here. The table was nothing more than a decoration. I attempted to take comfort in the idea that she was unlikely to sit here in the future and recall this moment. Such a possibility was a minuscule consolation.

With unsteady hands, I reached into my suit and pulled out three cardboard coasters. They'd been sitting inside my desk since she'd presented them to me days earlier at the Chinese restaurant by our office. I set them down one at a time, placing them side by side in their correct order. They were covered in my handwriting, *the words scribbled one drunken evening. Once they were out in the open, her lovely face that had flushed during our kissing was drained of color.*

"I'm guessing you remember these," I began.

She nodded and then shoved them back in my direction. "I don't ever need to see them again. I've reread them in my mind too many times to count. I know the words by heart," she said, her voice trembling.

I winced. I wanted to swipe the damn things onto the floor, but instead I let them sit between us. "You aren't one hundred percent right about these," I explained. "But you are right to be upset by them."

With lips delightfully swollen from our kissing, she sat up, straight and tall, preparing for an emotional sucker punch.

"If you're ready to hear everything from me, I'm ready to tell you now."

She nodded as she crossed her arms over her chest and avoided looking at the coasters.

Our moment of ultimate truth had arrived. This was what she had asked from me for longer than I'd been able to appreciate. I wasn't prepared for her to kick me out of her life as soon as this awful conversation ended, but it was a possibility. I only knew I loved her enough to let her know all of me, the good as well as the bad. She deserved a man she could trust and respect. She had held me in high esteem in the early days of our relationship, so much so that even I believed in the false value of my own worth. If I was ever going to become a better man, it meant taking the ultimate risk of losing her for good. I took a deep breath, not sure how to begin. Kathleen was always so brave, and while I was anything but, I peered into her worried green eyes and asked a question.

"Do you remember how you felt when you told me about your mother?"

She wrinkled her forehead with concern. "Yes."

"Were you afraid of my reaction?"

"Yes."

"I'm petrified of yours."

She stilled for a few moments and glanced around the apartment before settling her gaze on me. When she did, her expression was no longer uncertain. It was decided. She rose from her chair and extended her hand in my direction. This was an unexpected invitation to touch her, and I didn't hesitate. I rose and wrapped my fingers around hers.

Without a single word, Kathleen led me to her spare bedroom.

chapter
Thirty-Seven

KATHLEEN TOOK me to the queen-size bed and dropped my hand. We'd made love there just before Heide's accident. It had been the last time we'd made love in Bend. I held my breath.

She moved to stand behind me and pulled my blazer from my shoulders. As soon as she helped me out of my jacket, she walked over to the other side of the bed and removed her shoes, followed by her skirt and her blouse. Within moments of entering the bedroom, she stood in her bra and panties. I took in the sight with gratitude.

"I miss you so much." My voice cracked with weariness and emotion.

I was stunned and breathless as she leaned forward, offering me more than a glimpse of her luscious breasts when she pulled back the bed covers and arranged the pillows flat on the mattress. She then lay down on the bed, rolling onto her side to face me. She patted the empty half of the mattress and smiled shyly.

And just like that I understood her intentions. I sat down and removed my shoes and socks. When I stood back up, I took off my dress shirt, undershirt and pants. Since she had left her underwear on, I did the same and crawled into the bed wearing only my boxer briefs. I moved toward the center of the mattress, reflecting her posture.

She extended her hand to me once again, and as soon as our fingers entwined, her legs wrapped around mine. I was beyond *grateful but lacked the words to express myself. Instead, I allowed our newfound serenity to embrace me.*

As a welcome calm settled around us, she broke her silence. "I was scared to share my secrets, but you protected me. I was safe in your bed, and so I told you everything." Her green eyes locked on to mine, poignantly. "You're safe with me, Jack."

I nodded and then looked down at our reunited hands. "You were right about something."

"What?"

"What I wrote on those coasters was a memory. Not a fantasy." I waited longer than necessary to continue, wanting to give her the opportunity to speak. She received this revelation with utter silence.

I cleared my throat. "You told me I was recalling an encounter with Allison. You suspected I wanted to go back to her. That's where you were wrong."

"How so?"

Here is where the conversation took its most difficult turn. I counted down from five and forced myself to say the words I dreaded most of all. "I wasn't writing about Allison, and I wasn't writing about you. I was remembering a night with a different woman."

"Was it the girl you lost your virginity to?" Her voice was shaky but held an optimistic tone.

I was disappointed to let her down once more. I shook my head and tightened my hold on her hand. I didn't want her to retreat again. A prolonged silence stretched out between us. I allowed her time to accept this fact and was hopeful she would allow me the opportunity to explain myself.

"Her name is Elyse. She was a coworker of mine."

"A coworker?" Kathleen repeated the words in shock.

"Yes. She lives in Baltimore. We began working for the firm at the same time. We bonded because we were in the trenches together and trying to grow our careers. We were both single.

Unattached. We used to leave work and go to dinner together. Enjoy a couple of drinks and commiserate about the demands of the job. One night after dinner, she asked me to follow her home, so I did. I spent the night with her."

I went silent again as she processed my disclosure. "What you wrote on the coasters didn't happen at her house," she murmured.

I swallowed. "That's true."

"So... it happened with her more than once."

"Yes."

"You were in love with her?"

"No. I wasn't." I lifted my eyes to lock with Kathleen's. "And she wasn't in love with me. What I shared with Elyse is far different than what we've experienced together."

She pulled her hand back from mine and found a loose thread in the bedding to occupy her fingers. My heart was full of fear and pounding. She deserved to know everything, but it was a struggle not to lose control of my words.

"Elyse was always more focused on her career than anything else. She was never looking for a husband. She never talked about having children. She was a woman with certain needs, nothing more."

"I see. And you obliged them."

I grimaced. Her words and the disapproving tone she used to deliver them stung like a slap to the face. I gritted my teeth. "I admit it was the way of things for years. Then I met Allison."

Oddly enough, the mention of my ex-wife's name struck a certain chord with Kathleen. I watched as her bitterness gave way to a look of contrition.

"I apologize, Jack. I have no right to be upset."

I nodded, but I wanted to end my confession as soon as I could. The agony of the moment was deep. After months of evading the truth, I needed to finish what I'd started.

"I remember telling you that I fell in love with Allison almost immediately. She was so different from Elyse. She was a challenge.

One I thought worth fighting for. But it was never easy with Allison. When I look back now, I realize that it took a great deal of persuasion on my part to get her to date me. And that perhaps I was just trying to break away from the monotony of sleeping with a woman who didn't want anything other than my cock."

She blinked at my vulgarity but didn't interrupt me. I reached for her hand and she allowed me to reclaim it. I was thankful.

"What I experienced with Allison was more than I'd ever had with Elyse, but it was nothing compared to what I feel for you."

The rational side of Kathleen's brain was in full control. If she experienced any emotion over my earnest declaration of love, she hid it.

"I don't understand," she said. "You told me you would have proposed to Allison even if she hadn't become pregnant with Heide."

"I said I'd propose eventually. Who knows how long that would have taken? And if I'm being honest, I don't know if she would have said yes under any other set of circumstances."

"You don't think so?"

"We were attracted to each other, but we also frustrated the hell out of one another. I wasn't getting what I wanted from Allison, and Elyse knew it." A large lump formed in my throat and I swallowed it whole, more committed than ever to speak the truth. "She knew it. She took advantage of it. And I let her."

"What are you saying, Jack?" Her voice was low. Cautious and scared. It was the one time I chose not to look at her. It was cowardly, but I refused to take in her reaction when I answered her question.

"I was sleeping with both of them. I wasn't honest with Allison about it, and I didn't end things with Elyse until Allison told me she was pregnant."

"You dated Allison for six months before that happened."

I nodded.

"Did you ever stop sleeping with Elyse after you met

Allison?"

I shook my head, still unable to meet her eyes. "I'm not proud of it, Kathleen. But it's the truth about me and you deserve to know."

"How long did you work together?"

"Until I moved here."

"Oh."

I waited for her to say something more, to ask me more questions. But there was silence. I waited until I couldn't stand to.

"There is more I should tell you," I informed her. "But if you want me to leave now, I'll go."

"Have I heard the worst of it?"

Her hand was still in mine, although her grip had gone slack and her palms were clammy. I glanced down at our legs and realized they were still locked together. She was upset, but she hadn't pulled away. I was safe in her bed, just as she promised I would be. My heart ached for her ability to absorb great emotional pain and push beyond it. My stress pulsed throughout my body and my face grew hot at the understanding that I was just another loved one to break her heart.

"I believe so. Yes."

"All right," she sighed. "Go on."

"When Allison told me that we were going to have a baby, I broke it off with Elyse for good. But she knew my relationship with Allison wasn't solid. She tried to undermine it whenever the mood suited her. Once Allison agreed to marry me, I never looked back but our happiness didn't last long."

"What happened? Did Elyse tell her?"

"No. Nothing as spectacular as that. Allison was a television news reporter. She's a good journalist, and she just noticed certain things. She pieced it together and then confronted me about it. I mishandled the whole thing. It was a relief to get it out in the open, but she never trusted me after that. Nothing I ever did going forward was going to make up for what I did in the beginning. Our *marriage was weak from the start, because of me. There's one more thing you should know, but it's the one thing I'm most fearful of telling you."*

"You told me I'd heard the worst." Kathleen's voice was accusatory. This time she did pull her hand away. I surged forward with my last admission.

"The first time Allison and I were together in a room with you, she saw our connection. She accused me of seeking you out as a replacement for Elyse."

She was silent. I turned my eyes back to her face. I watched her reaction, knowing how she'd justified much of her recent behavior. She was under the belief that she was an interference in the potential reconciliation of my family. And I'd just confirmed her worst fears.

"I can't blame Allison for jumping to that conclusion," I continued. "I earned her suspicion and I've had to accept it. But I promise you, I was never going to put Allison through that again."

"How can you be sure?"

"Because Elyse wanted to sleep with me at my farewell party. If I'd wanted to, I could have done it. I could have slept with her and then disappeared to the other side of the country. But I'm not interested in a fuck buddy. There's no challenge or reward in that kind of relationship."

I paused once again to give Kathleen a chance to speak, but she didn't.

"I came to my senses far too late to save my marriage, but when I walked away from Elyse it was because I wanted to be a better man going forward. I moved us here because I always thought about what could have been with Allison without Elyse's interference. I had nothing left to lose, so I tried a last-ditch reset."

"Allison left because of me," she said.

I shook my head. "Allison left because of me. We both forced ourselves into a doomed marriage. I thought it would fall behind us in time. And when that didn't happen, I got the idea to put it behind us by distance. That was a failure, too."

"You told me the first time you were attracted to me was at the holiday party at Robert's house."

"Until you left for Denver, there was no doubt in my mind about that. But I've been thinking a lot while you were gone. I looked back to the very beginning, and I need to be honest with myself and with you. I was attracted to you from the moment we first met. I see it as clear as day now, but at the time I didn't. Given everything else I've told you, I know it may be hard to accept, but you must know that I wasn't trying to seduce you. Not before Allison left me, not after she went back to Maryland, and not our first night together."

I paused and considered making my exit from the bed, from the condo, from Kathleen. I'd leave if she told me to, but it would be the most difficult thing I would ever do. She was quiet. I had to remind myself to breathe while I awaited her verdict.

"I was the one who kissed you that night," she said. "You may have been attracted to me, but you were always a gentleman. Neither of us planned on any of this."

Could I dare hope that she would forgive me? I was stunned by her conclusion but recovered, savoring the opportunity to salvage our relationship.

"I'm not a perfect man. I used Elyse for sex. I cheated on Allison when we were dating. I never understood what real love was until I fell in love with you. Please believe that I would never disrespect you like that."

"Is there anything else you need to tell me?"

I shook my head. "I couldn't bare it if there was."

"Ditto."

An awkward pause settled over us, but I didn't allow it to fester. I wanted to keep the dialogue open between us.

"Tell me about Denver." I didn't want to know anything about Colorado, but eventually, I'd have to accept what was unfolding

between us.

Kathleen lifted herself on one elbow and looked at my face with scrutiny. Even so, she wore a tender expression that only softened as the seconds rolled by. She reached out and moved her thumb along the underside of my eye and expanded her focus to massaging the creases in my forehead.

"You're exhausted," she declared.

All I could do was nod.

"Me, too," she said. "And not just from this week."

I'd heard Allison say something just like this when she decided to leave me. I braced myself for a death blow, but to my astonishment, Kathleen set her hands on my chest and pushed me onto my back. She then placed her head down on my chest and burrowed in.

"I could just go to sleep right now," she announced.

"Do you want me to go?"

"Does this feel like I you want to go?"

"No."

"Then stay. Just like this."

"Are you sure?"

"I sleep so much better with you. Maybe that makes me weak."

With great caution, I wrapped my arm around her back, allowing my hand to settle near her hip. "Far from it. I can't believe you're not kicking me to the curb after what I've just told you."

She placed a light kiss on my chest. "Don't overthink this. Forget logic and forget heartache and just let me hold you."

chapter
Thirty-Eight

SOMETIME LATER, I stirred awake, realizing I never told anyone where I was going or how long I would be gone. The afternoon daylight had disappeared from the spare bedroom. We'd been sequestered from the world for some time. I carefully detached from Kathleen's arms and retrieved my phone from my discarded blazer. I ducked out to the living room and called Allison.

"Is everything all right?" she asked with a curious tone.

"Yeah. I'm sorry," I mumbled. "What time is it?"

"Almost eight o'clock. Where are you?"

"I'm with Kathleen, but it's not what you're thinking."

"What is it, then?" Allison's voice was playful. Her teasing surprised and disarmed me.

"We were talking this afternoon, and we're both just worn out. We've been sleeping for hours. She's still asleep. I'll wake her up and come home soon."

"Things are fine here. Don't stress it."

"What do you mean?"

"It's good that you're both talking. You should stay. Please don't rush out of some misplaced obligation to me." I detected no sarcasm in Allison's voice. She was speaking with sincerity.

"What about Heide?" I asked, amazed.

"She's fine. We're having a girls' night."

I sat down on the arm of Kathleen's sofa. "I don't

understand."

"What don't you understand?"

I ran a hand through my mussed hair and glanced in the direction of the spare bedroom. *"You're both being so good me. Why?"*

"What happened today?"

"I told her everything, Allison. She knows what I did to you."

"That sounds like progress to me. Good for you."

"How can you be so nice to me when I did such a horrible thing? I was an awful husband."

"No one here is awful, Jack. We got in over our heads. We did the best we could."

"I'm sorry I couldn't do better."

"You were there for me when I went back to Maryland. You never blamed me for leaving. You never belittled me or made me feel guilty for not coming back."

"I care about you. I always I will."

Allison ignored my declaration and charged forward. *"Do you want my advice? If Kathleen knows everything and still has this big decision looming in front of her, then wait. Stay there until she's ready for you to go. Don't storm off and don't slink away. Help her make the right choice."*

"I don't want her to leave." My voice cracked as I vocalized my fear.

"Then tell her that."

"Would you have stayed if I'd asked you to?"

"No."

I couldn't help but chuckle at her swift answer. *"Why not?"*

"Because I know you, and I know when you don't believe what you're saying."

"I would have stayed with you."

"I know that, too. But you would have fallen in love with Kathleen anyway."

I couldn't confirm her hypothesis any more than I could deny *it.*

"What you need to realize, Jack, is that she never would have fallen in love with you if I'd stayed."

"You're right about that."

"No matter what happens, support her the way you supported me."

Once again, I couldn't respond. I was a million times more frightened of losing Kathleen than I ever was of losing Allison. I couldn't tell Allison that, and I was terrified of what Kathleen's departure would do to me.

"Life is unpredictable," she went on, unfazed. "We found that out when we got pregnant. We were reminded of that when Heide almost died. Some marriages work. Some don't. Ours didn't, and that's okay because I think we're better friends for it."

"We have Heide," I said. "And I'll always cherish you for bringing her into this world."

"Thank you. And thanks for checking in with me. I'll see you sometime tomorrow?"

"Yes. Kiss Heide good night for me?"

"I will. Good night, Jack."

"Good night."

I disconnected from the call and let my phone drop into my lap. I stayed on the sofa, thinking about the surreal turn my life had taken over the course of a single day. I'd left home that morning thinking Kathleen was still in Denver and wondering if I would ever figure out a way to win her back. By afternoon, Kathleen had welcomed me back into her arms, and I'd told her everything I'd been holding back since the day we first met.

Did I dare hope that the worst was now behind us?

"Jack?" Kathleen called my name from the guest bedroom. Her voice was strong, but frightened.

I moved quickly, standing back up and taking long strides across the living room.

"I'm here," I called, just as she stepped into the hallway, still

clad in her underwear.

She flinched at the volume of my raised voice, and her hand covered her heart. *"You scared me."*

Her choice of words was poignant. I'd managed to trigger her fear twice within a matter of seconds.

"I didn't leave you," I replied in a measured and contrite manner.

We stared at one another and endured a prolonged silence as the implication of my statement settled upon us. Although I was an expert at it, Kathleen was the first to change the subject.

"How long did we sleep?" She dropped her head and raked a hand through her long hair, avoiding eye contact.

"All afternoon."

"Are you sure? I should feel more rested."

"You do look tired," I agreed.

"I want to go back to bed," she confessed.

"Do you want me to go home?"

Kathleen lifted her eyes to mine and we exchanged another look of significance.

"I want you to stay," she said. *"But I guess you need to go."*

"Only if you need me to go. Otherwise, I want to stay."

Kathleen absorbed my offer with a fair dose of confusion. *"Heide needs you more than I do."*

"Heide is fine." I lifted a hand and showed Kathleen my cell phone. *"I spoke to Allison. They're having all kinds of fun without me."*

Kathleen kept her thoughts to herself, but the nervous state of her posture shifted into a more relaxed stance.

"I'd like you to eat some dinner," I said.

A grin, albeit a shy one, appeared. *"I don't have anything here."*

"You look too tired to go out."

"I am."

"I'll go to the store and get us something for tonight."

"Something for breakfast, too?" Kathleen's timidity was in stark contrast to the boldness of her statement.

I smiled and approached the greatest love of my life. I caressed her face with rapt attention, my smile fading away as I lost myself in the soft touch of her cheek. Soon, my fingers descended to brush against the strap of her bra. I watched her expression as my cautious fingers slipped underneath the thin line of silk. She didn't object in the slightest when I tugged the material down and away from her shoulder. I lowered my lips to her bare skin and allowed my experimental kisses to linger on her body. She didn't push me away.

After a summer of uncertainty, my confidence where she was concerned was strengthening. I wrapped my arms around her slender back and unclasped the bra. Then I retreated a step as she allowed her lingerie to fall to the floor. I couldn't help myself. Overwhelmed by the heady mixture of the uncertainty of our future along with the certainty I had regained her trust, at least for this incredible moment, I fell to my knees in front of her and pulled her close in a tight embrace.

Kathleen reciprocated my hug. I trembled inside her arms as she leaned down and rested her cheek on top of my head. We held one another, both weary and emotional. Neither of us spoke, yet we understood one another. Minutes ticked by as I experienced the first peace of mind I'd had in months. We stayed this way for some time and I cherished every single heartbeat of it.

When my soul was fully nourished, I brought myself back to my feet.

Kathleen's posture remained unchanged. Her arms grasped onto mine after I rose from the floor. She kept her eyes lowered. And it was then that an epiphany struck me. Kathleen had known precious little about emotional security. She'd been denied something fundamental since childhood. I wanted Kathleen to feel every bit of happiness I was feeling right then, but now I understood something essential. Her peace of mind would take years, decades, perhaps the rest of her life to restore.

I processed this realization as I studied her exhausted body. I wrapped an arm around her waist and guided her down the hallway toward her own bedroom. She didn't fight me. She complied. We paused at the side of the bed and held on to one another as I pulled back the sheets with my free hand. I moved her to lie down on her back and she lifted her hips in complete submission as I removed her panties. I stared at her naked body without shame while I dropped her underwear to the floor. Then, I pulled the flat sheet up over her torso until it covered her breasts.

"Get some more sleep." I ran a finger through a stray lock of her long, blond hair. "Dinner will be ready in a little while."

Kathleen rolled onto her side, facing me. "Thank you," she mumbled as her eyes drifted closed.

Her slow, rhythmic breathing set in just as I closed the bedroom door behind me.

chapter

I WANDERED through the grocery store longer than usual, searching for inspirational ingredients. I wanted to make the perfect meal for Kathleen, one that would give her nourishment and comfort. After perusing the aisles and rejecting one idea after another, I settled on a "less is more" philosophy.

I made my purchase and returned to Kathleen's condo without delay. I entered her home as quietly as possible and was relieved she hadn't woken from her nap. I took the groceries to the kitchen and cut up vegetables for a homemade chicken noodle soup. Once everything was simmering, I switched on the natural gas fireplace in her living room before preparing grilled cheese sandwiches.

When our meal was ready, I plated her food and set it on the kitchen counter. She woke and sat up in bed when I opened the door to her room. Without speaking a word, I offered her a bathrobe and led her by the hand to the love seat nestled close to the fireplace. Once she was settled, I returned to the kitchen to fetch our meals. Together, we sat on the small couch and focused on the coziness provided by the heat of the fire and the warmth of the food. There was no conversation. It had been a long day for us both.

Afterward, I took away the dishes and she returned to her rest. I cleaned the kitchen slowly, even though I was brimming with impatience. We'd been apart for long enough. I needed to hold her in my arms, but I wanted her to have a few minutes more to herself.

I'd revealed everything to her, and she hadn't thrown me out of her life. At least not yet. Perhaps, she only allowed me to stay in her condo because she was too exhausted to send me away.

Much had been revealed, but little had been resolved. With this understanding in mind, I went back to Kathleen's room. She had discarded her bathrobe on the floor next to the bed. Following her lead, I removed my clothes as she watched from the center of the mattress. I turned off the bedroom lights and settled myself underneath the sheets. I pulled Kathleen to my chest with little effort. It was late, past our usual bedtime, and I was elated to hold her in my arms until morning.

I peered at the ceiling when I spoke my next words. "Just before that golf game with Robert, we talked about my father. Do you remember that?"

"Yes."

"You told me I was a great man like him." I shook my head. "You were wrong, but I wasn't brave enough to tell you so."

"I said you were a great man because you're a wonderful father. Don't underestimate how vital that is."

I contemplated her words, sliding my fingers up and down the upper part of her arm. "I don't feel great. I'd be a better father if I knew how to be a good partner. The day we made love on your sofa, I promised I would give you anything you asked of me. Instead, I broke your trust with my behavior."

She squeezed my torso. "I don't trust others easily. Or well. I'm trying, Jack."

I kissed her forehead and tightened my hold on her as I recalled Robert's words of advice: "Maybe Kathleen doesn't know how to keep the vault door from locking any more than we do. Maybe putting some distance between the two of you keeps the door open."

"You are trying," I said, hoping my words would reassure her. "I've never met anyone like you. When you told me about *what you'd been through with your parents, it made me fall more in love with you. You're so brave. So strong."*

"You're not the first person to say that about me, but you're the first person who may actually convince me of it," she said.

Within the dark confines of our surroundings, I grinned. Broadly.

"Heide is the strongest one though," she added. "How is she? I miss her."

"She misses you. We talked about you a couple of days ago. She'd like to see you."

"Yeah?" She raised her head from my chest and rested her chin on her hand. She looked at my face.

I reached out and twirled a strand of her hair between my fingers. "She asked if you were still my girlfriend."

"What did you tell her?"

"I wanted to say absolutely, of course she is," I admitted. "But I also wanted to be honest with her. I told her we were trying to figure that out."

She shrugged. "That's fair."

I dropped Kathleen's hair to place a comforting hand on her shoulder. "I didn't share that because I'm trying to get a commitment out of you. I don't need you to answer the girlfriend question until you're ready. I'm not going to put that kind of pressure on you."

Her shoulder relaxed. "Thank you. If it makes you feel better, I don't cuddle naked with my other friends."

I'd never heard more hopeful words from her. "Just me?" I pressed her with an egotistical grin.

She nodded and set her head down on my chest. "I'm ready to sleep again. Is that all right?"

"Only if I can join you."

"Yes. Please."

The following morning, I woke up early. As was my custom, I left her to sleep just a bit longer. I showered in her master bathroom before putting on yesterday's clothes. I gathered what few things of mine were scattered around her condo and then returned to her bedroom. When she stirred awake, I made sure I was sitting next to her on the mattress, stroking her hair.

"I have to go home and change." She'd never understand how sorry I was to leave her side.

"Don't want to show up in yesterday's suit?" she teased.

She stretched and smiled and I laughed. She lifted herself up onto one elbow, closing the distance between our bodies. Her eyes drifted away from mine. She opened her mouth to say something, then closed it. She'd changed her mind. Or lost her courage. The mood shifted between us. She appeared sad, and I resolved never to see her that way again. I bent down, kissing her forehead, and then her lips, cupping her cheek with a steady hand.

When her anxious green eyes met my steady brown ones, I said, "I love you." I then whispered, "No matter what."

"I love you, too," she said. "No matter what."

"You need to speak to Robert first."

She stared at me with an uncertain look.

"Get ready for work. Go to the office, and talk to your father," I reiterated. "Tell him what needs to be said. Then come and talk to me."

Her expression morphed from nervous to determined. She nodded, so I stood up and left her condo.

chapter

Forty

THE SUN hadn't risen quite yet, but ebony darkness had given way to predawn light. There was a scratching at my bedroom door, and I realized it was Kitty Hawk trying to find a way into the room. She was accustomed to sleeping in the master bedroom and roaming between my office and my bed during the night time. Worried that the cat's neurotic actions would rouse Heide from her own sleep, I pushed back the covers. I stood up from the bed and put on a pair of boxer briefs.

I opened the bedroom door quietly and the cat wandered in. She offered a few chastising meows before pausing in the middle of the floor. The cat stared up at the bed where someone had taken up residence.

I rolled my eyes and decided to check on Heide while Kitty Hawk worked out her own issues. I found my daughter sound asleep and smiled at her before returning to my room and closing the door. The cat was now lying at the foot of the bed, although not in her usual spot. Her ears were flat and her posture was tense. I scratched under her chin, hoping to lull her into a better mood. As I finished, I swept my gaze up the mattress.

Kathleen had pushed the covers aside, her naked body radiant in the emerging light. I was transfixed and nervous she'd leave my bed soon, never to return. I wanted to remember her forever and began taking a mental inventory of her body.

Beyond her appearance, I wanted to remember every emotion of our night together. Every whisper. Every moan. Every caress and kiss and thrust that gave her pure pleasure and emboldened her to encourage me further. I wanted to remember every time she said yes or spoke my name with desire.

Daunted by the mental task of preserving the details of our first time together, I sighed and pulled my gaze away from her long enough to spot my tablet resting on my bedside table.

Everything I yearned to remember about the magical night could be recorded there. And I could return to my memories any time I needed to. I'd worked in advertising long enough to know how to hone my creativity, but I'd never tried to write anything so detailed, so essential and so personal.

It was going to take some time.

I went back to my side of the bed and climbed back in with care. My worries were for nothing, however. Kathleen was sound asleep and unaware of her surroundings. I adjusted my pillows, leaning back against them and pulling the covers back up to my waist before reaching for the tablet. Recording my memories any other way meant I would have to turn on my bedside lamp or leave the bed to write in my office. With the tablet, I wouldn't have to leave Kathleen's side, and I was certain I was doing what I should be in that moment. I could study her with leisure and allow myself time to come up with the perfect words that would freeze this moment in time forever. It was the type of exercise I had always wanted to take advantage of, but never did. Until experiencing Kathleen's delicious kiss for the first time.

I wasn't a young man. I'd slept with other women. I'd been another woman's husband, but I'd never been so determined to hold on to anyone like I wanted to hold on to Kathleen Brighton. I didn't quite understand the fascination, but I adored her. My life had been in chaos for years. One exquisite night with her had changed everything. In her loving arms, I felt her want wrap around me. In her embrace, my worries evaporated.

I began typing about my feelings, not knowing if I would communicate everything that needed to be said in three sentences or three thousand. I refused to check myself. I just allowed the words to appear as they hit my consciousness. The more I wrote, the more I had to say. The process of molding my thoughts into something tangible was cathartic.

At first, I paused every little bit to check on Kathleen. I didn't want to wake her. From all indications, her night had been an emotional one as well. I took pride in the fact that she was exhausted from our lovemaking. She deserved hours of good rest. I realized that my actions wouldn't disturb her and turned my full attention to my project. The sunrise infused the bedroom in soft light, but even so it wasn't enough to break my focus on my essential task.

I wrote until I recognized that I was using new descriptions of illustrating what I'd already recorded. So, I went back to the beginning to examine my writings. I moved slowly, making changes here and there as it suited my mood. I thought about each sentence carefully, racking my brain to make sure nothing was being left unsaid. I was lost in the task, consumed by my desire to recall it with perfect clarity.

At some point, Kathleen rolled toward me. Except for one startled breath, I held stock-still, fearful that I'd disturbed her sleep. I waited, not even daring to look at her face, just in case it would jar her awake. She didn't sit up or speak, so I returned to my thoughts, seeking to complete my mission before more pressing matters intruded. Kathleen's breathing returned to its steady rhythm, confirming I'd made the right choice in not pulling her out of a much-needed sleep.

The oncoming day was bright and warm, and I looked around my bedroom, taking inventory of the various ways the sunshine flowed through the space. There was a tangible feeling of happiness that surrounded the two of us, and I was drawn into my electronic journal yet again, wanting to record it and ponder its meaning for the days to come.

I read and reread my newest observations until my daughter's familiar knocking on the bedroom door signaled that my time was up. I avoided turning toward Kathleen once again. I detected no movement from her side of the bed and was relieved. Neither of us had prepared for such a wake-up call.

"Yes?" I answered Heide's call for attention and prayed that I didn't sound cross.

"It's me." Her mother had taught Heide never to barge into our bedroom. It was a lesson I appreciated at that moment.

"Do you need something? Are you all right?"

"Can I play the Wii?" We never allowed her to play on the gaming system on school mornings. The rule sometimes made it possible for me to take a little bit of extra time getting dressed on the weekends. Yet another godsend this Saturday.

"Sure. Go ahead. I'll be out in a little bit."

She turned and ran toward the living room before she could offer up a response. "Okay!"

I set the tablet aside and rose from the bed, knowing that if I squared away a couple of things, I could return to wake Kathleen within a few more minutes.

We'd both been swept away by our passions the night before. We'd been fortunate to enjoy one another's bodies without interruption or distress. But as I was aware, everything had its moment. Every experience, no matter how joyous, had to end. My reality had knocked on the door, signaling it was time to resume my responsibilities.

As I dressed, I thought about what was to come. Kathleen would have questions about how to move forward with our morning. I was prepared to give her anything she needed and hoped like hell she wouldn't bolt from my house at the first opportunity. I wasn't ready for her to go home for the weekend, although it was inevitable. I wanted to do whatever I could to ensure that she would see me again. And soon. She hadn't yet left my bed, and I'd glimpsed how much I would miss her once she was gone.

I would offer her the chance to shower or bathe—by showing her how much her personal comfort was important to me. I would not make demands on her to lie to Heide about anything. Kathleen had brought me such ecstasy and such enjoyment. I would do nothing to make her feel unappreciated. I cherished her and wanted to do anything within my ability to prove to her just how much she was revered.

chapter Forty-One

I'D DRIVEN home from Kathleen's while Allison was driving Heide to school. I entered the quiet house and went to my bedroom to change my clothes for work. I took my time choosing a suit. I wanted to make an impression on Kathleen, and I knew I should spend a few minutes with my ex-wife before disappearing again.

Beyond that, I made no attempt to predict how the rest of my day was going to unfold. Robert had warned me about the danger of entertaining theories. It was sound advice.

When Allison pulled into the driveway, I was in the kitchen. She studied me thoroughly as she settled at the breakfast bar. I poured us each a cup of coffee and joined her.

"Did you enjoy the rest of your girls' night?" I asked, trying to keep the conversation casual.

She nodded but didn't share any of her adventures. "Were you able to work things out with Kathleen?" Allison worded her question in a manner that set limits for us both. We'd grown as friends in our post-divorce relationship, but even so, I wasn't inclined to share the details of my intimate night with Kathleen any more than Allison was inclined to hear about them.

"We talked. More than we ever have. I love her. And she loves me back."

"That's good." Allison sipped her coffee thoughtfully. "If Heide's next doctor appointment goes well, it will be time for me to go back to Baltimore."

I paused with my cup in midair. This was the first unpredictable statement of the day. "Only when you're both ready," I stipulated.

"I need to get back to what I started," Allison said. "We should set a date. I'd like to avoid another ill-conceived departure. We should be prepared."

Allison's return under the shadow of Heide's accident had been stressful on everyone. We'd argued in those early weeks, but I'd grown accustomed to her company over the months. As much as I wanted to be able to focus my attention on Kathleen, Allison was always going to be a part of my family life. And I was going to miss her.

"I suppose so," I replied, setting my coffee on the counter. I was concerned with the upcoming separation of mother and daughter. It was important to continue with compassion.

"The holidays are coming up," I mentioned. "If you'd like to stay until after Christmas, I'd understand that."

"Maybe."

I angled my body to face hers. "You don't want to?"

Allison was contrite. "Of course I want to, but Kathleen needs you now. And you need her."

She gazed at me pointedly. "This is a good thing, Jack."

I returned to my coffee. "Please consider staying a bit longer. Neither of us wants to put Heide through the stress of travel right now, and after everything we've been through, this would be a good way to move forward. I'd like the three of us to spend Christmas together."

I smiled and reached for Allison's hand. As our fingers came into contact, I marveled at how different holding her hand was compared to touching Kathleen's. Allison's grip was comforting, but Kathleen's touch was a homecoming. I squeezed her fingers and withdrew from her.

"I'm grateful we could work together for Heide's sake," I said. "I wouldn't change that."

"Me, too." Allison's eyes glistened in the morning sunshine as she offered me a beaming smile. *"But the worst is behind us, and we need to move on with our lives."*

"Kathleen's going to Colorado." I blurted the words without even realizing they were hovering in my thoughts.

Allison was astonished. *"Why?"*

I tapped a finger on the countertop. *"I can't explain the specifics, but she's dealing with more than just the challenges I've presented her. She may not break up with me, but I think she'll still have to go."*

"You think *she'll go?"* Allison was incredulous. *"Has she actually told you that she's taking the other job?"*

"She was going to this morning, but then she changed her mind."

Allison's eyes narrowed in doubt. *"What makes you so sure?"*

"I just am." I shrugged.

"What will you do if she goes?" Allison's tone had shifted from irritated to concerned.

"I'll do my best not to get wrapped up in hypotheticals."

Allison quirked a confused brow.

"I'll take it one step at a time." I took a final sip of my coffee. *"Speaking of which, I should get to the office."*

I rose from my seat, grabbed my things and waved farewell to Allison. *"Let Heide know I'm coming home right after work. We can cook dinner together."*

Allison nodded. Her expression was stoic, although her eyes betrayed her worry.

I was calm as I drove to work. I pulled into my usual parking space, grabbed my messenger bag and entered the front doors of Aurora Advertising as though it was just any other day at the office. My mood was perplexing in its way, but I didn't fixate over it. Kathleen's car was in the parking lot. Simply put, having her back in Bend did wonders for my emotional state.

When I entered the reception area, Tracie was sitting at her desk. She offered me a knowing smile as soon as we made eye contact. I didn't pause to say hello, but I mouthed my thanks as I moved past.

I peered at Robert's office. The door was closed, but the lights were on. It was still early in the workday by his standards, but he was already in the middle of a private meeting. I knew without checking that Kathleen was in there.

I went to my own office to hold vigil. I set about my usual tasks, occasionally checking on the status of Robert's closed door. Kathleen spent most of the morning inside her father's office, and this told me that a simple conversation, an easy decision, wasn't playing out between them. The prolonged, private discussion solidified my expectations, as had Kathleen's hesitation to say something to me earlier that morning.

I accepted this twist of fate alone. The longer their meeting dragged on, the more difficult it was to keep my mind on the work. When my efforts became worthless, I found myself reaching inside my messenger bag to retrieve my tablet. I turned on the device and trailed my fingers down the display until I discovered the file I was searching for.

I hadn't opened the document in months. My intense concentration that morning had distracted me from Kathleen. After realizing that she'd felt invisible because of my impulse to memorialize our first night together, I'd been unable to go back and read what I'd written. But at that moment, I was nostalgic. Our breakthrough from the night before emboldened me.

I sat back in my chair and absorbed the recollections I'd journaled months ago. I remembered many sentences word for word, but others had drifted from my memory, stunning me with their rawness. As much pain as my actions had caused Kathleen, this essay was everything I needed as I waited for her to finish talking to her father. It was the perfect way to remind myself what I was fighting for. I read the passionate words and gathered my strength for the new reality unfurling within Robert's office.

My usual lunchtime rolled around just as my cell phone pinged with a text message. I set the tablet down on my desk and picked up the phone.

Kathleen's smiling face greeted me on the display screen. "I've talked to Robert. I'm in my office. I need you."

I didn't waste time replying. I got up and marched over to her corner of the building. I stepped inside her workspace and closed the door as Kathleen rose from her chair. I strode around her desk with purpose but stopped just short of pulling her into my eager arms.

"Will you push me away if I touch you?" I asked, and not for the first time.

She was flustered, but then she shook her head.

I reached out and ran my hand through her hair. Her eyes fluttered shut, igniting both pleasure and memories of an intimate moment on a cityscape terrace.

Despite the tension, I smiled and capitalized on her openness. "I want you," I said with undeniable need. I leaned forward and skimmed my lips over her earlobe. "It's been so long."

We stood in this precarious pose, both too frightened to make the next move. Gradually, I wrapped my arm around her waist and spread my hand across her back. I encouraged her to lean into me, but she stiffened with cautious reserve.

I hoped to alleviate her fear. "I want to kiss you now, but I know I can't."

She leaned back and opened her eyes, grasping the broad slope of my shoulder and waiting for my explanation.

"If I kiss you, I won't stop. I'll take you right here on your desk."

"I'd let you," she confessed, her voice infused with as much desire as mine. "But we need to talk."

I settled for placing a chaste kiss on her forehead. I pointed to the chair in front of her desk. "Should I take a seat?"

"I'll leave that up to you."

Having been away from her for so long, I couldn't bring myself to step away from her. Instead, I perched on the corner of her executive desk and held one of her hands in both of mine.

She looked into my eyes. "I've been offered a job at Ryan Murray's firm in Denver."

I held stock-still. The rest of our lives would unfold during this conversation. I couldn't fuck it up. As I struggled to hold my composure, I focused on the emotion in her confirmation.

"You sound surprised," I said.

"Yes." She was unable to suppress a glimmer of pride. Despite my personal fears, I smiled and reached up to rest my palm against her blushing cheek.

"I'm not," I said with conviction. "And I'm sure Robert wasn't surprised either."

She nodded. "He was ready for it."

"You were in his office for most of the morning," I added.

"We were going over the angles. He was helping me."

Her voice communicated her astonishment, but I'd learned enough about Robert Brighton, as a man and as a father, to understand where he was coming from. Fighting his daughter would only poison their fledgling reconciliation. I was grateful to him. Perhaps his efforts to keep the peace with her would also help me shore up the damage I'd caused.

"He's willing to put his family before himself or the firm," I said. "You see that, don't you?"

"Yes," she answered.

I glanced down at our entwined hands. "Allison wants me to tell you something."

"What?" Kathleen's amazement was undeniable.

"She's returning to Baltimore after the holidays. We're both in agreement about this. Heide's moved far enough into her

recovery. She's out of immediate danger, and it's time for us to move forward with our lives."

Kathleen didn't respond other than to lean farther into my palm and squeeze my other hand.

"I'm not telling you this so that you'll turn down the job," I continued. "When Allison leaves, I'll need to dedicate more time to Heide's care. It's still going to be a long road for her. She'll need me."

"She will," Kathleen agreed. "You have no idea how much."

Sitting on the corner of her desk, I looked back upon the mistakes of my first marriage as well as the long-term effects of Robert's mistakes in raising Kathleen.

She was in her thirties and an accomplished, beautiful woman, but this was the first time she was embracing her own opportunities. I was committed to doing the right thing for us all— Heide, Allison, Robert, Kathleen and me. Even if that meant giving Kathleen the chance to build a new life elsewhere. Her happiness was paramount to our success.

"What do we need to talk about?" I encouraged her.

She squared her shoulders but didn't break our physical contact. "I haven't called Ryan since leaving Robert's office. I wanted to speak with you first."

"But you want to take the job?"

She faltered, but only just briefly. "I want your honest opinion on this."

"All right." I swallowed my emotion. It was so difficult to hear. But I would rise to the occasion rather than destroy it.

"I've worked out a compromise with Robert and Ryan. One that I hope will be acceptable to you."

"A compromise..." I repeated the word with wonder. Her declaration was unexpected, and I wanted to be certain I hadn't misheard her. "What do you mean?"

"I've accepted Ryan's offer, and Robert has agreed to give me a leave of absence."

My chest swelled with hope. "For how long?"

"A year."

I nodded. In my youth, a year may as well have been an eternity; but now, twelve months disappeared in the blink of an eye. I could survive one year. "And after you've been in Denver for a year? What then?"

"I'm not moving to Denver."

There was no disguising my reaction to that. I dropped my hand from her face and stood up from her desk, reclaiming both of her hands in mine. I looked down into her confident eyes. "I don't understand."

"Ryan offered me a position based in Portland. He has a VIP client there, and he's constantly traveling back and forth to manage just one individual. Ryan wants me to manage this client on his behalf. I've promised not to steal the client away. I won't disclose my background here, and I won't be working for Aurora in any capacity while I'm working for his firm. I may have to spend some of my time in Colorado, but I won't have to move there."

"I don't want to sound unappreciative, but I have to ask. Why go to Portland at all?"

"Robert is worried about my grandparents. My grandmother told him that my grandfather's health is declining."

"You won't be in Bend, but you won't be in Colorado full time either," I marveled. "I have one other question."

"What is it?"

"Why do you have to leave Aurora? Why go to work for him?"

She paused and shuffled her weight from one foot to the other. "If I can work from Portland, I can look after my grandparents and it will keep Robert from traveling back and forth so much. And the leave of absence will me give me time and space to figure out what to do next."

"What do you need from me?" I heard the vulnerability in my own voice, although I'd planned to convey nothing but strength.

"It wouldn't be like it was." She dropped her hands from mine to travel up my forearms. *"I'm not running away from you. I could come down here on some weekends, and whenever you bring Heide up to Portland for doctor appointments, you can stay with me. We can both do what we need to do, and we'd have time to work on our relationship."*

I could hardly believe my ears. It would be tempting to focus on the negative side of the situation, but instead I saw her compromise for the opportunity it was. I'd just been given a year to win back the love of my life.

I fell quiet for a time, allowing her suggestion to settle in.

"Do you hate me?" Her pained question drew my full attention back to the present.

I pulled her into my arms. "You know I don't," I murmured against her golden hair. *"Where did that come from?"*

"I don't know."

"All I need is for you to be happy."

She shook her head against my chest. "I'm afraid."

"Of me?"

"Of everything."

I leaned my cheek to rest against the top of her head as understanding washed over me. "I've been afraid that telling you my secrets may finish us, but I know that not telling you means I'll lose you for sure. I'm sorry I'm not the man you thought I was."

There was a pregnant silence between us. As I held her in my arms, I had more comfort to offer, but I also had one final confession to make.

"I was lost after my father died," I said. *"That's when I started sleeping with women. It was a terrible habit. My father would have been so disappointed in what I'd done. Maybe I wouldn't have done those things if he might find out about them. I don't know."*

"You were trying to cope."

"Becoming a father changed me. I became a different man the moment Heide was placed in my arms. I tried my best to make my marriage work, but I failed Allison early on. I've failed you, too. She left me, so how can I be so surprised by what's happening now?"

She lifted her head and looked up at me. Tears were burning my eyes and she could see them.

I managed to hold them back, but my voice betrayed my emotions. "It's almost the same. Her leaving for Maryland, and you leaving for Portland. But I don't want it to be the same."

"I won't be in Portland all the time."

Kathleen snuggled back against my chest. I wiped away a tear, and then I wrapped my arm back around her with a sniffle.

"Why don't you want it to be the same?" she asked, trying to help me work through my sadness. "What's different for you now?"

"As opposed to when Allison left me?"

She nodded against my chest.

"I let her go."

"You're letting me go, too."

"No." I grinned. "You don't understand, Kathleen."

"I guess not."

My embrace tightened around her even more. "I let go of Allison, body and soul. I will never let go of you."

To Be Continued...

Acknowledgements

My long list of thanks begins with Kris and Morgan, who read this book in all its various stages. They selflessly contributed their time, advice and encouragement, and their wholehearted support of Jack and Kathleen's story convinced me I *could* write a trilogy.

Melissa and MJ are my amazing and hard-working PA's. They both came on board just when I needed them most. Their time, talents and enthusiasm made it possible for me finish the most challenging book of my writing career, and I'll be forever grateful for their friendship and support. This is why Chaos has been dedicated in their names.

Thank you to my online colleagues at Argyle Empire. Coco, Iris, Mango, and MJ were amazing as I devoted my attention to writing Chaos rather than blogging for AE. They've all been amazing friends since the time we met, and this instance is no exception.

Special thanks also go to Autumn for reading the nearly complete version of the manuscript and offering a cover quote. I owe her one yummy cocktail!

I am grateful to Colleen, who provided editorial direction despite her own hectic schedule. I asked for her help, assuming it was a longshot, and she eagerly took on the project. Her fingerprint is definitively on this series and the story is better as a result.

I also enjoyed my collaboration with Janine and Greg at Write Divas. Their professionalism as editors is unequivocal and I'm so happy to be working on this series with them. I'd also like to express my gratitude to Marla of Proofingstyle, Inc. for her amazing copy edit skills. Carol (aka the Blurb Bitch) did a tremendous favor by drafting the synopsis for this book. Without her help, I'd still be trying to summarize this novel into a few eye-catching paragraphs. Lindsey Gray took on the task of formatting this book and it's been a delight to have someone who wants the inside of the book to be as appealing as the cover.

Jada D'Lee, Gel and Victoria all did something for this story that I never could. Jada's cover design, Gel's tempting illustrations and Victoria's illo have transformed my black and white words into vibrant pictures. The three of you were my top choices as visual artists for the Constellation series and I'm honored you found this story worthy of your incredible talents.

Christine from The Hype PR has been wonderful to work with and has provided me with amazing connections beyond my own personal circles. I love how we've worked together as a team and I can't wait to release other books with her help.

Since 2010, I've become close to many readers, reviewers, bloggers, artists, and authors. The people I've met both online and in person provide me with daily inspiration. I can't name you all here, but if we've ever spoken to one another please know I'm speaking of you now. Because of your friendship, I am happier than I've ever been. My life has been a fantastic whirlwind since you welcomed me into the community. Thank you.

In that place we refer to as real life, I have a full-time career. While many authors fear losing their day jobs and conceal their published works from their employers, my personal experience differs. Not only do my work colleagues encourage my writing, they also allow me to do so under my own name. I wish to express particular thanks to Carrie, Molly, Valencia, Bri, and Wanda. You may not realize it, but the support you have so effortlessly provided is indeed an aberration in my publishing circles.

I need to express my love and appreciation to my children and my mother, who all patiently allow me to pursue random story ideas and all that comes along with my writing endeavors. It isn't just about spending hours lost in a word doc or spending time on social media. It's also about me leaving home on occasion to attend author events and other assorted shenanigans. You are all very good to me, and I hope I'm as good to you in return.

Finally, I wish to thank my husband. Morgan has been by my side ever since our introduction on a dance floor in 1988. Several years ago, he saw a spark of creativity in me and encouraged me to rekindle my connection to storytelling. Thinking about writing a novel is one thing. Sitting down to do so is quite another. Without Morgan's enthusiasm, love and effort to draw me into the spotlight, I guarantee you never would have heard a peep out of me.

~ Jennifer
April 12, 2018

Author Bio

Jennifer lives in the Pacific Northwest region of the United States. She married her high school sweetheart, Morgan, in 1995. She is the mother of two children, a son and daughter.

Prior to publishing her first novel, she was a contributing reviewer for the Bookish Temptations book blog. She is also a founding moderator of Argyle Empire, an approved fan site for New York Times and International Best Selling Author, Sylvain Reynard.

Represented by Stephanie Phillips of SBR Media.

Connect with Jennifer on …

Facebook
https://www.facebook.com/MorganandJenniferLocklear/

Twitter
https://twitter.com/RandomCran

Bookbub
https://www.bookbub.com/profile/jennifer-locklear

Instagram
https://www.instagram.com/random_cran/

Goodreads
https://www.goodreads.com/author/show/8202703.Jennifer_Locklear

Newsletter

http://locklearbooks.com/

Want to join Jennifer's Facebook group, The Stargazers Squad? Jennifer posts silly videos, shares sexy teasers, hosts author takeovers/giveaways and posts other pieces of story related items. https://www.facebook.com/groups/TheStargazersSquad/

Books by Jennifer Locklear

Co-authored with Morgan Locklear
Exposure

The Constellation Series
Constellation
Chaos

Team Chaos

Write Divas   http://www.writedivasediting.com/

Proofingstyle, Inc.   http://www.proofingstyle.com/

The Blurb Bitch   http://www.blurbbitch.com/

Lindsey Gray Formatting Services
http://www.lindseygray.net/formatting-services

Jada D'Lee Designs   http://www.jadadleedesigns.com/

Tempting Illustrations
http://www.temptingillustrations.com/#sthash.bFewra3c.dpbs

Ruffles and Restraints   http://rufflesandrestraints.com/

The Hype PR   http://www.thehypepr.net/